MAESTRO

A complex scent of ripe fruitiness and decay greeted my nostrils and the warm, misty air had a delightful quality of enclosure. Could I trust Signor Cavallo not to harm me? The lightning revealed a jungle of huge, thick leaves and creepers, white lilies, a path. I ran my hand over my chest, feeling the congealed blood. I knew that, sooner or later, I would have to step deep into this forest. As I stood there, immobilised by doubt, it seemed that I heard, beyond the rain and insects, a long drawn-out cello tone – and in my mind's eye I saw once again the deep, peaceful blue of his steady gaze.

I had to trust. He was my Master and would take care of me. I need fear no evil.

MAESTRO

Peter Slater

For John and Richard

First published in Great Britain in 2000 by
Idol
an imprint of Virgin Publishing Ltd
Thames Wharf Studios,
Rainville Road, London W6 9HA

ISBN 0 352 33511 4

Cover photograph by Colin Clarke Photography

Typeset by SetSystems Ltd, Saffron Walden, Essex
Printed and bound in Great Britain by
Mackays of Chatham PLC

SAFER SEX GUIDELINES

We include safer sex guidelines in every Idol book. However, while our policy is always to show safer sex in contemporary stories, we don't insist on safer sex practices in stories with historical settings – as this would be anachronistic. These books are sexual fantasies – in real life, everyone needs to think about safe sex.

While there have been major advances in the drug treatments for people with HIV and AIDS, there is still no cure for AIDS or a vaccine against HIV. Safe sex is still the only way of being sure of avoiding HIV sexually.

HIV can only be transmitted through blood, come and vaginal fluids (but no other body fluids) passing from one person (with HIV) into another person's bloodstream. It cannot get through healthy, undamaged skin. The only real risk of HIV is through anal sex without a condom – this accounts for almost all HIV transmissions between men.

Being safe
Even if you don't come inside someone, there is still a risk to both partners from blood (tiny cuts in the arse) and pre-come. Using strong condoms and water-based lubricant greatly reduces the risk of HIV. However, condoms can break or slip off, so:
* Make sure that condoms are stored away from hot or damp places.
* Check the expiry date – condoms have a limited life.
* Gently squeeze the air out of the tip.
* Check the condom is put on the right way up and unroll it down the erect cock.
* Use plenty of water-based lubricant (lube), up the arse and on the condom.
* While fucking, check occasionally to see the condom is still in one piece (you could also add more lube).

* When you withdraw, hold the condom tight to your cock as you pull out.
* Never re-use a condom or use the same condom with more than one person.
* If you're not used to condoms you might practise putting them on.
* Sex toys like dildos and plugs are safe. But if you're sharing them use a new condom each time or wash the toys well.

For the safest sex, make sure you use the strongest condoms, such as Durex Ultra Strong, Mates Super Strong, HT Specials and Rubberstuffers packs. Condoms are free in many STD (Sexually Transmitted Disease) clinics (sometimes called GUM clinics) and from many gay bars. It's also essential to use lots of water-based lube such as KY, Wet Stuff, Slik or Liquid Silk. Never use come as a lubricant.

Oral sex
Compared with fucking, sucking someone's cock is far safer. Swallowing come does not necessarily mean that HIV gets absorbed into the bloodstream. While a tiny fraction of cases of HIV infection have been linked to sucking, we know the risk is minimal. But certain factors increase the risk:
* Letting someone come in your mouth
* Throat infections such as gonorrhoea
* If you have cuts, sores or infections in your mouth and throat

So what is safe?
There are so many things you can do which are absolutely safe: wanking each other; rubbing your cocks against one another; kissing, sucking and licking all over the body; rimming – to name but a few.

If you're finding safe sex difficult, call a helpline or speak to someone you feel you can trust for support. The Terrence Higgins Trust Helpline, which is open from noon to 10pm every day, can be reached on 0171 242 1010.

Or, if you're in the United States, you can ring the Center for Disease Control toll free on 1 800 458 5231.

Part One

One

Signor Cavallo's Narrative

I ignored the knock at the door. I go to bed early and tolerate no variation to my routine. My preparations at the end of each day go according to a set pattern, a habit developed over the course of years. I take a bath (the room lit only by a single candle on a shelf above the tub), go downstairs and eat a light supper of fish. Then I go to the music room and play my cello for an hour – usually something by Bach or, perhaps, Marcello. Finally, in the silence that has been informed and made intelligent by the music I sit and wait for the first furry signals of sleep to invade my limbs before making my slow way to bed. Sleep comes quickly. My soul is untroubled – although sometimes in my dreams I see wild boys racing naked on horseback through the forest, or splashing in the waters of the lake; and, after such dreams, I awaken with a palpable sadness.

I live practically alone, here in the Langhe region of Piedmont, in one of those small *castellos* that dot the countryside hereabouts. The Castello Caccini dates from the fourteenth century and, I suppose, looks much like the imposing fortress it was orginally designed to be with its three round towers and the apertures at the top of the brick walls through which boulders could be thrown on to the attackers below; but when I first bought the building it was in a state of considerable disrepair (and therefore not so very expensive). I have restored something of its former glory. The grounds are tended by a small team of dedicated workers from the nearby village, supervised by Callipo, my young aide-de-camp. Callipo is my only contact with the outside world. He cooks and fetches my shopping and gives me news of local gossip and world events. I have a fondness for him, but what he says holds no interest for me. I have severed my links with the world – wars are of no more interest than Signorina Lavacci's lost kitten. But I make a pretence of listening in order to be polite and cause no offence. Callipo is good-hearted and I could not manage without him.

No, I have no other contact with the outside world; and want none. I have no radio, much less a television. I never read newspapers. Some may call me eccentric – I'm sure many do. After all, I am not a poor man: I can afford anything I desire; and, in my youth, I lived a life of considerable excess. There were the fast cars, the yacht, the chateau in France, the parties and the boys. I was famous, you see – or as famous as one in my profession can hope to be. I am Ernesto Cavallo, the cellist. Sir Georg Solti once called me 'the greatest cellist of this or any other generation', and Herbert von Karajan always sent me his private jet when he wanted me to play in one of his concerts. 'The music of Bach has waited three hundred years and only in your hands has it at last found true expression,' Herr von Karajan once said to me – happily in front of the rolling TV cameras prefacing a concert for the President at the White House. I also composed the music for a number of major movies: there's an Oscar somewhere around here, in one of the cupboards amongst all my other junk. All that past life means nothing to me now.

The knock came again: discreet yet peremptory. I did not resolve not to answer it, but simply knew that I would not. I sat in my candlelit silence and breathed. The vast ornamental mirror above the harpsichord caught my reflection: Prospero in his cave,

I thought (not for the first time) — surrounded though by fine paintings, vases and objets d'art on small tables and with an intricately patterned Belushi carpet beneath his feet.

Go away! I thought. I knew there was no chance of Callipo's answering it: he had long since secreted himself in his remote wing. I could have summoned him by the bell-pull, but did not want to disturb him.

The silence was not utter, however: it rarely is. There is always the chirp of the cricket or the hoot of an owl at night, not to mention the mournful cries of the foxes and the soughing of the wind through the trees. But tonight there was another sound also: the steady thrum of rain on the gravelled courtyard and its clicks and drips as it slipped through drainpipes and holes in the complex guttering system that rings the *castello* with perhaps a slightly rickety exterior artery. The rain had also brought with it an unaccustomed chill to the air of this otherwise long, hot and dry summer. This was no night to be out and knocking on the door of a stranger: certainly no friend would call thus.

Perhaps in my latter years I have become somewhat cold — at least that is the aspect that I choose to present to the world — but I am not without compassion. I have known, as the youngest son of a desperately poor family growing up in the ruins of postwar Rome, true poverty. In those early years we rarely had enough to eat, and my family wore the most hopeless rags. I know what it is to be without. You may have heard of the Ernesto Cavallo Foundation in New York which dispenses generous bursaries to children of poor families who would otherwise be unable to fund their education in music schools. The Pope once remarked to me . . . Oh, but there I go again: name dropping. For sure I once was arrogant: all that is gone for good.

I heard the knock a fourth time before I realised that it was my duty to answer. Slowly I got up and went to the door. In my nightcap and gown and holding a candlestick I must have looked like an apparition from another century.

'Who is it?' I called from behind the closed door.

'Maestro!' came a frail voice.

How I have come to hate that word!

'Who is it?' I repeated testily.

'Maestro, my name is Ramon.' A long pause. 'My name is Ramon, and I am a player of the violoncello.'

'Go away!' I don't mind assisting someone in distress, but groupies I don't need ('Maestro, can I have your autograph? Can you sign my album cover? Do you have a signed photograph? What did you really think of Leonard Bernstein – is the famous story true about you and him?').

'I have come from Madrid.'

'I don't care if you've come from the furthest deserts of the moon. I don't want you here!'

Silence. Then came a crash of thunder and a stiff wind blew rain against the windows making a sound like the spattering of light gravel. It was an awful night, and the village was over three miles away. But no, I didn't want someone in here who was going to want to talk about my past life and dredge up all that stuff that I have been so happy to forget. To a poor, illiterate beggar I would have given supper and a night's shelter; but not to a wretched cello player wanting to add to his stock of future anecdote: 'I once spent a night with Maestro Cavallo!'

'You can shelter in one of the stables!' I called. 'I'm not letting you in here.' As I spoke I became more convinced that I was making the right decision. Who knew if this was not really a ruse to break into my *castello*? 'Ramon' might merely have been the front man for a gang of brigands.

'How will I find it? It's pitch black out here.' It was clearly the voice of a youth, boy-open and gentle.

'Turn around ninety degrees and walk in a straight line. You can't miss them. But surely you have a torch, else how did you find your way through the forest?'

To that there was no answer. I stood listening until I heard the shifting of feet and then the scrunching of gravel. Pressing my ear against the door I waited until I heard the creak of the door to the barn. Ramon had found it. Whoever he was, he would have shelter this night. In the morning I would take him some coffee and a little something to eat and explain patiently but firmly that I gave no autographs nor granted any interviews and wished only to be left in peace.

Two

Signor Cavallo's Narrative
(continued)

There is no time quite so lovely as the dawn of a clear summer's day following a night of rain. The world always seems renewed and refreshed.

On awakening on the morning after I had received my new visitor, I lay for some time listening to the dawn chorus – that glorious rush of sound: each bird's song like a thread woven into a vast colourful tapestry. After a while I rose and padded barefoot to open the window. My bedroom overlooks the great sweep of the garden with its wide lawn and brilliant flower beds, down to the lake where there is a rowboat moored to a landing-stage, and then the forest. It is one of the loveliest views in Italy. I have painted it many times, in different seasons at different times each day. I am a fair artist and can always make a faithful likeness; but, somehow, I always fail to grasp the *essence* of the thing. The *essence* of the thing: what every musician, too, hopes to capture when he plays and which few ever manage. Many people can play all the right notes in a sonata or a concerto, for instance; but only a very, very few can ever penetrate beyond that technical dexterity into the very heart of a piece of music. They said, once, that I was such a one able to realise the essence of music: its soul. But no more. I am sometimes apprehended by a memory of the past – a moment, a scent, a touch recalled; and it is always painful. I have rejected the life that has gone before. It means nothing to me now. And, above all, I have rejected love – or, at any rate, human love. I cannot shake my remaining passion for music; but even that is not now what once it was. Sometimes even my playing seems more habit than passion. I reduce the Bach sonatas to mere technical exercises; but who is to know? I am never less than note perfect and I can still astound Callipo and the other boys who work in the grounds with the nimbleness of my fingers.

My morning ritual is as ordered as the pattern I follow at night. I go downstairs in my nightshirt and cap and sip a mug of mint tea at the oak table in the kitchen. Then I return upstairs to shave and to dress. Breakfast is usually a modest affair: a roll with a little *dolce latte* and several cups of fiercely hot, sweet espresso.

How do I fill my days? The answer is: I potter about. A little painting, possibly. Some light gardening, a walk in the forest. I have taught myself to become an expert botanist and take pleasure in identifying and annotating the wildflowers that grow in these parts. Field Campion, Lady's Milkwort, the Freckled Butterfly Orchid: even the names of wildflowers give me huge pleasure. I read a great deal. At the moment, I am making my way through Spenser's *The Faerie Queene* – for perhaps the seventh or the eighth time – and in the original medieval English: I am fluent in seven or eight languages. How I love the poetry of that book! And I read musical scores in much the same way as the general reader reads a novel. Beethoven's violin concerto is a favourite, as is Dvořák's American string quartet. Ironically, I can 'hear' far more in a reading of a score than ever I can listening to an actual performance.

On this particular morning, however, my ritual was disrupted. The very thought of that youth in the stable upset me. I did not want to go downstairs in my nightgown and cap lest he should see me in such garb. It was not vanity, merely a desire not to be mocked. So, on rising, I dressed straightaway in brown corduroys and check shirt. It felt unusual to be wearing clothes at that early hour. I cannot deny that I felt as if I was getting the day off to a good, punchy start. There was nothing of that languid, idle feeling I usually experience on rising. And no returning to bed for that extra half-hour's doze.

Contrary to the popular gossip of the village, my *castello* is connected to the electricity supply. I did not, as has been suggested, defy a thunderstorm on my first night here and tear down the power cables with my bare hands. Yes, I prefer the warm, intelligent light of the candle and the oil lamp to the tedious uniform glare of the electric bulb and I do not require electricity to bring me the neuroses of the modern world through the media of radio or television. I prefer a log fire in winter to central heating, and the wood-burning Aga in the kitchen provides ample hot water as well as being a cooking-stove; but I am connected to the mains supply. It has its uses, after all, and one of these is to boil me a kettle of water speedily on summer mornings. In the winter I keep the Aga going day and night (the loveliness of the soft warmth of the kitchen on a cold, January morning!); but in the summer I light its fire only in the evening in order to have hot water for my bath.

I was in the kitchen, waiting for the coffee to brew and thinking that perhaps I might – as an amusing exercise – transcribe Bach's Art of Fugue for solo cello, when I heard a faint sneeze. Instantly, that sour mood I had experienced on first waking swept back in like mist closing over moorland. That boy, that groupie, was still around. Momentarily, I had been able to forget him. Forgetfulness, though, is a rare luxury. The sneeze came again. Should I take him some coffee? Oh, no, to hell with that! I was not going to be his servant. As I sipped my espresso, I tried once more to think of Bach; but could not. Here I was, dressed when I did not want to be dressed, unable to think my own thoughts and with, at the back of my mind, a sense of vague, unwelcome *responsibility*. There was someone on my property to whom, eventually, like it or not, I would have to give some refreshment and, perhaps, a little money before ordering him, quite firmly, to go away and never return. And, no, he would not get an autograph. *Curmudgeonly*; there was a word like a robber's cosh! Curmudgeonly Ernesto Cavallo. Yes, that was me!

I drank my coffee and ate my roll, enjoying the clear morning light as it washed in through the kitchen window above the porcelain sink unit and splashed on the kitchen dresser lined with plates, the stove and the black and white square-tiled floor. I love also the sounds of my mornings: the creak of the chair, the scrape of my knife as it spreads the cheese, the remaining scraps of birdsong following their great chorus and the cracks and groans of the old wooden boards in the *castello* as they slowly warm beneath the rising sun. As for any musician, hearing is the most precious of my senses. But not all sound, obviously, is welcome. And when a cough began to join that chronic, irritatingly arrhythmic and atonal sneeze, my flesh began to crawl with irritation.

I confess that when, at length, I went to the stable to check up on its young occupant and discovered him lying shivering in a foetal position on a pile of straw, his face pale notwithstanding the natural darkness of his skin, I confess I felt not pity but profound irritation. His clothes – black jeans and a loose-fitting white calico shirt – were obviously damp, and his black hair was plastered against his scalp.

He sat up when I added a cough of my own to announce my presence. I saw straightaway his extraordinary beauty. His lovely face with its thin lips and fine-drawn cheekbones reminded me of a young man whom my former friend Arturo Palazzo had once kept in his Tuscan villa: 'You may look, but you may not touch!' Arturo had warned when, on the first night of my last stay there that boy had appeared to serve us at table. Wearing only the shortest of togas and a bead necklace the boy fixed me with a stare that urged me to defy his master. And defy him I did. Arturo came upon us whilst I was buggering the boy on the kitchen table and my refusal (inability, actually) to stop until I had pulled out and ejaculated over the boy's tight, smooth arse, meant the end of our friendship. A pity. But it had been worth it . . . I digress again. The boy before me was far lovelier even than Arturo's slave. The wide black eyes that seemed to be flowing increased his beauty by adding to his physiognomy a look of innocent vulnerability – and yet also, paradoxically, they seemed to hint at an excess of debauched sensuality. His eyelashes were delicate and finely spaced and the brows seemed as if drawn by an artist's brush. And when the boy smiled, cautiously, and revealed perfect white teeth, my heart was thrown a fraction off course. A rogue part of myself overturned my annoyance and I wanted to kneel before the boy, stroke his dark hair, slowly unbutton his shirt: draw it first off one shoulder, then the other. A little hesitation, a questioning look, then I would lean towards those soft, slightly parted lips . . .

But no! I had put all that sort of thing behind me. My life now was self-sufficient. I no longer had any need or desire for sexual congress.

'I hope you slept well,' I said brusquely.

The boy nodded almost imperceptibly, and whispered, 'Thank you.'

He sneezed again, and I turned my head away to avoid the mist of germs he had doubtless sent in my direction.

'You must understand,' I said, 'that I can bring you some breakfast, and then you must go. I am not a charity. I ask you, respectfully, to consider my privacy.'

'But, Maestro, I . . .'

'And you must not call me that!' I shouted. 'My name is Signor Cavallo. Please. I'll bring you something to eat and drink.' I turned to go and was nearly out of the door, when the boy called, 'Would it be all right if I dried my clothes?'

'I don't care what you do, so long as you are gone from here within two hours!' I replied.

Feeling that I was being far too generous and wishing that I had evicted the boy immediately, I prepared coffee and rolls for him. I felt like a servant and my mood was foul. If I showed hospitality to this visitor, how many more might come in his wake? ('If you find yourself in Piedmont go and throw yourself on that old mug, Cavallo – he'll give you free board and lodging!')

The boy was out in the yard when I returned carrying a tray. He wore only pale-blue undershorts and was hanging his shirt and trousers over the washing-line. A chicken pecked in the dust close to his bare feet. I put the tray down on the wooden bench that stands just outside the stable, briefly indicated that I had done so, and walked smartly away. I had no wish to gaze at the boy's well-proportioned smooth chest with its large brown nipples, nor likewise did his firm legs dusted with fine dark hairs hold any appeal for me. If a passing fancy momentarily made me jealous of a housefly that was feasting on a bead of sweat just above his collar-bone, that was just what it was – a passing fancy of no consequence. I went back inside and slammed the kitchen door behind me.

I had intended to spend that morning painting. There was a patch of water-lilies newly come into flower at the edge of the lake, and I had been patiently working on a canvas involving them over the past few days – something in the style of the great Monet. But to paint one needs a depth of concentration and stillness. One can play an instrument – or even compose music – in a variety of moods. Painting, however, requires a steadiness of the spirit – and that was precisely what the boy had robbed me of.

I no longer knew what I wanted to do. All I truly knew was that I wanted the intruder to be gone from my life. I spent the next hour obsessively tidying and sorting through piles of music. Then I caught sight of the boy through a window. He was in the courtyard working through a series of t'ai chi exercises. Upset as I was, I could still see that the youth possessed poise and grace. He was lovely to watch, and I moved closer to the window and gazed out. Then he glanced over in my direction and our eyes met. I looked quickly away and moved from the window. I felt as if the boy had spotted in me an unpardonable weakness, and I was not going to give him the pleasure of feeling sexually superior. I did not want him. As I have said before, I have renounced all of that side of my life.

Time passed. I had finished my self-imposed chores and was sitting at the oak kitchen table literally watching the clock and waiting for the hour when I could go out and tell that boy to get out, when I heard the sound. In my life, heretofore, there had been just two moments of profound epiphany: moments of miraculous revelation. The first had come on hearing Glenn Gould play Bach's Goldberg Variations in Montreal in the winter of 1965. The piece itself had been remarkable and had reduced the normally coughing, whispering and sweet-unwrapping Canadian audience to awed silence; but the most extraordinary moment came in the pause between the final variation and the reprise of the melody. In that moment of silence seemed contained all the secrets of the Universe: it was a silence of joy and despair, pain and release, birth and ending – and all so brief. A second later, the beloved melody was played again, and my eyes were full of tears. The second epiphany was such an event that I cannot yet relate it – although I shall do so later. But now, here in my exile, I was hearing something that sounded very like a third epiphany.

This was Bach. His first cello suite in G. And I had never heard it played like this before. How can I explain when music is my chosen medium for expression and I have no natural facility for words? The music was being released by the player and allowed to become its true self. There is an archetype for all great music and, on hearing a piece performed, one can sense when the players reach or nearly reach or fail to reach that original. This is how we can judge the respective worth of interpretations. But what I was hearing, as I sat at my table on that summer's morning, was not merely a close approximation to the archetype of Bach; it was as if the player were reaching out and daring to rewrite the archetype. This was something entirely new, yet perfectly legitimate. This was a new Bach and closer to any fundamental truth than I had ever heard anyone approach heretofore. Including me. I was seduced.

But not quite. There were ragged edges. And a persistent wrong note. The player was practising the first movement and, in going over and over one sequential semiquaver passage, persistently playing an E instead of an F sharp. Admittedly, it was one of the most devilishly tricky passages in the whole of Bach's oeuvre, but nevertheless I was surprised that a player of this calibre would so frequently get it wrong. I had to intervene.

'No-no-no!' I said, stepping out into the yard.

The boy cellist, sitting on the bench in the warm sunshine ceased playing immediately. He remained practically naked, his bare legs wrapped around the instrument, its head resting against a cloth laid upon his shoulder. Lucky cello!

'Why can't you get it right? The forty-third bar of the first movement – it should contain an F sharp, and yet you keep making the note an E: da-da-*da*-da-da-da!' I sang.

The boy flushed as though I had caught him in the act of an even more horrendous crime (if such were possible). Then he said, 'Forgive me, Maestro, but . . . Forgive me, but I think you may possibly be incorrect.'

I was shocked – not so much this time because he had insisted on calling me 'Maestro' once again, but because no one had dared counter me on a musical point for over twenty years.

'What do you mean "incorrect"? Have you any idea how many times I have played this piece?'

'I'm sorry. I was wrong.' He bowed his head.

'You liar! You don't believe you're wrong, do you? Look at me! Look at me!' I tucked my hand beneath his chin and raised his head. His piercing eyes sent a trickle of lust through my stomach. My cock hardened and, despite my vows of renunciation, I wanted to fling him on to his hands and knees in the dust, tear off his shorts and fuck him furiously. But I could see that that was what he was expecting, and wanting – and my pride refused to give him the quiet pleasure in being right about this also.

'No. I don't believe I'm wrong,' he said softly yet forcefully.

15

I jerked my hand away roughly.

'I have the manuscript in my bag. Perhaps you have been playing this piece by heart and have not looked at the notes for many years. If you will permit me I can show you . . .'

There came a silence between us and we locked eyes. Gradually, I felt my resolve weakening beneath his steady stare. I knew that at any moment something was going to happen. And it did. Ramon laid his cello aside. As he stood up to face me, I noticed the growing bulge in his undershorts. He reached out . . . But I turned abruptly away.

'No! I don't want to see the manuscript! I believe you.'

Shaking with emotion, I walked around back of the *castello* and into the garden. Following a crazy impulse I wanted to row my boat far out into the centre of the lake. I had reached the water's edge when I heard the sweet sounds of the boy's playing once again. I stopped. I could not go on. His musicianship was uncanny. So perfect. And yet . . . And yet now that I was no longer disturbed by what I had perceived to be a wrong note, I felt there was something else not quite right. Some ineffable quality was missing – that extra touch that only the very greatest artists can achieve: those artists who are rarely with us more than once in a generation. Ramon was very nearly the greatest musician I had ever heard; but not quite. What was he missing? Standing there, looking out at the lake, I bit my lower lip and tried to work out what was wrong. I could not. I went back to him.

'Why have you come here?' I asked. I knew, now, by his playing, that he was not one of those silly fools who come hunting for an autograph or to research a newspaper article.

He did not stop playing immediately, this time, but rounded the phrase off to a neat, perfect improvised ending. It was well done, and I inclined my head out of respect.

'I have come,' he said carefully, 'to ask you to teach me.'

'What can I teach you? You know perfectly well that you're up there already among the very best. You've got a dazzling career in front of you. No one could possibly teach you anything.'

'Would you say, then, that my playing is perfect? Everyone else does,' he said frankly.

I hesitated before replying, 'Perhaps not quite.'

'I know it's not!' he said urgently. 'They beg and beg me to give performances, go on tours, become an international star, but I won't do it because I know I am not as good as everyone thinks I am. And I knew that you would know this also. Maestro, only you can teach me, only you can take me the final mile.'

I shook my head sadly. 'What you want I cannot teach. None can. You and I can both detect that there is a missing quality in your playing; but what that quality is neither of us can possibly explain.'

'No,' he said. 'That's not true. I know what is missing. It is a place in my heart that I know is there but which I have not yet reached. I cannot reach it by myself. I need help.'

I must have grimaced involuntarily at the mawkishness of his language – these Spaniards! – because he suddenly cried out passionately, 'This is true!' He fell silent for a time, then, 'Maestro,' he began in a frail voice, looking up at me with those puppy eyes so that I felt the balance of the world shifting. 'Maestro, I do not know what it is that I need, but instinct tells me that only you can help.'

I looked away and regarded the gravel.

'Maestro,' he began after some evident hesitation. 'If I might say . . . How can I put this? I do have some idea of what it is that I lack.'

'Go on.'

'Maestro. I am unschooled in love. I am twenty-one years old, and yet I have never . . . You must know what it is like! – practising for six, seven, eight hours a day and then I must go through the form of t'ai chi, which takes another hour, and there is my study of music theory and syntax . . . There is no time for anything else Maestro. Forgive me, I am Spanish and it is in my blood to be direct: I wish you to teach me the Art of Love!'

'No!' I said immediately.

'Maestro, you must!' He put his cello aside and knelt in the dust at my feet. His face only inches from my crotch, the urge to grab it and thrust it against me was enormous. But I took a step backwards.

He continued, 'Love, and the wisdom and experience that come from it – and only from it – is what my playing lacks. Only sexual experience with one such as you will transform me into the truly great player I know I can become.'

I saw straightaway the veracity of his words, and knew instinctively that he was right; but I wanted no involvement. I was finished with the world which he was now entering. My steely resolve, however, was dissolving moment by moment. It is not easy to live by ideals when a beautiful boy is on his knees before you. Suddenly, I saw a way out. 'If,' I said, 'you were a novice cello player would you approach me for lessons?'

'No, of course not. I would go to a lesser player. Someone of your standing could only be expected to teach masterclasses.'

'Exactly. And so it must be with love. You cannot expect me to teach you, or want to teach you, whilst you remain a clumsy virgin. No. You must work with others first, and only when – or if – you reach a certain level of proficiency will you then be permitted to come to my bed.'

He looked aghast. 'But who would want to do this? Who would want to teach me? Please don't send me away, Maestro! I have come so far.'

No, of course I could not send him away.

He stood up once again. How easy it would have been to reach out and take him in my arms. How wonderful to kiss those trembling virgin lips whilst my hands slipped gently beneath the waistband of his shorts, feeling the smooth skin of his arse, slipping into the warm, moist crack! Cautiously, he took a step forward.

'I know someone,' I said, breaking the spell. 'Someone who would, I am sure, be happy to give you your first introduction to the art of making love. He is not much older than you, and you may think him a little rough, but I am sure he is the right person. What say you?'

'Who is he? You can't expect me to make love with a youth I do not know and have never met.'

'He works in the garden. I'm sure if I ask him he will accede to the request.'

'Will I have to pay him? I don't have much money.'

'I'll see to all that side of things. Don't you worry.'

'He won't object?'

'He won't object.'

'When can I start?'

I smiled.

'I'll get Callipo to prepare a room for you,' I said.

Three

Ramon's Narrative

My lodgings were to be in a remote wing of the *castello*. Signor Cavallo led me through oddly narrow corridors and dark passageways painted with now-faded frescoes.

We passed through a vast room with mirrored walls and ceiling from which hung massive chandeliers. The effect was startling: one moment we had entered a room that was filled with a darkness so utter as to be almost tangible, then in the next a thousand lights had come on and were reflected ten thousand times. It seemed, as we walked through this room, watching our myriad reflections (or were they watching us?) that we were drenched in liquid light. And also, somehow, I fancied I heard the faint sound of distant laughter and chatter, the playing of a small chamber orchestra, the shuffling of feet as they danced across this ancient ballroom. We exited the room through double doors emblazoned with two heavy golden suns on either side with faces wearing bland expressions, and the Maestro turned off the lights. I glanced back briefly and the sudden darkness filled me with an unutterable melancholy.

My room was spacious and pleasantly light. A large four-poster bed was hung with curtains depicting birds and flowers of a tropical forest, and the quilt cover and silk pillowcases were patterned likewise. The walls were hung with pictures of birds and rivers. A large window overlooked the garden, lake and forest, and a refreshing breeze brought with it the scent of pine.

I placed my cello case in a corner and put my small valise on the bed.

Apart from the usual bedroom furniture there was also a harpsichord, painted with yet more birds. Maestro Cavallo sat down and played a few bars of Scarlatti.

'I shall be very happy here,' I said.

'You are probably tired. I don't suppose you got much sleep amongst the hay last night. I'll leave you to settle in and rest awhile.' He finished playing with a neat, improvised cadence ending in a tierce de Picardie: which musical device – turning a piece suddenly from melancholy minor into uplifting major – seems somehow always to promise infinite hope. 'If you need anything, there is a bell-pull,' he said, standing up and indicating a tasselled rope by the bed. 'Callipo, my manservant will provide anything that you want.'

The maestro gave a small bow and left me by myself.

It was the happiest moment of my life. I was exactly where I wanted to be, and I had longed for this almost from the first time I had started my music lessons at the age of seven. To be in the presence of Ernesto Cavallo! To be living in the same building! To have the promise of tuition! What would my old master, Herr Lindenbaum, have said? He would have been green with envy.

I took the opportunity to wash and brush up in the adjoining bathroom, and then settled down to practise my cello. There was no way that I wanted to rest, as the maestro had suggested. I was much too excited for that.

Shortly, however, after I had played my scales and exercises and a sonata by Pepusch, I did indeed feel a great tiredness come upon me. Last night had not been especially restful. The hay in the stable had been rather sparse and the floor hard; coupled with which I had had problems finding a place where there were no drips. My sleep could not have totalled more than a couple of hours.

I looked at the bed with its clean sheets and soft pillow and it looked most inviting. I yawned. Sleep. The certain knot of peace. That was what I needed.

I put my cello away carefully, undressed and climbed between the sheets. The pillow was of goose down and gorgeously soft. There is no greater pleasure than is to be found in those moments of deep tiredness before certain sleep. I shivered deliciously into a position of yet greater comfort and, smiling, fell asleep almost instantly.

I was awoken, I don't know how much later, by a whisper. My name trickled into my ear giving me, in my sleep, a delectable sensation of security and sensuousness: the word, more air than substance, curled lightly into the passages of my mind.

'Mm?' I stirred slowly to the surface of consciousness.

'Ramon!'

Suddenly I became aware that I was not alone. There was a youth, of about my own age, leaning over me on the bed. I jerked my eyes wide, startled.

'What do you want?'

His arms were either side of me, seemingly trapping me in a prison of strong limbs. His hair was thick and dark, and his face was handsome, well-proportioned and unshaven.

'Signor Cavallo sent me here.'

'Are you Callipo?'

What on earth did this strange youth want?

'No. My name is Domenico.'

He brought his head down ever closer and then, brushing the hair from my forehead, kissed my brow with strong, thick lips. Now with his right hand he began tracing the form of my body beneath the sheets. My instinct was to run.

Here was a youth conjuring my body into first life with a gentle exploring motion of his hand.

And I did not run. I lay very still.

Domenico's hand slid over the sheet, feeling the outlines of my legs and up over my chest. He avoided touching what seemed not only the centre of my body but the centre of my whole being for the longest time. Gently, he kissed my lips. At first I was unresponsive, but on the second occasion, I raised my head towards him when he teased me by backing away. His tongue slipped between my lips at the moment when his hand at last settled on my stiffening cock. He applied just the lightest touch of friction and I could not refrain from softly crying out. He raised his head and, gently massaging my cock, regarded me with a slight smile. I suppose my face must have registered a look of passionate bewilderment.

When Domenico pulled back the sheet and slipped into bed beside me, I saw that he was naked. I felt his thick, hard cock against my thigh.

Now he lay atop of me and we kissed deeply. His skin against my skin, his cock against my own. My hands explored the smooth skin of his back, the lovely roundness of his buttocks.

Domenico conjured me into life. My body arched with pleasure and my groans grew ever more unrestrained as he kissed me around the nipples and teased my cock and balls with skilful fingers. And when he finally reached my cock with his mouth, licking the length of the shaft and up and around the glans with flickering hummingbird tongue and then plunging the whole greedily deep into his mouth I writhed uncontrollably.

I was never going to hold back for very long on this first occasion of sexual experience and before long I felt the extraordinary welling deep inside that demands release.

'No!' I cried, wanting to pull myself away.

I struggled, but Domenico would not let go and I spurted deep into his mouth. Frantically, he tried to swallow as much as he could, but most of my spunk trailed out of his mouth and back down my cock and around my pubic hair.

I lay beneath him helpless and gasping and watched him sitting astride of me, masturbating. The warm feel of his arse against my legs was good. This great, strong boy seemed touchingly helpless as he manipulated himself towards orgasm. He threw back his

23

head, gasped roughly and shot his load over my chest. Huge splattering bursts of come fell on to my skin.

Still trembling and with his cock now subsiding, Domenico now gave me perhaps the loveliest pleasure by lying right against me and kissing me long and deeply.

We lay close, enjoying the feel of our sweat- and semen-soaked bodies, kissing quietly until, before long, our fires were stoked again and we began on a second round of lovemaking.

I lost track of the hours and the number of times we shared the most passionate intimacies. All I know is that it was dark by the time Domenico left me.

I returned to sleep.

A candle was burning on a table when I next awoke. Beside it were a bottle of red wine and a glass, a basket of rolls, some soft cheese, a bowl of olives, an empty plate and a knife.

It was a warm night. I put on my undershorts, sat at the table, said my grace and set to eating. A silver sickle of moon was poised in a corner of the window, and this, coupled with the frail light of the candle, added an ancient quality to all the objects in the room. Somehow, also, I experienced a sense of detachment from my body. Could this be the same body as the one which I had inhabited yesterday? Could my previous body have believed that such pleasure existed? I regarded my right hand holding the knife and cutting the cheese. This hand, this skin: it was as if I did not recognise it. It, too, was ancient and yet also utterly of the present moment.

After the simple repast I went, naturally, to my cello. I played for two hours or so before deciding to call it a day. As has always been my custom, I knelt by the side of the bed and said my prayers. I am, and always will be, a good Catholic.

Four

Signor Cavallo's Narrative

When next I saw Ramon I knew immediately that a great change had taken place. His eyes sparkled, his skin seemed to glow and he was much more relaxed and easy in himself. His body was on its way to gaining the sexual fluidity of youth that should replace the gawky clumsiness of childhood.

It was the morning of the following day and he was in the garden lying stretched out on the grass, reading a book. I recognised the green T-shirt he wore as belonging to Domenico. Perhaps the blue briefs, which were his only other dress, were also Domenico's. The T-shirt was too small for him and left a gap of a few inches between its hem and the top of the briefs. His buttocks were firm and well rounded and involuntarily I imagined them pinched tight and hard as he fucked furiously.

'So!' I greeted him. 'You've met Domenico?'

He turned round quickly and sprang to his feet, graceful as a startled gazelle, and it was then that I saw the change in him I have just described. He brushed a fall of black hair from his eyes and grinned winningly.

'Thank you, yes,' he said.

'It was what you hoped for? Come, let's go for a stroll around the garden.'

'It was all I hoped for. And more. He is very beautiful. May I ask you something. Have you ever . . .?'

'Slept with him? No, I told you: I have renounced love.'

'But . . .?'

'But don't worry. I will honour my promise to you. When the time is right. For one with such promise as you I can afford to make an exception.'

We cut across the lawn and along the path that winds through a tall bamboo thicket and into the rose garden. Amongst the bamboo there is the faint, dry scent of grass and the clear light is cut into spears by the wavering sticks and shoots; the rose garden, with grassy paths between the shrubs, is by contrast full of thick warm scent and the light falls flat and unbroken.

'When will the time be right?' he asked impatiently.

'When you no longer ask such questions. When you no longer want such a time but accept it gladly when it comes.'

I cut a stem of *Souvenir du Docteur Jemain* – a gorgeous, full-scented dark rose – and handed him the single flower. He took it with a smile, holding it delicately to avoid the particularly savage thorns (the loveliest roses always have the sharpest thorns). But his smile faded when I grasped his hand holding the rose and squeezed it tighter and tighter so that the barbs dug deep into his flesh. Beads of sweat appeared on his forehead and his face took on a blank expression. But he did not protest. A single tear budded in his left eye and then slipped down his smooth cheek.

I let go.

Slowly he uncurled his tight fist. The palm of his hand was a bloody mess. Torn skin, scraps of broken thorn and stem and green chlorophyll mingled with the blood.

'Why did you do that?' he asked. There was no hint of accusation in his tone: he was merely asking in the spirit of general enquiry, and I silently applauded him for his restraint.

'Without pain there can be no freedom from pain. Your

26

undamaged left hand now appreciates itself better, and it will convey that to your music.'

'Supposing my right hand becomes infected? Suppose I contract gangrene? My hands are insured, you know, for a million dollars, I . . .'

I threw back my head and laughed aloud. He had a lot yet to learn.

'Take a handkerchief.' I handed him mine. 'And clean your hand with spittle. You won't get an infection. Saliva and the natural salt of your sweat will provide all the disinfectant you need.'

Five

Ramon's Narrative

That evening, Maestro Cavallo gave me my first cello lesson in the music room. Through open French windows, a thin slice of moon was visible hanging at an angle to a cypress, and one could hear the insistent scraping and sawing of cicadas. The room consisted of shelves, packed with musical scores, a glass cabinet containing sheet music, a life-size statue of a naked boy playing a violin, a grand piano. Two tall vases, containing peacock feathers, stood at either side of a fireplace. The walls were painted with frescoes featuring various mythological creatures who looked either to be playing music, eating a picnic or having sexual intercourse with trees.

For all that he had said about my being able to improve my musicianship only through non-musical activity, the lesson was a revelation. We worked on a sonata by Marcello, and Signor Cavallo revealed to me new layers of meaning and passion that lay beneath the rather cold-seeming baroque exterior of the piece. It was a very familiar work, but within the first ten minutes of my masterclass, I felt as if I were encountering something entirely new. As is customary in a class of this nature, I first played the piece through to him in its entirety. When it was over, I confess I felt rather pleased with myself and smiled at the maestro's applause.

'Marvellous!' said Signor Cavallo. 'Glorious, wondrous, marvellous . . . crap!'

'I'm sorry, Maestro?' The smile slipped from my face. Heretofore he had been more than complimentary about my playing.

Signor Cavallo tilted his head. 'You play the piece as if it were a minor work by a minor seventeenth-century Venetian composed merely as a temporary adornment to a contessa's drawing room.'

I stared ahead, unable to look him in the face.

'Forgive me, Maestro, but perhaps I am missing something. This is a pleasant enough piece of music, but like you say Marcello composed to commission and churned these sonatas out on a production line to please the rather dim-witted aristocracy of the time.'

He began to pace the room, twirling his cello bow as he went.

'Musicians are not concerned with the history of fact, they deal only in the history of feeling. Production-line pieces can be every bit as deep and meaningful as those that take decades to write. When you slept with Domenico, last night, that was a transitory experience, was it not? – and yet its meaning was unfathomable. This sonata by Marcello. Composed in a week, played in twenty minutes – and its original audience probably chatted through the whole performance. It may have been born amongst shallow circumstances, but that does not mean it is music without depth. Think of the music as a living body. Where is its heart?'

'The slow movement?' I hazarded.

'Be more precise, for heaven's sake!'

I shook my head.

'Here!' He sat opposite me and picking up his own instrument played three bars from the Adagio.

And suddenly, hearing those bars freshly interpreted, it seemed that the whole piece was infused with new life. It was uncanny. I had merely glided over them before, and now I saw the damage that I had been doing to the entire sonata by my careless interpretation. Those three bars made sense of what had gone before and informed an understanding of what was to come.

'Now you,' he instructed. 'Starting from the B flat.'

I drew my bow across the strings (remembering, subconsciously, my hands caressing Domenico's back). The notes flowed into the silent air and this time the air itself seemed to participate in granting them their true potential.

'Better,' he granted. 'But still not quite there. To properly interpret a piece of music one must come as close as possible to the psyche of the composer. Listen.' He got up, went to the bookshelves and took down a musty, thick volume. '*Orlando Furioso*. Let me read you a passage. Marcello would have been familiar with this, these words would have been somewhere in his mind at the time of his composing this sonata: therefore you need them also.'

Accordingly he began to read from the epic poem. It was all in medieval Italian and I didn't understand a word, but I dared not raise my voice in protest. He read for over an hour, perhaps longer: it seemed much longer; and I began to experience a boredom so exquisite it was almost like passion.

Finally seeing my discomfort the maestro stopped his droning. He smiled.

'Tedium is one of the highest forms of Art,' he said. 'From it grows restlessness and the desire to move on, to create things anew. Boredom is the seedbed of discontent and discontent is the wellspring of Art. From this all concertos, symphonies, sonatas, operas, books, poems grow. Play me the opening Allegro of the Marcello.'

Joyfully I launched into the spirited music; and, yes, it took on new life. Perhaps it was merely relief that the dull poem had ended and the music begun, or perhaps it was deeper philosophical reason; whatever the cause, I felt as if I had never played this music so well and it took on a new dimension.

Six

Signor Cavallo's Narrative

That night Ramon was to be alone, and I could not sleep. My mind kept teasing my consciousness with an absurd assortment of mental junk. Old arguments that I had forgotten about years ago suddenly resurfaced: my dispute with a second flute in the Berlin Philharmonic over a Bavarian miller's son. The flautist was insane with jealousy and matters reached a head when, before a gala concert at which I was playing the Dvořák, he sawed halfway through my C string so that it snapped during the slow movement. I knew instinctively, straightaway, what had happened and my glare pierced through the orchestra and struck fear into his heart. I could see his eyes widen with terror: he knew that he had gone too far. My vengeance was swift. Within a fortnight I had exerted my influence and von Karajan had him sacked from the orchestra. He was obliged, so I heard, to take up a post teaching music at a convent school in the Black Forest. His loathing for adolescent girls was every bit as sharp as was his attraction to teenage boys. Justice! But that had all happened years ago: why should my mind resurrect it now to keep me awake?

And then I began to think of Dalapiccola's *Dialoghi*: that

outrageously complex work which I all but ruined on its first performance – not that anyone in the audience noticed. Most contemporary music could be played backwards and upside down and the average concert-goer would be none the wiser (such is the parlous state of music education, these days).

And old loves, lost loves, regrets began to tease me. Until . . . until I at last realised what my mind was trying to do. It was attempting to protect me, to get me to think of anything but the one thing that was most important to me and yet about which I could do nothing as yet. I wanted Ramon. Wanted him with such a fierce urgency as I had not experienced for over twenty years. And yet I knew that if I took him now I would upset my careful plan. Such a genius as his needs to be nurtured slowly and carefully. The approach to the pinnacle of perfection has to be soberly thought out and considered. Of course, I would not harm him now by giving way to my – and his – desires; but something ineffable would be lost. He would lose that fine sense of yearning, of exploration and eventual discovery that must inform the artist's playing each time he performs. There would be no mystery present in the playing. Sure, he would still make a fine soloist: perhaps one of the best; but not the best. I had to keep faith with the artistic ideal. It was not easy.

Seven

Signor Cavallo's Narrative
(continued)

We were in the music room and I was listening to Ramon play the Brahms cello sonata in E minor when I began to realise that there was yet more his playing needed other than merely having sexual intercourse with me or anyone else. As ever, he was note perfect and technically there was nothing I could reproach; and now, with his newly won sexual experience, the emotional side to his playing was deepening and maturing. But still there was lacking that ineffable something. Of course, I had every hope that this might emerge after I myself had made love with him; but now I began to wonder if this, after all, would be enough.

No, it would not be enough. It could not be enough. One cannot come to mastery of the cello – one cannot come to mastery of any instrument or, indeed, profession – through the medium of pleasure alone. True enlightenment can only be achieved through the intelligence of suffering.

'Ramon,' I said, when at length he finished the sonata and we were both sitting still inside the silence that, enriched by the preceding music, seemed to infuse each breath we took with the deepest joy. 'Ramon, do you trust me?'

'Of course, Maestro!'

'I wish you would not call me that! However. I'm pleased you trust me. And you earnestly believe that I, and I alone, can help you reach that lonely pinnacle of perfection which few before have ever attained?'

'Only you can do this. Is it to be now? Is it now that we two shall at last make love?'

He reached over and placed a hand on my knee. There was yet a gaucheness in the touch, and I gently removed his hand.

'No, not now. That time is still distant.'

'But it will come?'

His expression at that moment was so innocent, vulnerable and so full of yearning expectancy that only my strongest effort of will prevented me from reaching over to kiss his thin, moist lips – which action would have been the prelude to a day of unabated lovemaking. I held firm. I could not sacrifice the noblest cause of Art to the base instinct of a moment.

'Yes,' I said. 'One day, if you are still agreeable, we will make love together. But it is vitally important that your tuition takes a natural course, with nothing forced and all the elements in their rightful places. You enjoyed your time with Domenico?'

'Oh, of course!' His eyes lit up most charmingly and again a shiver of uncertainty and, yes, jealousy, trickled through me. 'But, Maestro Cavallo, he was so young! Lovely as it was to be with him, I felt as if he had no substance. It was all so, what can I say? *Physical.* I know he has great sexual experience and he taught me much in the way of the technical art of lovemaking, but he was in the way of love in the same position as I am in the way of the cello: technically perfect, but lacking that certain extra dimension.'

'Well observed, Ramon. By what you say I know that we are on the right track. And by what I hear also. You played that sonata most beautifully – in fact I have only on one occasion heard it better played, and that was by Casals himself in Verona on the thirtieth of October 1972. At eight twenty-five on that autumn evening, Verona was a different place than it had been at eight o'clock. Twenty-five minutes had transformed an entire city. Oh, the babies still cried, the drunks still guzzled their red wine, and the boys in the brothel still gave too much of their hard-earned money to the Cosa Nostra but an almost tangible essence of God had entered the atmosphere; and that persists to this day – I was there only a few months ago and still one can sense the spirit that Casals planted there on that noble evening. Do you think I'm crazy?'

'I think you are true, Maestro!'

I regarded him out of the corner of my eye. Would he ever lose that gaucheness, that clumsiness of character and expression? He would have to if he was to wear the crown that he so longed for; but, at the same time, would that not be a pity?

'Yes, well,' I muttered. 'I digress, however, Ramon. "Man has places in his heart that he does not yet know and into them enters suffering that they may be known." Léon Blum said that, earlier this century. He was a political leader in France, opposed to Hitler and jailed during the Occupation. But perhaps that is of no consequence, now.

'Ramon, it is time I took you on to the next stage of your education. Are you ready for anything?'

'Of course, Maestro.'

'Then you must come with me.'

Eight

Ramon's Narrative

The maestro led me through a part of the castle I had not as yet visited. We passed through dark halls, through melancholy empty rooms where the furniture was covered with dust sheets and up several flights of stairs. I did not pay much attention to his tales of warrior princes and wayward counts who cared more for seducing their page-boys than for managing the affairs of their vast estates: I was too absorbed in my new surroundings.

One room was an eerie chapel with pews and altar. From the walls hung tattered flags carrying the bullet holes and tears of long-forgotten battles. Misty beams of sun flowed through stained-glass windows depicting sheep and herdboys in landscapes of green hills and blue rivers. A fly buzzed lazily: the sound seeming to epitomise every slow late afternoon of high summer.

On we went. Along bare passageways, through other rooms. And now down flights of stairs. Always we were going down. Steadily, by degrees, down and down. Through a narrow window I caught a glimpse of a vivid green water meadow on which sheep were grazing. A willow tree overhung the lazily flowing river, and I yearned to be outside on this warm summer's day.

How lovely it would have been to sit on the grassy bank in the gentle shade of that tree, and read *Orlando Furioso*: why not? Perhaps in such lovely circumstances the poem would seem not quite so intolerable. Marcello might, after all, have liked it: how could anyone simple presume that he did not?

The lovely vista brought home to me that it was actually quite chilly in this part of the *castello*. Chilly and dank. This whole area had an unlived-in feel and one sensed that no one had so much as passed through for many months, possibly even years.

As if reading my thoughts, Maestro Cavallo said, 'This west wing is full of sadness. I avoid it as much as I can and even in the days when I used to throw lavish parties I would only offer the rooms for visitors to stay in if the rest of the building was absolutely full.'

We came to a picture gallery. Oh, I could have remained in this room for many an hour! The paintings – all oils with the exception of a few exquisite watercolours – were of beautiful men and boys. There were naked boys riding elephants or emerging from behind trees in the jungle; boys draped in gorgeous cloth and turbans revealing now a thigh, now a glimpse of pubic hair, the barest sight of a penis; boys making love on four-poster beds, on horseback, on the branches of an oak tree. Especially fetching was a pale youth on his knees giving fellatio to a strong, hairy man with low-hanging balls, vast thighs and wild, matted black hair. I saw myself as that boy. 'David and Goliath' the picture was called. Yes, I had heard the story that David had defeated Goliath not with his catapult (always unlikely, if one ever stopped for a moment to think), but by the charm of his sexual allure. The sight of the boy David, dressed only in scanty furs and clearly willing, would have reduced any giant to a state of delirious passion. According to that version of the story the moment Goliath shuddered his mighty orgasm into David's throat (causing a waterfall of spunk to spill out of the boy's mouth and down his smooth chest), Jonathan, David's lover, stepped out from the shadows behind the man and slit his throat. The giant died in ecstasy. They don't tell you that in the Bible; a pity, I'm sure the good book would have gained a whole new faithful readership if its authors had not been forever in the business of censorship.

Dominating the room, however, was a full-length portrait of a boy posing as St Sebastian.

The boy, naked and tied to a tree, was heart-stoppingly beautiful. He was perhaps sixteen or seventeen, perfectly proportioned with long dark curly hair flowing over his shoulders. His lovely penis, neither too large nor too small, seemed arrested just at that point of first tentative erection; and the artist had painted his skin with such tender care that one longed to reach out and touch it, convinced that it was warm with pulsing life. An arrow pierced his chest just above his right nipple and a trail of blood flowed around the nipple and down until it ended in his pubic hair. The boy's lips were slightly parted and, judging by the expression on his face alone, you might have thought him captured at the moment of orgasm rather than at the moment of death. And then his eyes caught mine – yes, it was as though they were alive and had actually moved to summon me closer – and I stopped dead in my tracks. They were of an exquisite blueness like the warm Pacific Ocean and surely they were more than a mere artifice of paint?

'Master, I'm sorry. But who is that boy?'

'Mm?'

Maestro Cavallo was several paces ahead of me. Clearly he did not want to delay in this room. He turned.

'His name was Pavel. He was a serving boy at the castle, oh, two hundred years ago. His history was not a pleasant one. Come, we must get along.'

I did not want to move. A part of me felt that I could not move whilst the boy's eyes were regarding me so steadily.

'What is his story?' I asked.

'I'll tell you someday.'

'I want to know now.' I felt an extraordinary urge to approach the painting and kiss the boy.

Maestro Cavallo sighed. 'Knowledge is not always a good thing,' he said.

'Without it can I ever hope to be a great musician? Nothing must be hidden from me. Those who create and those who interpret Art must know everything. They must have no barriers, no areas of silence. We carry the flame for all humanity, we live by proxy for all humanity, nothing must be denied us. It is our duty to know and to pass on that knowledge through the medium of our Art.'

'Or perhaps we merely have a fondness for gossip,' said Maestro Cavallo rather sourly, putting me in my place.

I blushed and lowered my head. Of course, deep down, the only reason I wanted to hear more about the boy was because I fancied him like mad. I felt, at that moment, that were he to be alive now I would sacrifice everything simply to be by his side. Art, music, the perfect interpretation of a sonata: what did all that matter beside utter physical passion?

'Come on! Quickly!' Maestro Cavallo was holding the door open for me. 'We haven't got all day. Do you think I can spend all my time waiting for you to quench your lust for a dead boy?'

It was the first time he had spoken to me so roughly, and I was naturally a little hurt. Passion is my temperament and I almost stalked off in the opposite direction. When I was younger many was the cello I smashed in a fit of pique; although they were all, needless to say, of inferior quality. My temper was never so uncontrolled that I would even contemplate destroying a Stradivarius or Guarneri.

I followed Maestro Cavallo out of the room. As the door closed behind me, I swear that I heard something very like a groan. I looked back quickly; but Maestro Cavallo had closed the door and there was nothing to see and no further sound.

'Did you hear that?' I asked.

'No,' he said. Then, 'The door needs some oil, that is all. I told you, no one has been in this part of the castle for many years. The hinges are rusty on all the doors. I must get Callipo to go round with an oil can.'

'Pavel,' I whispered under my breath. It was a lovely name. Saying it involved a delicious light curving back of the tongue, like part of a kiss. One could imagine a lover saying the name to his beloved as their lips joined in the first moment of passion.

Now we were walking through a long, narrow stone passage. We had entered through a rickety wooden door and, at the entrance, Maestro Cavallo had taken a wax torch down from a wall bracket and lit the end with a cigarette lighter. Fragments of light and shadow fell around us as we proceeded along this gloomy corridor.

I could not see much beyond the deeper shadow of the Maestro's back. Occasionally cobwebs caught in my face and hair. I hate spiders, their random quick movements and appalling stillnesses that always seem to presage a sudden leap on to a helpless victim fill me with dread. I became convinced that there were now spiders lodging in my hair and I swear I could feel them crawling over the bare skin of my chest and back. It even seemed at one point as though one particular creature with long, thin legs were creeping slowly over my cock and balls. Against my will, a part of me found this intensely erotic – a sort of horrific delight – and my cock gradually stiffened.

'How much further, Maestro?' I asked tentatively. 'I hate this place.'

'Don't ask so many questions!' Maestro Cavallo snapped.

He was angry with me. I longed to get down on my knees before him, hug him and bury my face in his crotch, beseeching forgiveness. How I wish I had not lingered before that portrait! Obviously there were some things that I was simply meant never to see or to understand. Perhaps Pavel had once been the Maestro's lover; but, oh, no, how could that have been? Hadn't he said that the boy had died over two hundred years ago? My mind was wandering and picking up any stupid fancy. Oh, please, what was our destination and when would we at last reach it? I knew now, however, that we were headed towards no place of luxury. What had my Master said about suffering? We were approaching a place of terrible suffering and were now very close,

I could sense it in my bones. Ironically, my erection grew stronger: it was now as firm and hard as bone.

The Maestro came to a final door. He lifted a giant hinge and there was the sound of a hollow clunk and grind. We were at the top of a flight of stone steps leading down God only knew how far.

'Are you afraid?' Then, in a lower tone of voice, he began to recite what I at first thought was poetry until gradually realising that it was from the opening of *Bluebeard's Castle* – that dark and terrible opera by Béla Bartók:

'"In vain I've dreamt too much of you, waiting too long, staring into the distance. In vain I lock you in my arms. Come no closer. Wild pain, wild and screaming pain. Who was it hurt you? Sometimes I see a stern face by the wayside or in the far corner of a crowded hall with chandeliers and I stare impatiently. It seems to say there is someone out there. I would cry out There is someone out there and I must go to them reach out to them with a hand's gentle caress ask them Did you too cry out last night? Did anybody kiss you? There is no way out of this magic circle. I too preserve your dreams and bloodily like a lacerated flood of birds your torn sounds will scatter on the wind."

'You must be taken apart, Ramon, and then put together again. But do not be afraid. You will suffer, but you will come to no harm. I would not harm you.'

He reached out and stroked the side of my face.

'You may turn back if you so wish. You may go now. I am not holding you captive. You are quite free to go.'

'And?'

'And become the cello player in a mediocre string quartet, or perhaps teach music to the children of American business people. Go on, go! You haven't got what it takes! Not by half!'

'Lead me on, Master. I am ready for whatever fate awaits me. I am not afraid.'

'A pretty lie. But follow me, then. Close the door behind you, and tread carefully, there is no safety rail. One slip and . . . The stone floor is a long way down.'

This was the dungeon. My eyes tried to pick out details of what might lie below as we made our progress down, but the light of our single torch was too frail; and, besides, the Master was holding it at such an angle that its glare blinded me rather than served a useful purpose. Terrified lest I fall, I pressed close against the stone wall on my left side. Once or twice I lost my footing, a few of the steps were slippery; and once I stepped on something that shot out of the way quickly and could only have been a rat. *Think of Brahms!* – I silently urged myself. *This is for Brahms and the cello suites of Bach! I owe it to them!*

Eventually we reached the bottom. Thankfully, shakily, I sat down on the bottom step whilst the Master lit a series of torches that were stuck in brackets along the walls.

The light illuminated a torture chamber.

I saw a rack, chains hanging from the walls, a cluster of whips standing in a basket, coils of rope on the floor. The Master opened a cupboard and produced a suit of leather complete with chains, high boots and mask. I watched him don this apparel and knew that shortly I should embark on the severest trial of my life. What was the theory? That through suffering one came to a greater understanding of life and music? At that moment I found it hard to believe; but I had to trust the Master. I was entirely in his hands. He could do with me whatever he so desired.

He stood before me and with a simple motion of his hand indicated that I should rise.

'Now remove your clothes,' he ordered.

I did so until I was naked. I had never felt so vulnerable. How I longed simply to fall into the arms of my leather Master, have him hold and protect me! Indeed, I took a tentative step forward, hoping that at the last he might relent.

But the Master took a swift step backwards and slapped my face with his leather-gloved hand.

'You fool!' he hissed. 'You thought it would be easy! You thought you could attain the heights simply by playing your scales like a schoolboy over and over. You thought that the path to Music was through music alone. Now you must learn the truth!'

'Show me, Master!' I whispered.

He slapped my face again. 'Do not speak unless I give you permission to speak, otherwise you must remain silent before me. Fool!'

What happened next surprised and puzzled me. I had expected perhaps to be tied up and whipped, or stretched face down on the rack exposing my arse to the probing of greased dildos and silver balls (all of which I saw laid out on a tray next to the rack). Or perhaps he would truss me up like a chicken and hang me suspended from the ceiling pulleys whilst he tortured me with feather or whip.

But there was apparently to be none of this. Instead, he led me over to the wall into which were drilled two wrist straps. He lifted my arms and locked now one hand, now the other, securely into place. They were padded and not uncomfortable.

And then, when I was firmly locked into place with no means of escape, he simply turned and left me.

'You will remain here for as long as is necessary,' he said.

But was there to be no torture? No pain? Seemingly not. Ah, how innocent I yet was at that time!

After an hour or so, my arms began to ache somewhat; but I knew that I could tolerate this position for many more hours, perhaps even days. My arms were strong as only a good cellist's can be and they could withstand a great deal that perhaps an ordinary person's arms could not.

Then I had an awful desire to piss. It was clear eventually that I could not hold out for my Master's return, so finally I allowed myself release. I cannot deny that the aesthetic sensation of at last giving way to this terrible desire and the feel of the warm piss trickling down my leg was delightful.

Time passed. I had no means of knowing how long I had been tied to that wall. The torches burned with steady flames and gave no indication as to when they might expire. I grew bored. I ran through various cello sonatas in my head to ease the passing of time; then the Bach suites; then the Brahms Double Concerto. To add a touch of variety, when I had been through the Brahms,

I returned to the beginning and resolved to follow it again but this time through the second flute part. I have a photographic memory and having read the score on a few occasions I had committed most of the orchestral parts to heart. It was amusing to imagine myself as second flute, and I daresay it did me good to see the piece through the mind of that instrument: no doubt the knowledge would add some extra small something to my interpretation next time I played the piece. I remember once, during one of the mighty climaxes in Berlioz's Requiem, I imagined the silence of the third oboe who, alone of all the instruments, had three bars rest. That was in the days when, as a teenager, great orchestral climaxes so thrilled me that I nearly always spontaneously came in my undershorts. Prodigious spurts of jism would slide down my left leg and I'm sure could not always have gone unnoticed.

For a time I dozed and when I awoke it was on account of a curious sensation. There was a feeling of great warmth around my cock and balls, and the lightest touch of – could it be a tongue? I looked down, half-expecting to see my Master returned, or perhaps some boy he had sent me. But no, there was no one there. I must have been mistaken, or it was a vivid dream. Nevertheless, in my fully conscious state I continued to feel that my genitals were being gently caressed. Was it a breeze? A light warm wind flowing in from the summer's day and possessing something of the mischievousness of the season? It seemed too tangible for wind. Perhaps, miracle of miracles, my cock had learnt to pleasure itself! It was certainly stiffening now.

And then the moment was past. There was no more the fancied caress of moist breeze or tongue. The sensation must merely have been the lingering of a deliciously vivid dream. I gazed around that desolate chamber of shadows and silence. A torch hissed, its flame like a flag fluttered in a draught, and a handful of sparks drifted into the air.

Despite the absence of tangible sensation around my cock, it remained stiff and desperately in need of attention. In vain, I thrust my hips forward and fucked the air; but this only served to increase my desperation. I tried to twist my body and half-succeeded in an awkward backwards clambering of the wall in order that my right hand might help me. Briefly, frustratingly, my cock came to within an inch of the tips of my fingers and no more. Up until that moment the size of my organ had never been of the slightest concern; now, though, I longed for an extra inch or even two!

Was this the suffering that the Master had predicted? It certainly felt like it.

I exhausted myself in the ungainly struggle and soon felt sleep approaching once again.

I awoke to the sounds of a struggle. It seemed that far off I heard breaking glass and, closer, the banging of a door and muffled shouts both male and female.

The door to the torture chamber was suddenly kicked open and down the steps came a struggling tangle of bodies. My first reaction was, needless to say, embarrassment. Several among this group of strangers were women, and I had not been seen naked by any woman since I was a toddler. And how on earth would I be able to explain my presence here – let alone my condition! Supposing these people were servants of Maestro Cavallo? – would he thank me for revealing to them that it was he who had left me in this state?

The group, however, appeared not to notice me. They had a far more important matter on their hands. I watched in horror as the terrible events unfolded.

There were four women in the white, starched uniforms of kitchen maids of perhaps a century ago, and they were fighting a boy who was putting up a fierce resistance. The boy wore the white smock and baggy trousers of a Russian peasant from the last century. It was soon apparent that the women had the upper hand and they were tearing the clothes off the boy. In no time he was naked and they swarmed over him in a sexual frenzy. It was a sickening sight.

Then from above came a sharp clap of the hands, and a deep female voice called, 'Desist!'

The vile women immediately sprang away from the boy, leaving him sprawled naked on the stone floor.

At the top of the stairs stood a tall, imposing woman clad in a voluminous blue gown patterned with myriad yellow stars, suns, moons and comets. Her hair was tightly bound in a green scarf. Neither young, nor especially old, she was absolutely captivating. As she slowly descended into the room, I could not take my eyes from her. Here was surely my rescuer. In a flash of perspicacity, I imagined that this was another of the Master's games. This woman would rescue me and then command that I make love with the boy who had just been stripped naked before me. Perhaps she would watch us – or even join in – and I admit that my sexual arousal was intensified by the perversity of that thought.

Alas, this notion of mine was not to be. Far from it.

On reaching the bottom of the steps, the woman kicked off her shoes and, approaching the boy, traced a silk-stockinged foot over his smooth skin. He lay quite still; and, although my sight of him was partly obscured by shadow, I could see that even when her foot lingered long over his genitals he was not aroused.

In a swift, graceful movement, the woman undid a clasp and her gown slipped from her body. Underneath, she was naked. With another twist of her fingers her hair was released from its band and it fell long and black right down to her waist. She had a fine body and from behind, with her slim hips and tight, taut buttocks, she most resembled a young boy. I grew yet more sexually excited and now, rather than fearful lest I be seen, I began to long for attention. See me, release me, let me fuck! At that moment I felt ready to fuck anyone – man, boy or even woman!

But if these actions aroused a certain dormant bisexuality in me, they plainly had even a greater effect on the boy. For, when the woman got down on her knees beside him and took his generous cock into her mouth, it stirred immediately. Whilst she gave fellatio, the other women returned and kissed and fondled the rest of his body.

Finally, the woman stood up. Now, surely, it would be my turn! I coughed modestly, but went unheard.

'Chain him to the wall!' she commanded.

Her servants followed her order. They hauled the boy roughly to his feet and fastened his hands into manacles that were of the exact same position and design on the opposite wall as those which held me captive. We faced each other at opposite ends of the chamber. For the first time I could see him clearly. He was most beautiful with lovely, clear eyes, long curly hair and a well-proportioned body. It seemed to me that I had seen him somewhere before. Perhaps in a masturbation fantasy when I had sought to conjure the loveliest of all possible images. I smiled at him and lifted a hand in greeting, so far as I was able.

He looked at me. Or, rather, it seemed that he looked right through me because it was as if he could not see me.

Now knowing that I was certain to be seen sooner or later, I spoke, trying to be as casual as possible.

'Hello,' I said. 'What is this? One of the Master's games?'

No one took the slightest bit of notice. The lady put her cloak back on and, after giving whispered orders to her maids, sat in a chair and contemplated the captive boy. With her legs wide apart and her fingers stroking the top of her thighs beneath her gown, she was clearly determined to be provocative. The maids left the room.

I gazed again at the lovely boy. No wonder the woman had attempted to ravage him! He was unutterably beautiful, perfect in every way. His eyes fixed on mine – still, however, with that peculiar quality of not-seeing (was he perhaps blind? or perhaps he was merely pretending not to see me in order not to draw the attention of the predatory woman towards my vulnerability). I felt my insides melt and my stiff cock pulse.

Until, in a moment of recognition, I suddenly realised that I had, after all, seen this boy before.

This was Pavel. The boy whose portrait so enchanted me in

the gallery. But hadn't the Master said that Pavel had died over two hundred years ago? What was this? What was going on? Was this maybe a descendant of his?

'Pavel!' I called.

Oh, come on! I didn't care if I was seen! The woman was attractive to me. I would not struggle to avoid her attentions. And, besides, if I could distract her from him then I would clearly be doing him a favour.

'Pavel!' But my mouth was dry and my voice clearly not strong enough to be heard across the room.

Just then, the high door to the chamber opened once again.

The cohort of maids was back and with them another youth. This boy, however, was already naked and tightly bound around the chest with rope. Two maids led him by rope from the front and two held a rope behind.

The youth was dark-skinned and curly-haired. He had a fine, noble face with a hint of stubble, and his broad chest was dusted with hairs. His cock and balls hung low. There was something quite Hispanic about him, and I could easily picture him aboard a pirate ship in the Caribbean: naked, as now, but maybe with the sole addition of a bandana around his head.

A cruel smile flickered across the woman's face.

'I don't need you now, Pavel, darling. This is Manon. He is the stud I keep for whenever I want a fucking. He lives in my stables. Do you see the straw in his hair? I like him to sleep rough and to live rough because it preserves the animal in him.'

She rose to greet her stud and gently released him from his bonds.

'Manon is quite wild. My maids, you see, had to restrain him; but with me he is quite calm because whenever he sees me he knows he will fuck.'

Again her gown fell from her and she curled, sensuous as a snake, against her stud and ran her hands all over his body.

'Do you like what you see, Pavel? This is more your sort of thing, isn't it? You precious little fairy boy! Wouldn't you just love this bull to fuck your tight little arse! That would make you scream, eh? Ah, I can see how much you do like my stud! He excites you, doesn't he? Would you like him? Ask, and you shall be given. Don't be afraid to ask. He'll do anything for you. That's his job. Come on, Pavel. Say please and I will set you free and give you over to Manon. Isn't that what you want? Don't you ache for my prize stallion? Manon, help rouse our young friend a little further.'

She pushed Manon towards the young Pavel, and the stud got down on his haunches before the boy and proceeded to give him fellatio.

Never before had I heard such unrestrained moans of pleasure as those now emitted by the boy. I was all the more astonished – and excited – because, although aroused, he had been so cold and silent previously. I too began to groan. I was desperate now for some attention. Surely someone would hear me and release me? I wanted to be fucked senseless by Manon and as a prelude he could give me a blow-job in the way he was now favouring Pavel. But no matter how much noise I made, no one seemed to hear.

In a sudden, swift movement, the woman grabbed Manon by the hair and tore him away from Pavel, then she herself mounted the boy's erect organ. Her screams as she fucked against him were almost terrifying in their intensity, and neither did the cries of Pavel die away. It was clear that a base part of his character was savouring this perversity; and, when two of her maids unfastened his hands, he fell eagerly upon the woman. They sank to the ground and copulated with the intensity of animals. When they were both satiated – and it seemed that with every thrust both attained a fresh orgasm, or part of an orgasm – the boy rolled over and lay on his back exhausted. His cock, however, remained erect, and Manon crouched down to lick it clean. When he had done that, he did the same for the lady and, finally, mounted her. Once again ecstatic screams filled the chamber.

My frustration was huge. It was a physical ache. But it was only when I called out again, in as clear a voice as I could summon, and went again unheard, that I finally realised what the true situation was. Of course! How had I not understood the facts before?

The chamber was haunted. I was watching the actions of ghosts. That lovely boy was Pavel, and not merely a descendant. Did Signor Cavallo know of the chamber's being haunted? A cold sea water of absolute fear ran beneath my skin. Never had I been so afraid. It was appalling to be in the presence of the dead and be unable to escape. Would they remain for ever in this moment of bodily incarnation, or would they perhaps start to decay before my eyes? If I saw them at one moment of their physical lives, why not at another? Why not see them as they had been in their coffins, with worms in their eyes and maggots crawling from between their cold lips?

Was this the reason for my being kept here? To let me know the twin passions of extreme terror and desire? This was indeed a further limit of human experience; but, whereas previously I had always delighted in the experiences Signor Cavallo gave me, this time my emotions were very different. The desire was as bad as the terror: a yearning that could never be fulfilled, an utter emptiness. To gaze on the picture of a dead boy and fancy that one would have enjoyed sleeping with him is romantic and not unpleasant. But to see that boy in the flesh, as it were, and be accordingly aroused and know that any sexual act would be with a corpse is . . . I don't know what it is. It gave me an indefinable feeling, a sense I suppose of unutterable loss.

The players of that terrible scene gradually began to fade, confirming, if any confirmation were needed, that they were indeed not of this life; and, as they gradually went from me, I reached out. Afraid as I was, I still needed to possess, to touch, to feel my beloved Pavel. Let him kiss me and if his kiss meant that I too would return to the realm of the undead then so be it. I called out his name, and my voice was, as ever, unheard. All human striving is useless, all hope is futile. Life can only ever consist of absurd, pointless longing. *Sehnsucht* as the Germans say. Into my mind came the slow movement of the Elgar cello concerto. For the first time I felt as if I understood what had been in the composer's mind when he wrote that piece. Previously it had always seemed to me only a hymn of sad regret – comparable to the feeling that one experiences when returning to work following a long holiday or when taking leave, temporarily, of an old friend. Now, however, I saw that the music was imbued with a much more powerful force. Whole new layers of meaning were revealed to me. When last I had played the piece I had been as a child. Now I would know what to do when next I picked up my cello.

If there was ever to be a next time.

I began to wonder if Maestro Cavallo might have forgotten me. I was growing hungry and extremely thirsty. Was Maestro Cavallo a madman? How did I know? He was certainly crazy to abandon the world and live alone in this haunted castle. An international soloist with his pick of all the best things in life: why retreat to this desolate place of madness and regret? Beautiful and fascinating as it undeniably was it was surely not a place in which to spend one's entire life. How many boys had come here before me? How many other boys had he seduced into believing that they should be manacled naked to a wall and left alone in a torture chamber? If he was mad, then I was also a little crazy. Perhaps his plan was to starve me to death and then to fuck my corpse. Oh, don't think these thoughts! I railed against myself. Or maybe he would appear soon and give me a draught of poisoned water so that in death I would still be attractive.

It was the ghosts who had inspired my mind to think in this appalling direction. Great God, this was a terrible place!

I dozed and awoke, dozed and awoke. My strength was fading fast. Although I am young, I am an artist and do not have vast reserves of physical strength, except in my arms.

Then, at the very point when I had almost given up hope for good, and when I was urging my heart to stop beating in order that I be spared the agonies of slow death by thirst, I heard the creak of the door to the chamber.

I looked up. Fear once again swirled within me. If it was the

51

ghosts once more I would go mad. I would scream and froth at the mouth and howl like a mad dog.

But it was my Master. Dressed in his leather uniform, but without the mask, he progressed slowly down the steps. I gazed at him with love. I drank in the sight of him. Never, it seemed, had I loved anyone more.

Sternly he stood in front of me and raised one eyebrow.

'Master,' I managed to say with thick tongue and dry lips. 'I think I have accomplished what you set me here for. I have seen . . .'

He raised his arm and placed a hand against my lips. I was not to speak of what I had seen. I was not to speak.

Gently, he released me from the manacles and I fell gratefully into his warm, strong arms.

Nine

Ramon's Narrative
(continued)

I am not the sort of person who can recover easily from stress. Following my ordeal – and to this day I have no idea for how long it lasted – the Master carried me to my bed and there I rested and slept for many days and nights, disturbed only by Callipo who brought me plates of sliced fruit and water. Maestro Cavallo had only briefly mentioned his manservant in passing and, somehow, I had formed the impression that the fellow was an aged retainer. But this was not the case. Callipo was young, perhaps a little older than me, and had the appearance of a dashing cavalier with black hair in ringlets and a sweet, good-natured face: deep brown eyes and dimples in his cheeks. He wore a loose-fitting white blouse and black pantaloons. On his visits, however, I had not the strength to engage in the conversation, or flirtation, that I might have liked to do under different circumstances. I would sit up in bed, eat and drink like an automaton, and then fall back amongst my pillows and instantly return to a thankfully dreamless sleep.

One morning I awoke early. I rose and, naked, stood gazing out the window at the sloping lawn, the flower beds and the lake. Wreaths of mist swirled over the surface of the water and in them I fancied I saw strange shapes and figures. A peacock appeared from behind a rhododendron bush and, with characteristic jerky hesitancy, picked its way on to the lawn. A flock of white doves flew low over the garden. The smudgy yellow sun, obscured by frail cloud, rose slowly behind the broad casuarina tree, coating its branches with liquid gold.

I wanted to stand and gaze for ever, but I was not strong enough and returned to bed within a few minutes.

My period of convalescence ended one night during a great thunderstorm. I had been feeling somewhat recovered during that afternoon and had been sitting in the armchair reading an obscure choral work that I had found in manuscript form on one of the bookshelves lining my room. It was a bizarre piece, of immense length, scored for boys' choir, thirty flutes and percussion. The text was taken from a set of medieval lyrics concerning the licentious behaviour of monks and boys at a monastery in Pisa. I was engrossed both by the words and the delightful musical writing which was tuneful, inventive and witty. The composer, Benedetto Marcavalli, was alas unknown to me.

Whilst I read the score, distant thunder rumbled over the lake. I looked up once or twice and saw the surface of the water wrinkled like a cloth and breaking into white waves against the shore.

The music so captivated me that I did not hear Signor Cavallo enter the room until by a slight cough he identified himself.

'I see you have found the *Missa Ragazzi*.'

'It's wonderful, signor. I think it's a masterpiece. The scoring is so wonderfully intricate and ingenious!'

He inclined his head. 'Perhaps. It only ever had one performance, in Trieste in 1803. It ended in a riot when one flute player accused another of making eyes at his lover who was a member of the chorus. Their fight escalated until finally it involved the entire concert hall. All the parts were destroyed in the subsequent fire and now the only trace of the work that remains is that original full score which you hold in your hands.'

'But you must make a copy! Supposing this were somehow to be lost?'

'What would the world lose? No one knows the piece apart from myself. It simply sits on the shelf here, gathering dust.'

'The world would lose some of its potential!' I said.

'Ah, you misunderstand. That the work exists is enough for the world. It does not need to be performed. There is more to music than its tangible realisation – which is at best absurdly transitory. Simply by being, by sitting on my shelf unread and unperformed, the *Missa Ragazzi* does service for the world.'

'What can it do?'

'It can wait. It has its own patient power.'

'I don't understand.'

'Do you understand the moment of silence before you begin to play a Bach suite? In that moment, the piece may not after all exist. Who can prove that the player will perform it, that it will ever be heard again?'

'Yes, but the chances are . . .'

'Chances. Chances are not facts. What does the existence of a piece of music mean to most people? When it is played, they do not really hear it, not the thing itself; rather they hear the surface of it, the easy tunes. And then, when it is no longer being played, what is it to them but a few scattered meaningless fragments of melody drifting haphazardly through their minds, probably in an assortment of different keys and very likely with fistfuls of wrong notes. The *Missa Ragazzi*, a silent, perfect score, is as valuable to the world as is the tropical butterfly alighting now on a leaf in Borneo but unseen and unregarded by all sentient life. Music and butterfly, they quietly help to keep the universe in balance.'

'But . . .'

'Shush!' commanded Signor Cavallo as a fresh crack of thunder shook the windows. 'Don't try to understand just yet. Take it in stages. I came here just now because I thought you might be hungry. Are you quite recovered?'

'Perfectly.'

'I'm sorry that your time in the chamber proved such a trauma.'

'Yes,' I said. 'I have some questions.' Suddenly the memory of that terrible time came flooding back. 'Who was . . .?'

'Shush!' Signor Cavallo said again. 'If you have questions I will answer them later at the appropriate time. Not now. Now you must come with me.'

He held out his hand in order to assist me to rise. I had dressed in a green silk suit that I had found draped over the back of a chair. As I stood it rustled warmly against my bare skin. We suddenly found ourselves standing close against each other. The belt fastening my blouse fell to the floor and the loose cloth parted over my chest revealing my left nipple. For the first time, Signor Cavallo reached out and touched my breast. Was it to be now? Was this to be the moment when at last we would make love? With a simple movement he could easily slip the blouse from my shoulders. I imagined it falling gracefully, like a soft cloud, to the floor. I would yield myself to him without question or restraint. My body would be his to possess and teach in whatever way he so desired.

But he turned abruptly away.

'Come! It's time to eat.'

Once again I found myself being led through the labyrinthine passages of the *castello*, along corridors, down stairs, up stairs, through wide rooms. This time, however, in contrast to the route we had travelled before, every floor was carpeted and our progress was soundless without so much as the creak of a floorboard. The green silk blouse felt like a pleasant breeze flowing against my skin. We could still hear the distant rumble of thunder.

Presently we stopped before a set of double doors. Signor Cavallo produced an extraordinarily large key, unlocked them and swung them wide. The darkness within was so intense as to seem almost liquid: it might have flooded out in the manner of light. I took an involuntary step backwards.

We entered the room, not without a certain degree of trepidation on my part. There were malevolent spirits in this castle and I hated to step where I could not see.

Signor Cavallo closed the doors behind us. I felt myself swaying without sight or touch to guide my balance. I seemed to drift through the vast, empty but somehow intelligent silence of outer space. My skin was tense with the expectation of contact. Where was my Master? Near at hand or far away? Fear metamorphosed into desire. I was ripe for fucking and anxious to spill my own seed. At any moment I expected a touch that would at last mark the beginning of my sexual relationship with my Master.

Alas, that moment was yet to be.

'Ramon.' I heard Signor Cavallo's voice at a distance at last giving geometry to the room. From the tone I recognised a large room, probably with a minimum of furniture.

Signor Cavallo lit a candle.

And then another and another. It was a chandelier hung low. It seemed in the as yet frail and uncertain light as though an ancient painting were gradually being revealed. A moment in time forever in the past.

I saw, first of all, the side of his face, illuminated and golden. He looked more than ever like a wise and noble god. Then I could make out a plain long wooden table set with crusty bread, cheeses, bowls of green salad, olives, fish with disturbingly bright eyes, bottles of wine, goblets, plates patterned with the spare brush of a Japanese master: each stroke a sigh. Two high-backed chairs were placed at either end of the table. Each object, and part of an object, possessed tiny rags of flickering yellow.

Signor Cavallo pulled a cord, the glittering chandelier rose – a hint of sulphur filled my nostrils – and the shadows rushed to different positions in a great scurry of scattering darkness. As I had predicted, there seemed to be little other furniture in the rest of the large room, but there were paintings on the walls that I could faintly discern.

At Signor Cavallo's silent invitation I sat down. Callipo

appeared from nowhere, it seemed, and poured me a glass of wine. At the other end of the table Signor Cavallo raised his glass.

'To music!'

'To music!' I returned the toast.

The wine was remarkable, its rich white fruitiness conveying a sense of a long-ago Sicilian autumn: somehow I seemed to hear the distant voices of children and the bleating of goats on a far hillside.

I ate my fish, bread and salad ravenously. I had a wonderful hunger that matured into that most delightful of conditions, a hearty appetite, after my first few bites. I ate and drank myself into a state of wonderful contentment. All was right with the world. Here I was where I wanted to be, in a place with someone I loved. Callipo ensured that my glass never remained empty.

The meal was simple and unfussy and we chatted about trivialities. Signor Cavallo unexpectedly shared my passion for football and we talked about transfers and fixtures and the variable fortunes of Arturo Zippi: by coincidence our favourite player and, in my opinion, the greatest striker the world has ever known. Following the fish course, Callipo brought in bowls of fruit: apples, mandarins, papaya, lychees.

We sat back in our chairs, eating the fruit and sipping the wine.

Resting his elbow on the table and his chin in a notch made by his thumb and curled fingers, Signor Cavallo suddenly changed the subject:

'So you have met Lady Isabella?'

Wide-eyed, I tilted my head in silent question.

'Lady Isabella,' he continued, 'the monster who has trapped numerous moments of time in various parts of my home. Who ravaged poor dear Pavel.'

'Then it wasn't a dream? I saw things, you know, down in that chamber.'

'Of course you did. I'm sorry that you had to see such things, but it was part of your education. A great musician must see everything.'

'So it was Pavel? The boy in the portrait?'

'Worse things happened later. In another part of the castle there is a far more grotesque haunting. Perhaps you need not go there. We shall see. Lady Isabella lived in the castle, oh, when? two hundred years ago or thereabouts. She had insatiable appetites and was ultimately crushed to death by a bull she had had rigged in a harness and hoisted above her bed. Oh, don't laugh, it was a blessed occasion. She terrorised every young man within a range of a hundred miles. No one dared resist. And Pavel who, because of his nature, could do little other than resist, she had put to death. Or, rather, she executed him herself. That portrait of him as St Sebastian was painted from life, if that is the correct expression in this case. Lady Isabella fired the arrow that pierced his heart. She remarked afterwards in her diary that this was the finest, the truest consummation that she had ever experienced. She wrote, "As the arrow quivered from the bow I felt a similar shudder engulf my body more overpowering and glorious than that of the sexual climax." That marked the beginning of a new period of even greater terror. Like a monstrous black widow spider she copulated with a youth then murdered him almost immediately afterwards. Even Manon, her favourite, who you must have seen in the chamber, was not spared. Although in his case she regretted her action and had a wooden stake inserted into his penis so that she might fuck him after death. According to an account by her personal chaplain, she continued to have relations with Manon long after his body had started to decay. The more perverse her passions became, the greater her ecstasy. In other rooms, on certain nights, you may hear her screams of perpetual orgasm.'

There was a silence between us for a time, and I could not help but seize what might have been an opportunity.

'Master,' I said. 'I have been doing as you instructed. I have slept with Domenico and learnt many things, I have suffered physical pain and terror, I have learnt the meaning of *sehnsucht*. Surely now I am ready for the final stage. Surely now must be the time when we two will make love together.'

'No,' he replied, quite simply. 'Not yet. You have only just begun. There is much more that you have to learn.'

'But how do you know how much I've learnt already!' I protested. 'Give me a trial, and I can show you some tricks that will astound you!'

He laughed. I was offended at the time, but looking back I can see the naivety of my expression.

'No, I don't want to see your tricks. If I want to see tricks I'll buy a ticket to the circus. Or hang out on Times Square. The Bach C minor suite – which is the most important note?'

I was suddenly tired of his games. 'Why do you no longer perform?' I asked.

'Answer my question!' he snapped.

'I'm always answering your questions. Now you answer one of mine. You suddenly renounced your career when you were at your prime. There was not a better cellist in the world. Why did you abandon everything and take to the life of a recluse?'

'I will answer your question. But not now. There will be a time for that. You must wait. And waiting, I know, is something that you find extremely difficult. Good. Sixty bars rest, four-four time, Adagio.'

I was about to say something, when I realised that he had commanded a silence. I complied. And in that silence I seemed to understand that my time in the castle was something like a long symphony with its periods of melody, rest bars, climaxes and quiet moments. Signor Cavallo was orchestrating life into music.

'In the jungle of central Africa . . .' Signor Cavallo's voice stole softly into the vacant soundless space. It was like the return, after the long bewildering absence, of the divine melody in the first movement of Tchaikovsky's violin concerto. One felt a mixture of relief, joy and blessed recognition. '. . . I have heard the singing of native people like a great organ filling a vast cathedral. Western music pales by comparison.'

He stopped speaking. Something extraordinary was about to be born into this pregnant silence.

Suddenly the air was filled with a gorgeous swarm of massed

singing. There must have been a thousand voices. Gentle but insistent and powerful waves of music ebbed and flowed. Strange echoes and parts of echoes reverberated in corners of the room like stray sparks from a fire; seconds clashed with the force of water breaking on stone. Cadences constantly restored balance only to have it upset again moments later. Water or light, the music was everywhere and overpowering. I stared at my feet, almost expecting to see skidding skeins of notes sliding across the floor. High thin threads of women's voices curled above complex, beautiful inner harmonies supported by a deep-flowing bass. And also there seemed to be – although I could not quite be certain – an accompaniment of piping forest birds and whirring insects. The music contained everything and was everything. I was in no doubt that I was hearing the music of the universe itself. When finally the wondrous noise came to an end, I sat in a daze, all my senses upside down.

'Now you are ready for the next stage,' Signor Cavallo whispered. 'Wild boy.'

Ten

Ramon's Narrative
(continued)

A strong hand took hold of my arm. It was Callipo. I looked questioningly at Signor Cavallo, but he continued to sip his wine as though nothing were happening.

Callipo led me from the room.

'Where are we going? Where are you taking me?'

He did not reply.

Presently, in yet another part of the castle with which I was not yet familiar we entered a white-tiled bathroom. Whilst he removed my clothes with his usual grim efficiency, I felt once more an intense desire.

'You must have some feeling,' I said, as he knelt beside me to remove my trousers. I swung my erect cock against his cheek, but he merely turned away. I did not believe that he was as cold as he made out. Why, after all, did he insist on undressing me? I was not helpless, and could do the deed myself easily enough. 'Come on, Callipo. Just once. Why don't we do it?'

'Signor Cavallo has forbidden me,' he said.

'Oh, but that makes no sense! We could do great things together and Signor Cavallo would never know. Please, Callipo! No, don't stand up! Just stay there. Suck my cock.'

'The signor would find out.'

As he spoke I felt his warm, moist breath upon the skin of my cock.

'He'll never know. How could he find out?'

'He knows everything. I don't want to lose this job. Please, Ramon. Let's do things his way. He knows what he's doing. And . . . And it's as hard for me as it is for you. Perhaps harder. Who knows? Tonight, Signor Cavallo has some extraordinary thing planned for you. You'll see. Have patience. You won't be frustrated by the end of this night, I promise.'

'So long as I don't have sex with you, I shall always be frustrated.'

'Nonsense!' he said scornfully.

But I could see, by the trace of the first smile I had ever seen him wear, that he was pleased at the thought.

Callipo moved away and began to fill the deep, square bath. I watched him as he poured in the bath oils and bubbles. Beneath his customary, shapeless white jacket and baggy trousers, he clearly had a trim, well-proportioned body. He tested the water with an elbow before pronouncing it ready for me.

As I stepped into the water, I asked what perhaps I should have asked long before. 'Tell me, Callipo, are you and Signor Cavallo lovers?'

'No, of course not! You know perfectly well that he has renounced love.'

'So he says. Only I can't quite believe it. How can anyone – least of all someone of Signor Cavallo's artistic, romantic temperament give up the pleasures of the flesh?'

Having only recently lost my virginity I suppose I was putting on a worldly, sophisticated air.

'You don't know him. The signor is a man of immense strength. If he puts his mind to anything, then he can do that thing. There are no limits to his power.'

Although I proffered the sponge to Callipo he declined to accept, so I soaped myself. Once I had finished washing and had dried, however, he took me over to a bench covered with a white cotton sheet, and bid me lie down. When I was comfortable, face down with my head resting on my arms, he began to massage me with a warm, sweet-scented oil. His hands were firm and sensuous, soothing the tensions in my muscles and spreading little sprays of pleasure throughout my body. When his fingers teased the sensitive, usually hard-done-by skin of my feet and toes I gave small gurgles of outright pleasure; and when, at length, he began to explore the crack of my arse I moaned. He turned me over. My desire for him was evident; but, apart from a rather cursory caress of this part of my anatomy, he paid no heed. If Signor Cavallo had iron will power, then his servant possessed no less a strength.

When the massage was over, I felt a new person. Perhaps that had been the purpose. I was about to be given a new identity.

Giving me a towel to wrap around my waist, Callipo took me through to an adjoining bedroom and sat me down at a dressing table. In the mirror I saw reflected a double bed and a harp. There were some watercolours on the walls. On the dressing table stood an array of cosmetics. My first thought was that Signor Cavallo had instructed Callipo to do me up in drag. I would not have been averse to the idea. The notion of becoming a pretty little señorita for a night was attractive. And what sort of man might have wanted to seduce such a señorita? The thought of being fucked by a straight man was desperately exciting.

But it soon became clear that this was not to be my fate.

Callipo sat next to me and drew me close in between his wide-spread legs. First of all he applied a little mascara to my eyelashes and brows. It was the work of a few moments, but when he was done I glanced at my reflection and could see that even in so short a space of time he had added a fresh touch of sensuality to my beauty. Then he selected a blue ochre marker and traced a curved line stretching from the bridge of my nose to my right jaw. He repeated the decoration on my left side. During the next half an hour, Callipo painted my face and chest with intricate patterns of red, blue and yellow. When he had completed the work to his satisfaction he tied a bandanna around my head. I had become an Indian.

'A forest Indian,' said Callipo.

He asked me to stand and, removing my towel, replaced it with a loin cloth.

'There!' he said. 'Now you are ready! You are an Indian of the Telameni tribe. They live in the Amazonian rainforest. On reaching manhood, every boy is taken out into the forest where he must fend for himself for several days. Eventually, older men of the tribe start out to look for him. When they find him they initiate him into sexual intercourse. A boy can only become a true warrior when he has the seed of a man planted inside him.'

'Sounds good to me!' I said lightheartedly, but Callipo frowned at my joke.

'This is serious,' he said.

'Why? What are you planning to do? – ship me out to the Amazon and dump me there?'

'You'll find out.'

Suddenly, without the least prior warning, he pierced my left nipple with the pin of a gold ring. He then pricked me to the side of the nipple, so that my flesh itself was torn. Fierce pain jaggered through me and I let out a huge scream.

'Shut up!' commanded Callipo, and he slapped my face with such ferocity that I was astounded into silence. 'What's physical pain? Can't you bear it?'

'No,' I said, the tears streaming down my face.

'You're smudging the fucking paint!' he cursed.

I ran from him, then. I could stand this life no longer. I had come to Signor Cavallo on a pilgrimage. I had hoped for masterclasses in the art of cello playing and gentle lessons in lovemaking; but what I had received instead was torture, ghosts and sexual encounters with strangers – which, however wonderful, was not what I truly wanted. And now this ghastly physical and verbal assault from the one person I had begun tentatively to think of as a friend. It was all too much for me. I wanted to go home. So what if I would never make it as a musician of the first rank? I was still good enough to pass as an average concert soloist. I didn't need any more of Signor Cavallo and his castle of nonsense.

I ran out of the room and fell headlong into the arms of Signor Cavallo. I struggled to break free, but he held me firmly.

'There, there!' he soothed, as I began to calm down. He stroked my hair. 'What is it? What's the matter?'

I sniffed and swallowed, unable to speak. Now I started to cling to him. I wanted to remain buried in his arms for ever. This was the only peace I knew.

Gently, he detached himself and, holding me at arm's length, dried my tears with a glowing white handkerchief. There was, I saw, blood on his white shirt. I looked down at myself. My chest was streaked with blood.

'We are only doing what is necessary,' he whispered. 'You do understand that? All this pain and suffering is not meaningless. You are working towards a goal, and that goal is worth it. You do understand?'

I shook my head in bewilderment. 'It's just . . .' I was lost, not knowing how to complete the sentence.

'Not like the music academy in Madrid?'

I was unable to share in his joke, which he obviously found very funny.

'I'm sorry,' he said.

Callipo came up behind me and put a hand on my shoulder.

'We have to go.'

I looked beseechingly at the Master. He stared into my eyes, and I melted under their hypnotic power.

'Go with Callipo. It's for the best. In time you will understand. What are a few moments of discomfort compared to the lifetime of glory that you will thereby attain? Go.' And then in a whisper that was more air than sound, 'Wild boy.'

I stood perfectly still as Callipo lowered a rope noose around my neck.

The storm was at its height when Callipo led me out into the garden. The rain, however, was warm and because I was naked apart from the small cloth around my loins I was spared the discomfort of wet clothes sticking to my skin. Lightning illuminated the trees and shrubs making them appear brittle and insubstantial.

We walked to a far part of the garden that I had not previously visited and there came upon a magnificent glasshouse. It was an extraordinary structure, as large as a palace: indeed, from what I could see in the flashes of lightning, it most resembled old pictures I had seen of the Crystal Palace in London: an architectural hymn to glass.

We climbed a series of steps, guarded by stone lions, to the front entrance. There, Callipo removed my noose and bid me enter. Alone.

'But aren't you coming with me?'

'Of course not. This is your trial. Go on. Go in. Search carefully and you will find a place to sleep and plentiful food and drink should you need it. And whatever comes, you must accept willingly. Remember . . .'

But whatever it was that he desired I should remember was drowned out in a mighty crack of thunder. When the noise died away, I turned to ask him to repeat himself; but he had gone. I was alone. Ultimately we are always alone.

I crossed myself, muttered a speedy prayer to the Virgin and to Giacomo of the wood doves, my patron saint, and entered.

A complex scent of ripe fruitiness and decay greeted my nostrils and the warm, misty air had a delightful quality of enclosure. The rain thrummed on the roof and it was pleasant to feel protected from it. I stood close by the door for a long time, fearing to move from the security of escape. The lightning revealed a jungle of huge, thick leaves and creepers, white flowers like lilies, a path. And when there was no lightning I saw bursts of phosphorescent from what must have been fireflies. As my senses became more accustomed to the different circumstance, I began to hear the steady whirring and clicking of insects and a pak-pak pak-pak-pak as of wood on wood.

I knew that, sooner or later, I would have to step deeper into this jungle; but how real was it? Were there wild animals? Might there be jaguars, lizards, snakes? Could I trust Signor Cavallo not to harm me? How could I be certain that he was not mad when most of his actions thus far might easily be construed as those of someone insane?

As I stood there, immobilised by doubt, it seemed that I heard, beyond the rain and the insects, a long drawn-out cello tone and in my mind's eye I saw once again the deep, peaceful blue of his own steady gaze. I had to trust. He was my Master and would take care of me. I need fear no evil.

I ran my hand over my chest and, feeling the congealed blood, my mind became aware again of the pain near my nipple. That pain, ironically, gave me strength. I had survived physical pain, my body was streaked with blood: I was strong, a warrior. Nothing could harm me. Wild boy.

So I took my first cautious steps into the jungle. I followed the twisting path deeper and deeper into the unknown. Soon, I knew there was no turning back.

As I walked, I sensed that there were eyes watching me from behind the trees. I heard the crack of a twig, the shuffling of leaves. And once it seemed that I heard the steady, shuffing sound of breathing.

Outside, the storm died away. The thunder became more distant. A thin yellow moonlight spread over the forest giving everything the quality of an ancient sepia print.

I grew tired. After all, I was not long recovered from my last ordeal and the meal I had eaten together with the wine had a natural soporific effect. Searching for a place where I might rest my weary limbs, I was overjoyed to find the perfect spot. A bower, it was, with a roof made from banana leaves, palm-woven matting on the floor. I crouched down to enter and brushed against a wreath of flowers that gave off a frail sweet scent.

Gratefully, I lay on the mat, rested my head on my hands and, curled into the safe comfort of an embryo, was instantly asleep.

I awoke into a gorgeous rush of birdsong and light. Stepping out of my bower I felt like the first man on earth experiencing the first morning of consciousness. Naturally I was erect and, removing my loin cloth, pissed through my erection on to the forest floor, curving backwards the while into a great stretch of my limbs.

I was hungry. Was I to be expected to go hunting for breakfast? Hearing the sound of trickling water, I went in its direction and came upon a small stone fountain beside the path. Bending down to drink, I saw, spread out on a large, thick, rubbery banana leaf, some food: an orange, a papaya and a small cloth bag containing nuts. I sat comfortably with my back in the hollow of a great tree and ate the handsome repast. Looking around, it was easy to forget that I was in a glasshouse: all I could see was vegetation, and the dense mass of birdsong was all that one might expect from a tropical forest. Through the great swirl of sound, one could make out occasional more individual warbles and a high piping *sees-seees sees-seees!* I searched for these creatures and eventually saw two tiny, vividly colourful birds perched side by side on a high branch. Then, as my eyes became more accustomed to their surroundings, I began to distinguish camouflage from leaf and flower and gradually made out parrots, cockatiels, a toucan and numerous other small birds.

Fully rested and fed, it came time to explore.

Who had Callipo said that I now was? An Indian of the Telameni tribe. And this adventure was part of an initiation rite. There were others, then, in this forest. Perhaps I had not wholly imagined those eyes on the previous night. Were those same eyes watching now?

I spent the next few hours wandering at random in the jungle. It was a remarkable place, full of unexpected delights: there were more birds, flashes of rainbow colours appearing high in the tree canopy, or fussing amongst leaves on the forest floor; large butterflies, blue like scraps of fallen sky, or else yellow, red and green; a tree liberally fruited with oranges, and another hung with a ripe fruit that looked like a cherry but tasted of strawberry. By a pond, I crouched and watched a troop of iridescent dragonflies hovering over white and yellow waterlilies and dabbing the surface of the water at regular intervals. In the water swam numerous fish and by the water's edge toads rasped a throaty call.

It was impossible to judge the area of the forest. I kept discovering new paths and fresh vistas; and, when I did come up against the glass, the view outside also seemed to consist of trees. This was a forest inside a forest. Despite all my efforts, I was unable to locate the door wherein I had entered.

From time to time I came upon fresh offerings of food. Like a grazing animal, I ate these on the spot before continuing on my way.

The sun was high in the sky when, in a clearing, I spied two boys playing some sort of dice game in the dust. They were, like me, forest Indians, and wore only loin cloths. Had they been sent to hunt me down and put me through the initiation promised? Meaning to stay hidden, I was dismayed when the cracking of a twig announced my presence. They looked up immediately. I ducked down, but knew that I had been seen.

'*Tana la bayan taka!*' one of them called. '*Tana la bayan taka!*'

Whatever the exact meaning of the words, the summons was obvious. I stepped out into the clearing.

They rose to greet me. They were in their early twenties, brown-skinned, painted and exceptionally beautiful. Their faces were round, in the manner of many Asians, and their dark eyes were of an exquisite almond shape. Both had long hair that trailed right down to their slim waists. If they were in the employ of Signor Cavallo they gave no sign of being anything other than natives of this forest region. It was not clear, initially, whether or no they were pleased to see me. A fly landed on the shoulder of one and started to drink a bead of sweat before he angrily brushed it aside.

When I was close, one of the boys – still unsmiling – reached out a cautious hand. He touched my face carefully, tracing the tips of his fingers over my stubble. His friend did likewise and it was then that I noticed that their bodies were completely hairless. They swapped comments in their obscure language. When they began an examination of my entire body, so genuine seemed their apparent wonder that I began to feel as though this was not, after all, part of the scheduled plan. Surely I, too, was supposed to be of their tribe? If they had been briefed properly, this sense of amazement at my Western features surely would not have formed part of the script?

Crouching, one of the boys removed my loin cloth. His delicately probing hand stroked behind and around my balls and up gently into my arse crack, then back to my cock which he began to massage gently. The other boy moved behind me and, bidding me spread my legs and bend forward slightly, began to lick inside my arse with a tongue of such ingenuity and delicacy I could not help but let out an involuntary groan of pleasure. Meanwhile his friend, having secured the desired erection, began to nibble the side of my cock with pristine white teeth.

Now appeared another Indian. This man was obviously much older and a strapping figure with a leather loincloth and a headdress of brilliantly coloured feathers. His face bore the marks of ancient scars. He stood at some distance watching us, before removing his loincloth and headdress and coming over. Pressing his erection hard against my side he seized my head somewhat roughly and bit into the sensitive skin of my neck. Thus assailed in my most erogenous area, I squirmed and cried out and, had the boy giving me fellatio not removed his mouth at the crucial last moment, I would have spilt my load there and then. When he was done with my neck (he must have left it black with lovebites) he kicked aside the boy who was giving me a rimming and, without further grace, pierced my arse with his long, thick rod.

For a moment I stopped breathing. Pain and ecstasy mingled in equal measure. I wanted this moment to end, I wanted it to go on for ever.

'Please!' I gasped, meaninglessly.

The man did not begin the rhythm of fucking immediately, but waited awhile as if gathering his strength. He bit the back of my neck, sucking and tearing at the skin. The two boys stood either side of me, watching my face carefully and holding me firm in my bent position.

Then the man began to fuck. I gazed at the boy on my right side with an expression of awed wonder and he returned a look of equal puzzlement. Although the fucking began gently enough, it quickly gathered pace. Soon the man was pounding into me with heavy bull-like grunts and I could feel his balls slapping against my arse. The boys had to hold me steady to prevent me toppling over. They kissed and stroked me tenderly, murmuring unknown words of reassurance in my ear.

Eventually, the man pulled out. With strong arms he turned me round and forced me to my knees before him. I needed no invitation to suck his cock and, as I did so, I was joined by one of the boys and we worked on either side of the massive tool. The other boy stood tongue-kissing the man who worked his cock furiously. It was this boy who came first with a series of thin, fierce spurts and a high, aching moan. Next came the man with string after string of jism shooting into the air. Finally, my cocksucking companion and I rose with mouths pressed together and tongues intwined and masturbated each other until simultaneous climaxes juddered through our bodies, drenching our fists, cocks and thighs in plentiful rich come.

The Indians disappeared into the forest whilst I, lulled by the birdsong, sank exhausted through sexual effort, curled up on the dusty floor and fell asleep.

In my dream I was the innocent Telameni youth sent out into the forest to lose his virginity and become a man. I raced through the shadowy forest, clutching a bow and arrow. My bare skin was dappled with flickering light. Spying a bird high in the branches of a tree I took aim with my bow and fired. The bird fell dead at my feet.

Then I was close by a river. A group of boys was swimming in the clear water, splashing and wrestling. I longed to join them, but knew I could not. Then, close at hand, I spied two boys who had separated from the rest. They were seated side by side on a flat rock and caressing each other with gentle hands. As I watched them kiss and stroke, I was filled with a sense of overwhelming sadness and lust. Dreams do not bother with preliminaries. Suddenly, my cock was buried deep in soil and I was fucking the earth with all my might. And now the Indian who had fucked me earlier was on top of me, his root tightly inside my arse, occupying my whole being. This was my initiation. I was to be filled with the seed of a man and would thus become a man. A drum beat a steady rhythm in time with the man's pulsing inside of me and my pulsing inside of the earth. There were cries all around, from the boys on the rock, the birds in the trees, the man inside me and from myself. We were all one, united with each other and with the copulating rhythm of the universe. There was nothing else but to be and to fuck, to fill with seed and to be filled with seed. The man was so strong, so overpowering I could only fuck in time with his own thrusts. This was all that mattered, this small tight world that was for this moment (that was eternity) everything. As the pain increased, so did an extraordinary profound joy. The man pumped faster and faster. I knew the time was fast approaching when he would release his very essence into me. I felt the shudders rippling through his body in the long seconds before his orgasm erupted into me, and they set off my own climax. He howled like a wild stallion, jerking crazily into my body, the warm come filling my insides as my own come was filling the earth itself.

I awoke. My cock, pulsing and stiff, had ejaculated on to the soft earth. Idly, I rubbed my finger in the jism, consciously burying the seed. So vivid had been the dream, I felt too as though there were seed inside me, and I looked around to see if my lover was actually nearby. Of course, I was alone.

Warm, ripe and full of seed I drifted back to sleep.

There was music.

Or was it? I could not be certain. I sat up. The song of the birds was rich as ever, a glorious tapestry of woven sound threaded with sighs and pipings and whistles. There was a raucous cackling and a sharp crack of wings. A careful repeated fluting of three notes repeated over and over was especially charming. But, beyond all that, another sound insinuated itself. Something about this particular sound suggested that it emanated from a human source. It was a tapping, as of wood on wood, in harmony with the birds, but also standing a little outside. I remember in my student days when I used to play in an orchestra, often the sound of my fellow musicians breathing or the soft shuff of their clothes whilst they bowed would seem to me as much a part of the music as the score itself. This dry tapping had the same effect: a part and yet different.

I went in search of the source of this music.

The glasshouse was a remarkable edifice. It must have encompassed at least two acres.

I came to a raised wooden platform on which was seated, cross-legged, an Indian man, his bare chest painted, long dark hair braided and tied with beads. He was beating out a rhythm on a small drum with his fingers. As I stood watching nearby, a boy came up and, sitting beside him, started to play a nose flute. There was no melody as such, but I was entranced.

This is the song of the forest, I heard the voice of Signor Cavallo in my head. *Do you hear how perfectly it fits in, a natural part of creation. The rhythm, the tone, the harmonic balance. This is what we must learn. How music can place itself exactly into the heart of all things. So many Western musicians have lost this Art. The music plays in the dry concert halls before the dry audiences; but it is a dead thing: a simulacrum of what it should be. Listen to the Indians. How they play without effort and consequently how their music captivates us and seems to guide us to some understanding of the life source itself. Listen and learn, Ramon.*

Time had no meaning here. I listened for a period until I felt it was the moment to move on. I walked slowly away.

And found a door, outside of which stood Callipo. I almost turned back, not wanting to leave this enchanted forest; but he shook his head and beckoned me forward.

'You can never turn back,' he said, as I stepped out into the still warm but less steamy atmosphere of a Piedmont late afternoon. 'Remember Orpheus.'

Even the trees came to life when they heard Orpheus play his lute. I had always known the story; but only now did it begin to make sense. The trees came to life because, when Orpheus played, they *were* the music.

Eleven

Signor Cavallo's Narrative

The next time I heard Ramon play, I knew that we were on the right track. It was three in the morning. I do not always sleep well and had been sitting at the table in my room pondering a particular chess problem that had puzzled me for years, when I heard the sound of Bach. The music seemed to be offering a tentative suggestion – not, alas, the answer to Kuchinsky's gambit – but rather a hint as to the careful ordering of life. *Follow this pattern* the music seemed to be saying, *and all will be well.* There is nothing that cannot be found in the Bach suites for solo cello.

I sat back in my chair and listened.

Then, without apparent thought, I moved a knight on the chessboard, and the problem was solved. Oh, Herr Bach, your range extended to that small corner after all!

Was Ramon ready for me? I gazed into the candle. A yellow flame flickered around a tiny brown heart. Was he ready? Or was it simply my lust that was urging me now to go to him and take him as I had been wanting to do from the very first? If it was simply lust then I would have to subdue that instinct. Only if Ramon and I were united when he was fully ready would his musicianship truly benefit. A consummation too soon and something precious, albeit ineffable, would be lost for ever. Quite simply I did not know what to do. His playing was near perfect. He had learnt a great deal in his time at the Castello Caccini. I had never heard Bach played like this before, and yet I knew that it was the only way that Bach should be played; all other interpretations – my own included – seemed blasphemy by comparison. Could such playing be bettered yet further? Dared mortal ears hope for more before the very gates of Heaven? Would the gods become jealous if Ramon took so much as another step towards perfection?

I took the candle and went along the corridors to Ramon's room.

It was obviously not possible to knock and interrupt the music, so I entered his door as silently as I was able.

My lovely boy was sitting playing in the very centre of the room. He was naked. If it were possible to make love to a musical instrument, this was what he was doing. He had lit candles all around the room, and the gentle light and soft shadows seemed to wrap the music in a gentle embrace.

I sat on a high-backed, elegantly carved eighteenth-century chair, splayed one leg at an angle and rested my arms on the sides.

Ramon looked at me but his face betrayed no sense of recognition. Was he lost already to the gods? This sometimes happens to the very greatest artists. They reach such a pinnacle of perfection they no longer have any need for the usual stuff of human existence. Ramon may have reached a point where he no longer needed me after all. Perhaps a part of me was relieved as well as heartbreakingly disappointed.

The music finished and one understood the true purpose of all music: to make silence intelligent. The silence in which we both sat now seemed vibrant with all truth, all understanding. This was the silence of deep space between the stars; the silence of the moment before creation; the silence of the first morning before the first intelligent cell of evolution made the first purposeful sound. When did the first man speak? And what was that word?

When did the first man consciously utter the word 'love'? To exist! What a fantastically impossible concept that is! How can we ever take it for granted? We exist and every extra moment that we can wrench from life is a privilege. And if any one of those moments contains love then we can say that we have lived life to the full.

'Maestro!'

It was I who uttered that word.

Ramon's eyes met mine and he shook his head slightly.

'Maestro,' I repeated.

'No,' said Ramon.

There was a long silence, then Ramon said, 'If you will forgive me, Maestro, but I know that I do not yet deserve the appellation. Forgive me if I suggest that perhaps something is clouding your judgement.'

He was right. My critical faculties were impaired by the fact of his beauty. I was overcome by the combination of fine playing commingled with the extreme loveliness of the boy. The playing was great, but it was not yet the greatest. It was getting there – almost impossibly close – but not yet there.

So that now should have been the time when he and I would make love. But I had spoilt that moment by succumbing to maudlin emotion. Whilst I was in that state I could do him no good, no matter the lovemaking skills I might impart.

As Bruckner once behaved before Wagner, I got down on my knees.

'Please, Maestro,' Ramon said softly. 'It is not for you to do this.'

He was right again. I was exposing my weakness. I returned to my chair.

'When I was your age,' I said, 'I was fêted in every city in the world from Rome to Paris to New York to Nairobi. Everywhere I went people threw garlands at my feet. Presidents gave speeches in my honour, the most beautiful women proposed marriage, the loveliest boys offered me their beds. If I knew in my heart that I did not deserve such honour I said nothing. Who would have done? The public loved me, other musicians loved me – great musicians. Herbert von Karajan himself said – oh, but I think I've told you that already. Only one or two people really knew that I failed consistently to reach the heights that were ascribed to me, and their writing was dismissed as sour grapes. I might have become great, of course; but for that I would have had to have gone into retreat for many years. And once you have tasted the joy of worldly success it is an addiction that cannot easily be abandoned. As a young man in my twenties I was never going to do that. So I carried on. Books were written about me, there were TV documentaries and countless magazine articles. I was attractive and giggly and self-deprecating. I hosted a game-show in Nebraska and for a time there was a whole cable TV channel in New York devoted entirely to me. I wrote the scores for two movies. So I became very rich. And the richer and the more famous I became the further I retreated from true Art.

'You asked me once, Ramon, what was the reason behind my suddenly abandoning my career and sloping off to live in this remote castle. I can now tell you why. I was in Cremona. It was a holiday and I was with Christian, a pretty Portuguese lover of mine. He was a devout Catholic, which meant that he knew no boundaries in the acts of love so long as he could always confess them on the following Sunday. Roman Catholic priests, I'm sure, have the material to make several fortunes out of writing erotic, as well as Mafiosi, fiction! When we travelled, Christian and I made a point of visiting every chapel and every church. I myself never abandoned the faith, although I was never fervent. Anyway, one time, we were in a tiny chapel. It was a Wednesday morning as I recall and blazing hot outside. In the chapel, however, it was deliciously cool. I was sitting in a pew, Christian beside me praying on his knees, when a boys' choir filed in and embarked on their practice. The music was exquisite, at first, if unremarkable. Then began the *Miserere* of Allegri. You know the piece: the choir sings a melody whilst high above soars a descant treble. If the boy hits the right notes the effect is always wonderful; but this time the singing had about it a purity, a sense of the very divine. This I knew, in a moment of epiphany, was what all music aspired to be, and what it should be and could be in the interpretations of the greatest performers. And as I knew this, I also understood that I had blown my own chances of great achievement. I had ripened too young. Gone too far too quickly. I was ruined. Knowing what I might have attained, and therefore what was for ever lost, I broke down in tears. And never again performed in public. CAVALLO SUFFERS NERVOUS BREAKDOWN! was the headline in the world's press. No, my whole previous life had been one of nervous breakdown. My career was over. I was thirty-three years old. But, with my tears, I entered at last a time of sanity.

'In you, Ramon, I see the self that I have lost. Play me some more.'

'You stopped your whole career because of that one moment?'

'Of course. Nobody would have understood, so I did not tell them. But you, Ramon, you understand, don't you? You are the only person I have ever met who could possibly understand. Tell me that you understand.'

Ramon nodded slowly.

'Play me some more,' I whispered again.

But instead of obeying, Ramon laid his cello aside and started towards me. His pretty, slender penis was already beginning to become erect and I was momentarily paralysed with awe. Once again I felt the urge to fall to my knees. Sheer lust swirled beneath my skin.

No. I was made of sterner stuff. If once I had had the courage to abandon an entire career on the altar of true Art, I knew that despite my advanced years my devotion to that Art had not lessened any. The time was not yet right for this.

'Not yet!' I held up my hand. 'Stop! Stop in the name of God!'

Nothing, however, was going to make him stop.

I rose quickly and ran from the room. Once outside, I had the presence of mind to lock the door behind me.

★

The next day I ordered Callipo to take Ramon and lock him in a high tower. There was to be no furniture in his cell, aside from a straw mattress, and he was to be allowed neither books nor music. He must also be deprived of his cello. The one thing to keep him company would be a canary in a cage. Let him learn something from the sweet singing of this creature. The canary sings all the sweeter when it is imprisoned.

The truth was, I felt lost and desperate and confused. I knew, in my heart, that Ramon was nearly ready for me; but I did not know what the next stage in his development should be before the time would be ripe for our making love. He had been through pain and suffering, wildness and excess; he had had wonderful sexual experience. His playing now reflected this, but there was still a certain gaucheness in his execution, a lack of some fundamental essence the like of which I could not exactly pinpoint. So. What next? What now?

The answer came to me, as do the solutions to most of life's problems, in a dream.

In my dream, I saw Ramon playing in the courtyard of the Castello Caccini, and around him were positioned eight small stones, shaping a mandala. I knew – one always knows in dreams! – that the layout of these stones was not accidental: it had teleological significance; they were placed in a certain pattern for a reason. I once studied such matters in Alexandria, and learnt, for instance, the means to decipher the patterns of the flight of birds and the correct interpretation of the movement of leaves in wind. My teacher, Father Abdurrahman, an ancient, bearded Druse who had spent most of his life in a cave in the Syrian desert, believed that one day, when all the people on earth were, by chance, arranged in exactly the right positions, the Great Transformation would suddenly come about. Peace or holocaust he could not exactly say; but he tended to believe that it would be peace. The slightest deviation from the right position, how-ever, and nothing would happen. With great hilarity, he recalled how, twenty-five years previously he had predicted such a moment for the twenty-second of September 1962 at 3.12 p.m. At 3.11 and 50 seconds p.m. a small child was distracted by a pigeon and chased it across a square in Tangiers (my Master was there at the time) and all was lost! Never again, he said, would he make a prediction. Predictions were for charlatans. Teleology can teach us the correct understanding of the present; it cannot tell us anything exact about the future.

But back to my dream. As I say, there was Ramon, wearing a loose-fitting linen suit, playing amongst stones, when a skein of notes, like a magic carpet, swept through the air and under my feet and carried me up high above the clouds. Father Abdurrahman had taught me about magic carpets – oh, they existed, in the days before cynicism! – and I was unsurprised and unafraid.

The world beneath me was of toy villages and roads, picture-book sheep and cows. I was a child and therefore knew everything. An aeroplane flew close by and the passengers gazed at me without interest: there goes another cellist on a musical stave. What's the key? G Major. No, you fool, it's E minor – look at the D sharp!

Below me there appeared three rivers winding their way through a town of red rooftops and church spires. I recognised the Marienkirche where J.S. Bach had worked for twenty-seven years. So this was Leipzig! I knew the city well, having made several pilgrimages there in my youth. Were we going to stop? No. My carpet swung southwards again. Soon we were approaching another German city. I knew this one also. That opera house! It was Bayreuth, of course, home of Wagner, second only to Bach in musical greatness.

On I travelled. To London, where Orlando Gibbons, who was the first to write great music for the viol, the noble ancestor of our violoncello, is buried. To Cremona: the town of Stradivarius. To Zaire – where the music of certain tribes fuses in perfect harmony with the music of nature. To the Arctic. What were we doing here? It took me some time to puzzle out this one, until it came to me that here could be found the most perfect silence: the ultimate purpose of all music, the ultimate purpose of everything. And on to a little village in Spain. Again, I could not immediately see the purpose in the music's taking me here until, through the windows of a mean, adobe house, I saw a small child struggling through a series of scales on the cello. This had to be where Ramon was born.

Finally, my magic stave whirled around in a presto whizz and I saw, in the distance, that city which even in real life seems to belong to a dream. A shimmering blur shivering into cautious existence as a mirage in the desert. Domed roofs, campanile, bridges . . . Venice. Of course. And then I knew. I knew what had to be done.

When I awoke, I was filled with a certain melancholy mingled with deep happiness.

I visited Ramon in his tower. He was seated cross-legged on the floor, meditating. Dusty motes of light swirled in from the narrow barred window and caressed his bare chest. The canary was silent, its cage covered with a black cloth. Ramon had been in this room for nearly a week. I had not visited him in all that time, for fear of being seduced and destroying everything.

Despite the heavy clanking of the bolt, Ramon had not appeared to be aware of my entrance and I had to cough discreetly several times and say his name aloud before finally he opened his eyes and looked up at me. Oh, those liquid black eyes! One cannot only drown in substance!

'Ramon.'

He did not return my cautious smile.

'You are not here for a punishment. It is only part of your education. The song of the canary . . .' I ventured rather feebly. 'And the chance to meditate . . . I hope it is helping. Callipo has been looking after you, I hope?'

He raised an eyebrow. A rather coarse gesture which I did not much care for.

'If you have any complaints, please tell me.'

'None,' he answered.

'My instructions for your food were perhaps a little strict?'

He had been on a bread, water and fruit diet.

'No problem.'

'Anyway, Ramon, I have come to tell you that your time in this room is now over. I hope it has been of use to you – and to me. Now I think you are ready to move on to the next stage.'

By the changed light in his eyes I knew the direction of his thoughts. How it hurt me to dispel them!

'You must go on a journey. A long journey. When you return, then you and I will embark together on the final stage of your education.'

So I told Ramon my dream and what I believed he had to do.

'There is a place in Venice. It is an academy of excellence where the very greatest artists may be trained. Entry to this academy is strictly by invitation only, but I have the right connections and I know that you will be admitted.'

He would have to make a pilgrimage to the Academy of the Silver Mandala. There, he would be taken through the rigorous last stages of his initiation. If he passed, he would be awarded the Silver Mandala, and with this he could return to me. If he failed . . . I would never see him again.

Even as I spoke, I wondered whether, pass or fail, he would ever return. I was sending him out into the world where he would meet so many other men and potential lovers. Perhaps one of these would capture his heart and he would choose to follow the path of love rather than true Art. He might never even make it to the Academy. And who would have blamed him? Take him now! urged the voice of the devil in my ear. Take him whilst he is here with you and willing. More than willing. Shaft him right here on the floor of his bare cell. Or do you never want to hear those high cries of orgasm squeeze from between his soft lips? Can your precious Bach stand any comparison by the glory of the moment of sexual consummation? But on I spoke, giving no indication of the turmoil going on in my mind.

Naturally, he was full of questions. What was this place? This 'Academy'? He had never heard of it. Had I ever been there?

'Alas, no,' I admitted. 'Although I was once invited. Had I

gone, had I taken up the challenge, perhaps I . . . But the world is full of ifs.'

'But what happens there? What is it all about?'

'Ramon. Your time with me has been an apprenticeship. You have been learning how to inform your Art with a deeper wisdom. In Venice they can take you on to the very last stage. I cannot tell you what your training will involve because, quite simply, I do not know.'

'But what is this place? Who goes there?'

'Very, very few artists and musicians go there. Perhaps just ten in a hundred years.'

'What?'

'But those who do go, and pass the trials, become the fabled Greats in the artistic pantheon.'

'Name one!'

'I cannot.'

'It's crazy! You're crazy! Locking me away here! Proposing I go to some asylum in Venice! I want to go home!'

'You have always been free.'

His next words, however, proved how wrong my last words to him actually were.

'How can you be sure that they will accept me?' he asked.

He was never free, but always a slave to music.

'I have the right connections. A word from me and I know they will not turn you away.'

'I have to know what will happen to me there! I mean, is it a formal music academy?'

'No. It is an institution dedicated to musical excellence, but very different from what you might consider a music academy. Your education will continue along the lines begun here. Your time here will stand you in good stead.'

'And what if I refuse?' He spoke the words, but I knew they were mere form.

'I can't make you go; but it would be a pity if, after all that you have been through, you were to give up now.'

'Supposing it's all mumbo-jumbo? What I have been doing

here, what I may do there? What can any of this have to do with music?'

'What can anything we have been doing connect with music in a literal sense? Music, Ramon, is inherently absurd. A bunch of sound that moves the spirit! That inspires men to love, to go to war, to cry. Mere sound can transport one into the realms of joy. It can make one understand, in a profound sense, any situation. Music can bring one close to the presence of God. This mere sound makes sense of life. And yet it cannot be explained. Scientists may say, "Oh, it's this part of the brain that is attracted by music. Similar emotions can be triggered by electrical impulses." But that is not a wherefore. There never can be a wherefore. You cannot reason with music, it is far beyond that. So in the same way you cannot reason the ways in which those of us who are musicians learn how best to convey our Art. There are countless thousands of musicians who go to music schools and achieve perfect technicality in their playing, but only one or two reach beyond that technicality and show us the depths of feeling and emotion that had hitherto been denied us. Why? Never ask why. Reason is incommensurable with the problem. Reason can teach us nothing. I had thought you understood. Clearly you had not understood. Perhaps it is time for us to have no further contact. I tried to help you. I failed. Go from me!'

'Maestro!'

'Do not call me that! How many times must I tell you?'

'Venice?'

I went over to the window and looked out. Two swans flew low over the surface of the lake, and an aeroplane made a thin vapour trail high above. The plane crossed the face of the sun and became an insubstantial silhouette. On the grassy banks of the lake, Callipo was searching for duck eggs. My life would always return to three-thirty on a summer's afternoon in Piedmont.

'Venice,' I said, more to myself than to Ramon.

'And if I should refuse?'

'Then go from here and never return,' I said in a soft,

86

inconsequential voice. 'And your playing will remain as crappy as it is now.'

He looked hurt. I wanted him to be hurt.

'I'm still the second best player in the world!' he protested petulantly.

I shrugged. 'That means nothing to me. Does it mean anything to you?'

'How will I travel? I don't have the money for flight tickets or expenses.'

'Of course I shall take care of all that side of things. Air tickets, though. I'm not so sure.' I studied my fingernails carefully: the half moons occasionally revealed secrets. 'You see, Ramon, your journey will be a pilgrimage, and I'm not so certain that pilgrims are allowed to travel by plane. You will go on horseback.'

'I don't know anything about horses!'

'Not so fast! You won't be alone. Callipo will accompany you. He knows all there is to know about horses.'

'How will I carry my cello?'

'Ah! You won't be taking your cello.'

'But apart from some of the time here, I haven't missed a day's practice since I was six years old!'

'Then it's about time that you did. Who can know the cello who only the cello knows? You may temporarily lose a little technical expertise, but you will quickly make that up once you get to Venice: where, I am sure, they have the finest Guarneri and Stradivarius instruments. It will be good for you to unlearn a little.'

'I won't go!'

'Oh, don't keep saying that, it's becoming tedious. You will go, and you will learn, and you will return. To me. And now if you have no further questions, I have much to do. I will send Callipo to you presently – when he has found his quota of Mallard eggs – and he will take you back to your room where you may begin your preparations to depart.'

'Why can't I make my own way back to my room?'

'Why do you ask so many questions?'

'Because you are a cranky old fool who keeps wrongfooting me. I never know where I am.'

'On the contrary. I think you know perfectly well where you are all the time. You must stop looking to me for confirmation. Join me for supper, this evening.'

I left without another word, and bolted the door behind me.

Twelve

Ramon's Narrative

'We are creatures of moisture,' said Signor Cavallo at supper, that night. 'Consider the blood that flows wet and warm beneath our dry skin.' He poured me another glass of red wine. I noticed how it splashed into the glass; drops stained the white tablecloth. 'Our hearts are always wet. All that matters about us is wet. Our stomachs, kidneys, liver.'

Callipo had joined us at table, and was clearly not enjoying the turn the conversation had taken. He toyed with the fish on his plate. My own trout gazed up at me with a lugubrious eye.

'Eat up, Callipo!' Signor Cavallo urged. 'Busy day tomorrow!'

Callipo belched.

'There!' said Signor Cavallo. 'That's it! That's the secret to life. The human body's greatest joy is to shed substance: in a belch, in the squeezing of a boil, in an ejaculation. Who does not enjoy pissing? It is probably the greatest pleasure known to man.'

He spoke for some time on these vile matters, extolling at great length on the so-called delights of base bodily functions. Finally, I had to interrupt.

'Forgive me, Maestro, but why are you saying these things?

89

You have imparted so much real philosophy to me on the nature of music and life, why must you spoil that wisdom with these horrible observations?'

He cut off the head of his trout, lifted it with his fingers and plunged it whole into his mouth. The crack and squelch of the bones made Callipo wince. Signor Cavallo looked at his servant out of the corner of his eye and smiled.

'Chill, Callipo!' he said, his mouth full of half-chewed gristle and bone. The slang word sounded strange coming from his lips. 'Ramon, my dear. What have I been teaching you in all this time? Connectedness.

'All things connect. Connection, the joining together, the breakdown of separation: these are the things at the heart of what I have been trying to teach you. Music, the universal language, is the one form that has the potential to join the whole world. It exists not only for itself but for everything, and can only come into true fruition with the input of everything. Everything connects, everything unites. There is nothing that lies outside music. There is no such thing as "base", neither is there such a concept as "noble". Music is catharsis, only another form of ejaculation. Music is jism by another name.'

Callipo and I exchanged weary glances, and in that look something very like love passed between us. Callipo. Of course Callipo. Why had I not noticed him before? I mean noticed in a sense other than his merely being Signor Cavallo's manservant. Callipo was lovely, and especially lovely tonight with his long curly hair trailing neatly over the top of his scarlet silk shirt. I wanted to reach my hand across the table and hold his. This was romance. Somehow, I did not feel the customary urge to fuck with a man whose presence and physiognomy pleased me, I just wanted to be with him all the time. I wanted his good spirit to curl around me and be with me and for me. He and I were the only sane people in the room. And, therefore, we might have been the only two people who mattered in the entire universe: because the universe is always ourselves. However generous our spirits may be, however empathic, we ourselves must always be the centre of any universe because to deny that would be to deny the fact of our very existence.

I looked across at Signor Cavallo, and by the expression on his face I suddenly knew that this was all his doing. Yet again he was proving that he was Master of everything and totally in control. His bizarre speech, just now, was designed not just to prove a point (a point I only later came to realise the truth of), but to draw me and Callipo closer together in the manner I have thus described. I needed another emotion, another experience to add to my stock, and this he had given me.

A bat flew in at one open window, darted swiftly the length of the room and disappeared out of another window.

'So our life,' said Signor Cavallo. 'A brief flash of colour and twist of muscle between two great unknowns.'

'And so each piece of music,' added Callipo, voicing the only scrap of philosophy I was ever to hear him give. Signor Cavallo gave him a sour look.

So began my love affair with Callipo, and a time of extraordinary happiness.

Over the next few days, Callipo gave me riding lessons. First of all, we worked in the courtyard. I sat astride Monteverdi, a bay stallion of gentle temperament, whilst Callipo guided him round and round on the end of a rope. Unused to this form of transport, my legs never felt so stretched as at the end of each day and my arse was always sore. It was wonderful, then, that each night Callipo laid me down on a bench and gave me a soothing massage. He rubbed delicately scented warm oils over my buttocks and between my legs; but, although sensuous, his touch never became sexual. At first I was ashamed and embarrassed by my erection; but after a while we both seemed to accept it as something inevitable and easily ignored. Indeed, so constant was it that it was like a priapism, and as unremarkable a part of my anatomy as my big toe. When I retired to my bed I could fully indulge my fantasies, the most delightful of which involved myself lying naked face down on bare horseback, with Callipo on top of me, his cock skewered firmly into my arse. He did not thrust, but rather allowed himself to fuck according to the rhythm of the horse's trotting. His orgasm I imagined as coming with no increase of pressure or movement: it simply flowed out almost unexpectedly in the normal run of things. His come spilt down my thighs whilst my own shot on to the horse's rough back.

When I was not riding or masturbating, I was playing the cello. I practised with furious intensity hour upon hour. The thought of having to leave my beloved instrument behind whilst on my journey was painful to me. Signor Cavallo was also kind enough to continue to give me regular masterclasses, and these were as inspirational as ever. If sometimes his insights into the music were a little eccentric they never failed to improve an aspect of my playing. 'These five bars: Marcello was obviously thinking of a certain choirboy when he wrote them . . . This note here: that was where Vivaldi paused for an extra fraction of a second before dipping his pen in the ink . . . That cadence: doesn't that prove that Beethoven was, at the very least, bisexual? . . . This tierce de Picardie, what does it tell you about Giuseppi Giordani? It's obvious to me, as it should be to you, that he spontaneously ejaculated in the moment of writing this bar. Each note is redolent with spunk.'

I learnt never to smile at his observations, let alone laugh. Once, when I could not suppress a giggle, he stalked off in a huff and disappeared for the rest of the day.

At last the day came for our departure. Signor Cavallo had planned the time and date of our leave-taking exactly according to the actions of a group of wagtails who had alighted on the lawn near to where he was playing one afternoon. I don't know the exact details of his divination, it was something to do with the number of times they took off and returned to the same spot and the sextant points of their direction.

It was a damp, early morning, with a fine rain that seemed to hang suspended in the air rather than actually fall. The mist was rolling into the courtyard across the water meadows from the river, and there was a repeated desolate cry from some hidden water bird far off. Our voices sounded hollow as we murmured suggestions and instructions: this tin in the right saddle-bag, that book in the left. Callipo did most of the work. He was wonderfully practical, even down to making minor adjustments to Monteverdi's horseshoes. Signor Cavallo stood, perfectly still, by the statue of Apollo at the foot of the steps to the front entrance of Castello Caccini. He wore a linen suit and held his hands folded in front of his stomach like a benevolent English vicar.

'He's in love with you, and he's going to miss you terribly,' Callipo whispered to me over Monteverdi's back.

'Nonsense!' I replied, seemingly casually; but the words started a shiver through me. Could the Maestro really be in love with me? It was too much to hope for. And also too awful. I had always assumed that he tolerated me merely for the excellence of my playing. Never had he shown me the least affection, and the promise of lovemaking on my return from this jaunt seemed only a duty that he felt obliged to perform for the sake of Art. He certainly had shown no enthusiasm at the prospect. I noticed Callipo's impish expression. Was he teasing? Callipo returned what must have been my look of naive puzzlement with a characteristic shrug and an attractive raising of the eyebrows. If I loved Signor Cavallo, my affection for Callipo was hardly any less. He was got up like a travelling troubadour, with a soft leather jerkin, green leggings and red leather boots. Around his neck he sported a red cravat. His hat, wide-brimmed and with a feather stuck at a jaunty angle, lay on the gravel path. To wander Italy with the lovely, good-humoured Callipo! What could be better!

Signor Cavallo approached us slowly.

'A brief word,' he said, with a decorative flourish of his right hand as though clearing a path for his 'brief word'. 'I cannot, of course, instruct or order beyond what I have already set out as your brief for this mission; but I might request something, perhaps. And, if you have any affection for me, you might wish to comply.'

93

His sentences were as baroque as any sonata by Armando Verspucci. And, as with the sonatas, I suspected a fur-lined trap to spring shut at any moment. I was not wrong.

'There will be times when you will find yourselves alone together . . .'

Plenty! I thought eagerly in the ellipsis of his sentence.

'I would wish that you refrain from union. That is all.'

I regarded the gravel, then Callipo, then Apollo, then Signor Cavallo.

'I'm sorry, Maestro. Do I follow your meaning?'

'Yes, you do. You may severally have relations with whomsoever you wish on your travellings. I merely ask that you do not share such intimacy with each other. I cannot enforce my request. I only hope. Ramon, you are aiming for the summit of Mount Parnassus. Trust me as your guide. Callipo?'

'Your requests have always been my orders, Signor.'

Signor Cavallo inclined his head and pursed his lips.

'Nothing is ever easy.'

We were ready to go. Suppressing my desire to embrace the Maestro, I shook his hand very formally. Tears budded in my eyes.

'We will be as speedy in our mission as we possibly can,' I promised.

'Time is not important.'

Callipo crossed himself and, getting down on one knee before Signor Cavallo, kissed his ring. He murmured the words of the Nunc Dimittis: '*Nunc Dimittis servum tuum, Domine, secundum verbum tuum in pace . . .*' Lord, now lettest thou thy servant depart in peace . . .

There was a last moment of silence and stillness, deepened by that bird's continued desolate cry, and then the noisy business of leave-taking began.

'Hup!' Callipo slapped Monteverdi's thigh and gave me a leg up into the saddle. He tightened the cinches, put on his hat, picked up his long staff, then took the horse's reins and led us away.

'Don't look back!' he whispered to me. 'Remember Orpheus.'

The mists began to clear. It was going to be a hot day. And we were headed on horseback towards Venice, where I had no idea what form my musical education might take, but was certain that it would not be conventional. What is Art, after all, but merely a refined form of madness?

Part Two

Thirteen

Ramon's Narrative

Whilst we remained on the lanes and side roads of the Italian countryside, our journeying was exceedingly pleasant. Callipo and I took it in turns to ride and our conversation was easy and amiable. I had played no part in the more mundane preparations for travel, and it was Callipo who held all our money and poste restante addresses in a leather pouch. When I asked him for details, however, he was not forthcoming. 'The signor asked me to keep certain things from you,' he explained. 'He said that if I were to mention Francesco Provenzale you would understand? A certain violoncello sonata in A minor. Does that make sense?'

I bit my lower lip. The sonata by Provenzale was indeed known to me. The melody of the slow movement flowed through my mind. Suddenly I saw the music not simply as melancholic, but rather full of mundane doubt and uncertainty.

Well, so what?

We stopped for lunch on a grassy river bank, and sat in the shade of an ancient gnarled olive tree. Whilst Monteverdi grazed contentedly we tucked into our bread, wine and olives. It may not have been a feast, but it tasted as good. Presently, with a sense of delicious drowsiness, we stretched out and prepared for a postprandial nap. The burbling of the brook and the snatching sound of Monteverdi's tearing at the lush grass was soothing. A flight of doves swept from one tree and alighted on another. This was hilly country and on the other side of the river rose a steep sandbank in which swallows and martins nested. I watched the birds going to and from their holes until, lulled by Nature, I fell asleep. The finest wine assures us of the happiest dreams. In my dream, a choir of angels sang Palestrina whilst Callipo and I made love on a cloud. There was a degree of perfection which cannot be experienced in the tangible world. My skin awakened my soul to mortal joy. But, alas, as I approached a climax and was about to shoot a bursting flower of spunk into Callipo's arse, I awoke.

Callipo was studying a map, spread out on the grass. Had I spoken in my dream? Had I given anything away? I yawned and stretched.

'Good sleep?' asked Callipo.

'Wonderful!' My eyes caught his. What his look signified I could not be sure. I only knew that I wanted to mate with him there and then, without preliminary, without grace: simply a bald, brute fucking. This was what I had so far lacked. Domenico's loving had been adept and graceful, each act of intercourse an aesthetic delight; and likewise with the men in the forest. But one could not be satisfied by that style alone: baroque music is glorious in its way, but one also wants occasionally a raucous medieval band of sackbuts, serpents and crumhorns. *Take me, Callipo*, I urged with my eyes. *I'm yours now. Say nothing. Just do it.*

I knew that Callipo shared my desire; but he was a faithful servant. He had made a promise to his master and was not going to break it. He turned back to the task in hand.

'We have many miles to go before we find lodging for the night,' he said.

'Show me,' I said.

Studying a map together would provide an opportunity for

closeness and touch. One finger pointing to a destination might be joined by another. Where? Just there.

But Callipo was impatient to be getting along, apparently, for he allowed me only a cursory glance at our route before folding away the map and going to catch Monteverdi and put him back in harness.

'Come on,' he said, when all the preparations were done. 'You'd better mount up.'

'No, you ride,' I offered. 'I don't mind walking for a time.' It was not so much magnanimity on my part as a desire to see him mount the horse and swing his leg over its back. In that brief instant, I could imagine that he was mounting me, swinging a leg over my back. Each moment is precious, as Signor Cavallo had said at one time.

So we pressed on. I took the reins and held Callipo's long staff to aid my progress.

We passed through a village, quiet and almost deserted in the late afternoon sunshine. A cat slept on a windowsill amongst pots of geraniums; a small child, squatting beside a doorstep, played an earnest game with twigs and leaves. He looked up when we went by, clapped his hands with great delight and called a greeting in that thick rural Piedmont dialect which, as a Spaniard, I had never been able to master. Callipo answered him cheerfully and the narrow street echoed with the child's beautiful laughter.

Soon, however, our progress became less pleasant. So long as we kept to the lanes and side roads of the remote countryside, we might have been travellers in another century. Cars had been few and far between. Now, Callipo informed me, we would have to travel along a busy road for several kilometres. No sooner had he said this than a truck whizzed by, trailing a cloud of dust and fume. The idyll was over. Generously, Callipo urged that we must swap places: it was my turn to ride.

So our going became hard.

There was a pleasant interlude, however, when a tractor and farm trailer loaded with bales of hay slowly overtook us. The young farmer shouted an amiable greeting: we shared a sense of solidarity in that he mistook us for agricultural peasants similar in station to himself and we were happy to fall in with his assumption. To be a peasant: I liked the idea. Then, as tractor and trailer trundled along before us, we saw in the back, hidden amongst the bales of hay, the loveliest dark-haired peasant boy. His bare chest, revealed beneath a loose-fitting jacket, was the colour of wood and his teeth when he smiled were the white of ivory. We could not help but stare and he returned our look with a steady gaze. Presently, he slipped a hand beneath the waistband of his trousers and began to masturbate. Our pace quickened in order to keep up. The boy eased his trousers down around his ankles and began playing with his balls. He took a swig from a bottle of water before pouring some down his chest and over his cock and balls. He licked the palm of his hand and resumed his idle wanking. Frustratingly, no matter how we increased our pace, the tractor was always that little bit faster. I could, of course, have urged Monteverdi to a canter; but that would have meant leaving Callipo behind, which would hardly have been fair: although I'm sure the dear soul would have voiced no objection. Speed became irrelevant, however, when the tractor and trailer turned down a side road leading to the farm. Should we, too, go down this track? We needed lodging for the night, after all, and a farmhouse was as good a place to try as any. No. There was still plenty of light left in the day for travelling and, besides, some experiences are more potent when left as mere voyeuristic encounters. The boy left a sweet memory lodged in our minds. That was enough.

In the distance, across fields muddled by pylons, shacks, allotments and rusting machinery, we saw the tall, smoky chimneys, factories and tower blocks of Turin.

The traffic grew even heavier. We were tired, dusty and hungry and longed for good food and rest. My mind conjured the image of a monk's cell: a single bed with clean sheets and a feather pillow. A glass of water on the table by my head. This was the image of heaven.

We were a long way from heaven. Now a group of rowdy youths shot past us on their mopeds. They blew whistles and yelled foul abuse. Poor Monteverdi was quite startled and it was all I could do to restrain him and keep him from galloping off in panic. How was all this supposed to make me a greater cellist? In my tired state I flew into a rage.

'Fuck Signor Cavallo and his mumbo-jumbo!' I shouted above the roar of the traffic. 'The guy's a crazy and what do I do? I go along with his mad scheme!'

'Sssh!' urged Callipo, holding Monteverdi's halter lest my temper set him off again.

I calmed down.

'I need to play the cello,' I said, more quietly. 'I ache to play. To make music: it's a yearning every bit as powerful as lust. You can't know what it's like. I need the melodies to slip through my fingers. They build up in me and I need to release them.'

The words of Signor Cavallo, talking about the joys of ejaculation and pissing and so forth came back to me. To release: that is what every human being exists for. We are conduits through which possibilities flow. If we block those possibilities – whether they be metaphorical or actual – then we suffer pain. Each of us is God, making actual what is potential, creating every moment of every day.

We found a seedy hotel on the outskirts of the city, where the owner agreed, albeit reluctantly, to stable Monteverdi in the yard. 'But if he creates a disturbance,' the man said, scratching a nipple through the grubby cloth of his singlet, 'then you're out!' Ash, from the cigarette lodged permanently in his mouth, fluttered on to the register on the reception desk. Far off we heard the wailing of a police siren, closer at hand the cry of a baby and a woman's voice raised in anger. There was the sound of breaking glass. We had come a long way since the peacefulness of our morning departure.

Our room was mean and dark: two single beds, a wardrobe, a table and a hardbacked chair were the only furniture. The bathroom was situated along a creaky corridor with peeling wallpaper. A dirty window overlooked the yard where we had placed Monteverdi. He had no shelter, but seemed contented enough, nuzzling his bag of hay.

'Signor Cavallo was not over generous in his allowance?' I asked, kicking off my shoes and stretching out on the bed. Oh, it felt good to stretch: a long, chromatic scale reaching to the very limits of the cello's range. I was myself a cello. Play me, Callipo!

'On the contrary,' said Callipo. 'He has arranged for us to have ample funds, but part of my instructions was to show you some of the harder aspects of life. Artists need to have had experience of all life, is his theory, as you know.'

'But I was born a peasant!' I protested. 'I come from a humble family. When I was growing up we barely had enough to eat.'

'To be poor as a child is no hardship, providing that one has the basic necessities. A child will play as happily with a few toy twigs as with the most expensive electronically operated toy. Poverty for adults is true torment.'

I lay back and listened to the mosaic of noise coming from the mean tenement in which we were lodged: the whine of a TV, that baby still crying, a man shouting now, the steady low drone of traffic and beeping of car horns. This was all a long way from Bach and Frescobaldi. Or was it? Surely Signor Cavallo would disagree. I heard his voice in my inner ear: *All things connect and combine. Music represents the essence of everything, and yet in itself is nothing: mere vibrations in the air. All sound is music. Listen to it intelligently. Be involved.*

We ate, that evening, in a gloomy restaurant where cockroaches would suddenly appear from nowhere and dart across the stained tablecloths. When we pointed this out to the sullen waitress she said that we were free to go or to stay, as we pleased. We were too tired and too hungry to go trudging the streets of this suburb where, on cursory inspection, there had seemed to be few places to eat, and those all as run-down as the present establishment. The pasta was overcooked and flavourless; but it served its primary purpose well enough and we bolted it down. The red wine, at least, was palatable: we drank a bottle each.

I suppose that I was a little tipsy when it came time to leave the restaurant. Callipo paid the bill and was right behind me as we exited. When, however, I turned to speak with him a moment later he had disappeared! Perhaps he had returned to pick up something he had left behind. I put my head back inside the door. The two waitresses were alone, sitting at a table and preparing a game of cards.

'Hey, dearie! Fancy a cigarette?' One of them proffered the pack when she saw me. 'Come and join us! How about a game of strip poker? Let's see what you've got down there! Or is it all promise and no substance like Biagio Marini?'

That this woman should name an obscure seventeenth-century composer startled me every bit as much as did her ready musical perspicacity. By coincidence, Marini was one of those composers who, when I first became acquainted with his work, filled me with indescribable delight. But later study proved that he was indeed obscure for a reason: the initial impact of his music thrilled one's superficial senses; but there was nothing in him to satisfy a deeper need.

'Come on, sweetheart! Draw up a chair! You know you want to!' She licked her lips and looked me up and down, her eyes lingering provocatively on my crotch.

I had not really looked at either of them before. I tend automatically to dismiss all women and their faces and bodies do not generally register with me. I can never forget a man's face; women I am always confusing. They were both in their late thirties and, although not beautiful, were attractive in a *belle laide* sort of way. One was dark, the other fair; one chubby, the other slim.

'Come on, darling! You're not coming over all shy, are you! Ain't he sweet? Come to Mummy! Mummy likes music, too. She heard you and your mate chatting, she knows the kinds of things you're into. Oh, come on!' she urged, with a touch of impatience, now.

'I was looking for my friend.'

'Ooh, you won't see him tonight no more,' the dark-haired

one said. 'He's gone off with the kitchen apprentice. Wasn't you watching?'

Frankly, I hadn't been. I hadn't had a clue that Callipo was cruising during our meal. I hadn't even noticed that there was a kitchen apprentice.

Without waiting for my acceptance of their offer, the blonde woman began dealing me a hand of cards.

'I really can't!' I apologised, holding up my hand. 'I . . .'

'Shut up and come over here! Or is your name Marini! Is it Marini? Biagio Marini, the eternal failure.'

'Oh, he wasn't that bad!' I took a step forward. 'I mean I think there's a place for shallow Art: it doesn't all have to be . . .' I stopped. They were grinning at me. After an awkward moment, I returned their smile.

'That's better, petty! Take a seat. What's your name?'

'Ramon. I'm from Spain.'

'You speak lovely Italian.'

'Thank you. My mother is Ital – '

'This is Maria and I'm Cantella,' interrupted the dark-haired one.

For all their initial wooing of me with esoteric musical knowledge, it soon became clear that their characters were fundamentally base; and their conversation was full of lewd references to walnuts and cucumbers and the local college football team. Each time they said something risqué they looked at me slyly. I confess that several times I blushed and kept my eyes firmly on my cards. The game confused me. I had thought that I knew the rules of poker, but they kept informing me that I was doing things wrong and I soon began to lose with every deal.

It was not long before I was called upon to remove my jeans. I stood up and turned away from the table, embarrassed by the all too evidently growing bulge in my briefs.

'Come on, sweetheart! Don't be bashful! You ain't got nothing we haven't seen before – although each fresh one's always like the first one ever, ain't it, Cantella? You never get jaded.'

106

I sat down again as quickly as I could. Both of them tilted at an angle to get a look beneath the table.

'All right,' said Cantella. 'To preserve your modesty a while longer, I propose that from now on, every time you lose you have to pay a forfeit. That way you can keep your knickers on. Agreed? Or maybe you'd prefer . . .'

'That's fine by me,' I said. 'Anything you say.' Although, in truth, I had the deepest misgivings about what they might have in mind. Perhaps I would start to win from now on, and could recover some of my clothes.

But of course I did not start to win.

The first forfeit was demanded by Maria.

'A kiss!'

I leant over and gave her a swift peck on the cheek.

'Oh, no, that's not what I meant!' she said, laying her hand upon my own. 'That wasn't a kiss! What I meant was . . .' Her lips met mine and her tongue slipped into my mouth. As she craned forward, her chair toppled backwards and she fell heavily on to me causing me also to fall. We landed heavily on the floor. She was on top of me, her mouth against mine, our tongues twining like copulating snakes. We rolled and, when our positions were reversed, I felt Cantella sliding her hand into the waistband of my briefs and then slowly pulling them down.

This was my first time with female love and my gaucheness must have revealed itself when I began to fumble with Maria's undergarments for she said, 'Here!' and sat up to unhook her brassiere for me. Her full breasts were not unattractive and their softness was delightful. Nowhere do men's bodies have flesh so comfortable. And when I began to tease her tits with my tongue she let out a desperate moan.

Meanwhile, Cantella was licking my thighs like a cat, and nuzzling into the crevices beneath my buttocks.

It became clear that they wanted to take total command of this situation, I was to act only as their compliant plaything. They turned me on to my back and stretched my legs and arms wide apart. I had never felt so vulnerable and yet, paradoxically, so utterly safe. Whilst Maria tongued me and tortured my erect nipples with fierce fingers, Cantella was absorbed with my cock. Now her mouth and tongue worked their way slowly up and down one side, now her tongue lapped around the base of the glans; now she took the whole cock into her mouth, taking its full length with a technique that could only be called swallowing. Her mouth pulsed around my cock, confirming its potential as a natural sexual orifice. I would have come had she not pulled away just in time.

I was pulled to my knees. Maria stood before me and Cantella, kneeling beside me, showed me the technique of cunnilingus. Soon, both of us were pleasuring Maria in this manner and it was not long before she shuddered into her first orgasm: a high, repeated piping that at length ripened into a drawn-out wail.

I was pushed on to my back again and Cantella mounted me. My cock slipped easily into her tight, firm cunt. It was moister than an arsehole, of course, and I was surprised that one could enter with so little preparation. I missed the build-up, but the fucking sensation was almost as good. She pushed her hands into my shoulders quite painfully, and her long hair trailed over my chest. As we fucked, Maria squatted over my mouth and I tongued her cunt as vigorously as I was able. I was surrounded by a polyphony of desperate cries; but could not have identified the source of any – not least my own.

When Maria came, she flung back her head and howled. Spittle trailed out of the corners of her mouth, and mingled with the blood where she had bitten her lips in the agony of ecstasy. She eased her body from mine and I ejaculated spontaneously, my come spurting from my cock, shooting high on to my chest.

Now I guessed that Cantella wanted to be fucked. She came down off my face and began to lick my cock clean, her tongue taking my spunk with obvious relish. If my cock had momentarily wilted, it soon came to life again under the expert care of her tongue combined with a little gentle manipulating with her long fingers.

The women lifted me to my feet. Seeing my long cock

swaying, taut and erect as ever, I conceived of myself as merely a machine for fucking. The sole purpose of my existence was to give these women pleasure. And I was loving it. They knelt before me, one on each side of my cock, and jointly gave me fellatio. From time to time their mouths met at the top of my cock and their tongues entwined in a deep kiss before separating again to return to their original task.

They rose again and, giving me a look almost of serious foreboding, Cantella took hold of my cock and led me to the wall. When she could go no further her expression seemed fearful as she guided my cock into her cunt. I entered her with infinite slowness, pulling out after every inch and then stealing in again an extra inch and so on. I manouevred my hips and imagined the tip of my glans penis scraping the dark walls of her cunt, scraping every tortured nerve end as it progressed deeper and deeper. Finally, my full length was inside her and she betrayed the excess of her passion by biting my neck and shoulders with teeth sharp enough to draw blood. Squeezing my buttocks tight I began slowly to build up a momentum of fucking.

Now Maria came alongside and drew my right hand to her so that whilst I fucked her friend I was also masturbating her.

Harder I fucked, and yet harder, ramming myself into Cantella who seemed one tight parcel of sexual being. Our bodies slapped and squelched and our voices knew no restraint. My second orgasm always takes much longer than the first and with her own hand rubbing at her clit Cantella shuddered her climax long before I was ready to explode. Consequently, I pulled out and penetrated Maria again, still masturbating her, and she responded by quivering into an almost spontaneous climax: I felt her small shudders shivering the length of her body. In response, I became gentler inside her. My cock teased out her orgasm by slow degrees and, when it had passed, continued to probe and explore her innermost self, looking for that moment in her physicality which could send her again to that region of fierce joy. Deep inside her cunt, I felt her love muscles cunningly caressing my cock like firm, moist tongues. We fucked slowly for an age, our selves becoming nothing more than cock and cunt. Sometimes we had little spurts of speed, sometimes slowed to an almost complete stop.

Presently, I heard Cantella's voice in my ear and felt her hand slip between my legs and stroke my tight ball sac. 'Come on,' Cantella whispered. 'Fuck her like you fucked me. Give her some of that hard bull fucking and let's hear her scream!'

Accordingly, I gave Maria a couple of tight, firm jerks. Her welcome response indicated that she wanted more of this, so I thrust into her again with yet more force.

'Come on, young Spanish bull,' hissed Cantella. 'Show her what you can do!'

So I steadily built up a rhythm, gradually becoming stronger and faster. From the depths of my body issued a low roar which found its echo inside Maria. Her fingers rubbed at her clitoris, wet and urgent.

We came together in a series of convulsive shaking. Tears stained her cheeks and my eyes also were blurry. Still attached we sank to the floor clutching each other tightly.

'There, there!' I heard Cantella's soothing voice and felt her hand stroking my skin. 'There, there!'

I was sobbing, although hardly aware of it. My body was not my own, and my cock retracted of its own accord from Maria's cunt. I only knew that it had shrivelled to its deep resting position by the sudden feel of cool air. The room was filled with the scent of come, cunt juices and sweat.

'Don't cry, my darling!' whispered a voice. 'Please don't cry!'

They licked and stroked and did their best to comfort me. I had no idea why I was crying, all I knew was that I could not stop. But I was not unhappy: rather, I felt a profound happiness.

Eventually, however, my spirit was quieted. Like contented cats, we lay on the warm floor curled in each other's arms and fell into deep sleep.

My sleep was profound.

When I awoke, next morning, beams of dusty sunlight were flowing in the wide window, the lower half of which was covered by a grey net curtain. I sat up, unsure at first of where I was. I was alone in the room. The chairs had all been put upon the tables, and the floor swept.

'Maria!' I called softly. 'Cantella?'

A group of schoolboys passed merrily in the street outside. There was the sound of high laughter and the scuffling of a football on the pavement. Instinctively, I covered my now rather shrunken genitals with my hand; but I was protected from sight by the net curtain.

I could not at first see my clothes and, as the memory of last night came back to me, I wondered if I had been robbed. Seduced and robbed. I got to my feet. No, there were my clothes folded neatly on one of the tables. A note was placed on top of them:

Don't worry about Biagio Marini. You're nothing like!
Safe journeying,
love,
Cantella and Maria

When I was dressed, I called their names once more. There was no reply. I went up to the bar and tried the door next to it. It was locked. There was an old poster on the door advertising a Spanish bullfight featuring Ramon Iglesias. The full-length picture of him, dressed in his matador's uniform pulsed with sexual potency. I smiled.

'Tor-e-a-dor-o!' I softly sang the phrase from *Carmen*.

Reading the note again, I concluded that it was a farewell. However much I wanted to say goodbye in person, no use would come of it. Folding the paper carefully and tucking it into my top jacket pocket, I went out of the front door and into the narrow side street. A pigeon flew up in front of me and, from a high window, one old woman watering her pots of geraniums shouted across to another on the opposite side of the street. There was the sound of dripping water. A red balloon, trailing a string like a spermatozoon, drifted idly along at waist height before gradually climbing higher and higher. The baker's boy entered his shop carrying trays of loaves. We gave each other amiable greeting. There was the scent of coffee. Another Italian morning had begun.

Fourteen

I found Callipo in the small café across the street from our pension. He was at a table by himself reading *Corriere della Serra*. On the table were a pastry and an espresso. I sat opposite him without his noticing and, ravenously hungry, began chomping on his pastry. It was delightfully fresh, topped with almonds and filled with a pistachio paste. Neither could I resist a sip of his coffee. From the radio came the sounds of a jolly sonata by Cazzati. Whilst I ate, I read the headlines on his newspaper:

INSTRUMENTAL MUSIC TUITION TO BE PROVIDED FREE
IN ALL SCHOOLS WORLDWIDE, FUNDED BY UN.

NEW OPERA HOUSES TO BE BUILT IN PISA,
ROME AND VERONA.

POPE DECLARES ALL MUSICIANS TO BE SAINTS.

BUSKERS TO RECEIVE UN PENSIONS.

AMERICA CONVERTS WEST POINT MILITARY ACADEMY
INTO A MUSIC COLLEGE.

Nothing radical happening in the world, then.
Without looking from the paper, Callipo stretched a hand out

to take his espresso. I could barely restrain a giggle as he lifted the empty cup to his mouth. His expression of puzzlement when he lowered the paper, in the instant before he saw me, was delicious to behold.

'Hello!' I said. 'Where did you get to, last night?'

'And how were things for you?' he asked, ignoring my question. There was a twinkle in his eye.

'Oh!' I said, putting the half-eaten pastry back on the plate. 'Oh! It was you, wasn't it?'

He tilted his head and adopted a blatantly false innocent look. 'I'm sorry?'

'You planned what happened to me. It was part of Signor Cavallo's instruction, wasn't it?'

'I don't know what you're talking about.'

'Does the name Biagio Marini mean anything to you?'

'You've stolen my coffee and my pastry. We need to order some more. Will you be joining me?'

'But . . .'

But clearly he was not going to be drawn on this subject so easily. He held his hand up and the waiter approached.

Only when we had our fresh coffee, did Callipo say, 'All the world, Ramon. Nothing must be hidden from you, you must have experience of everything. How was it?'

'Couperin. With a little Stravinsky and Ligeti thrown in!' I licked the end of my teaspoon and widened my eyes.

'No Respighi?'

Callipo's wit pointed out how essentially humourless Signor Cavallo was.

'Definitely no Respighi. But certainly some Shostakovich, I should have said.'

'Sounds good to me! Would you go back again?'

I had to think a moment. Then, more seriously, 'No. It's not where my heart is. But I'm pleased to have known it.'

He nodded. I leant across the table. It seemed the moment was ripe for a confidence that might better be shared with a degree of humour.

'So what about you, Callipo?'

'What about me?'

'Who are you?'

'Signor Cavallo's faithful servant. As I have been for many a year.'

'Yes, yes, sure! But what are you? Do you love men as he and I do, or do you favour women? I know nothing about you, Callipo, and I think it only fair that I should.'

He sat back and folded his arms.

'There's nothing to know,' he said. 'I have devoted my life to the service of Signor Cavallo.'

'Are you his lover?'

'No.'

'Would you like to be?'

'That is an inappropriate question.'

'Will you answer it?'

'Things are as they are. I see no reason why any situation might change. I live a celibate life, and am happy to do so.'

'But Callipo!' sighed I, only recently a virgin. 'That's almost a sin! Our bodies are sacred for the brief time we are on the earth and we must use them to their full potential.'

'That is an argument,' he acknowledged. 'But sometimes certain potentials can fail to be realised if we concentrate too much on the sensual aspects of our character. What sort of cellist would you have become had you found the pleasures of the flesh when you were sixteen? Would you have practised so hard? Would not at least some of your essential passion have been diverted into physical love? Potential is a complex concept.'

'And your potential?'

'To help you realise yours. I am a servant to Signor Cavallo and, therefore, a servant to you because he has asked me so to be.'

I pressed my lips close to his ear. 'If you are my servant then you must obey me and I command you to sleep with me!'

He flinched only slightly. Only later, much later, would I realise the turmoil that I had unleashed in his heart.

'I cannot sleep with you,' he replied. 'Signor Cavallo has expressly forbidden it. Please do not refer to this subject again. Come!' He slapped a few coins down on the table. 'It's time to go and we have another long day's travelling ahead of us.'

Feeling like a foolish schoolboy – another role, perhaps, but one that I was, however, already familiar with – I followed him out of the door.

'*Arriverderci*, signori!' The waiter waved us goodbye with a large red cravat decorated with musical notation. '*Bon voyage e auf Wiedersehen!*'

'What was that all about?' I asked when we were back in the street. 'Did you see his cravat?'

'Of course. It was from the score of Parsifal. The story of the search for the Holy Grail.'

'Oh, I'm fed up of all this significance!' I grumbled. 'Why can't we even get a cup of coffee without it being turned into a symbolic act?'

'Because we need reminders, whereas our musical ancestors accepted the numinous as part of the everyday. When Bach drank a glass of water, it was always a holy act. When he washed, when he shat, when he walked down the street he was in communion with God. Only when we recover that sense can we ever hope to understand Bach – or any music – properly.'

'OK, OK, but how come the waiter . . .?'

'No more questions.'

'But I . . .'

'Look at that peregrine falcon up there!'

Callipo pointed to the thin strip of blue sky visible above the narrow street. There was nothing there.

I had not realised quite how sore my body was until it came time to mount Monteverdi once again. My thighs and arse ached from all the riding yesterday, and my genitals were fascinatingly bruised from the bizarre exertions of last night. Motion eventually numbed the pain, however.

Large cities may be easy to escape from in a motor vehicle; on horseback the task is near impossible. The motorways are forbidden to one, and all the outer roads seem to double back into the centre of town. For hours we progressed in circles. When Callipo tried to draw a comparison between our situation and the labyrinthine scores of Messiaen, I lost my temper.

'Oh, for heaven's sake, Callipo! There is a world outside music, you know!'

'If there is, I have never found it,' was all he would concede. He was the best-hearted man I ever met.

In the end, a group of army cadets came to our rescue. They allowed us to clamber aboard the back of one of their trucks; and, as luck would have it, they also happened to have an empty horsebox for Monteverdi. They took us all the way to Mont Alba, a small village barely a hundred miles from our destination. The journey was delightful, if a little bumpy. We sang revolutionary songs from the time of Garibaldi and made good friends of all of them. When it came time for us to take our leave there were heartfelt kisses and embraces all round. I still treasure the memory of the boy who pressed his tongue into my mouth and scraped his hand over my crotch as a parting gesture. Such civilities cost nothing and society is the poorer for not accepting them into everyday custom.

Fifteen

A late summer's afternoon, and we were progressing along a quiet country road past endless fields of sunflowers. The sky was a clear blue stretched so taut one could almost hear it hum. The only actual sounds were the clack of Monteverdi's hooves, his heavy breathing and occasional snort and soft exchanges between myself and Callipo. Sometimes there was the idle drone of a bee, trailing a thin line of sound amongst a sheet of silence. An open-topped red Ferrari, drenched in metallic pop music, that overtook us served ultimately only to deepen the silence. Huge noise gradually dissolved into the air as the car disappeared over the brow of a hill. The music had been good: I was sorry to hear it go so quickly.

I had been on horseback most of the day, and the sun was clearly going to my head, for I imagined I heard again the voice of Signor Cavallo: *Only by contrast can we ascertain the true meaning of any situation. There was no silence before there was sound.* I scratched Monteverdi's neck and gave him an encouraging slap.

Callipo took a swig of water and, after pouring some over his head, began to sing a troubadour's rondel: it was jolly, delicious music.

118

'You were born five centuries too late,' I remarked, when he was done.

'Maybe that's true,' he said; and in his voice was such sadness I regretted having spoken. I wanted to climb down off the horse and embrace him. I wanted to make love with Callipo in the midst of all these sunflowers. Why should we allow Signor Cavallo to retain this power of prevention over us? I was falling ever more deeply in love with Callipo and ultimately, surely, *amor vincit omnes*. To put more love into the world: was that not a worthier aim than to put in an extra quality of music? We would kneel before each other, hidden amongst the tall forest of flowers, and I would decorate his naked chest with yellow pollen whilst whispering his name like an incantation. *Callipo, you are my life and my love. Let's run off together. Never return to Signor Cavallo.* The prospect was enchanting. My love and I together for ever. Suddenly, even music itself seemed dull, dry and laborious. What were the Bach suites but merely clever mathematical exercises? What was a sonata if not simply a pleasant enough means of easing the passing of time; but certainly nothing more? If you were a sad obsessive, you might read things into music that were not there; but if you had a life, and a love, then you could truly reach fulfilment. Signor Cavallo was nothing but a madman: living alone in that castle for all these years had driven him out of his mind.

I brought Monteverdi to a halt. This foolishness had gone on too long. I must have Callipo and hang the consequences! Playing the cello was a waste of time! All that mattered was making love with one whom one loved. I looked down at Callipo. A glimpse of his collarbone beneath his soft leather jerkin inflamed my passion yet more. In my mind I was already tearing the jerkin from across his chest – oh, I could rape him if needs must! – when he calmly pointed out a farmhouse at the end of a rutted track through the field.

'Come on!' he said. 'Why don't we see if we can find shelter there for the night?'

His calm voice and normal manner, so far removed from my

own feelings at that time, served to bring me to my senses. I was suddenly ashamed that I had allowed such a fever to hold me in its grip. The opening bars of Ligeti's cello concerto came to my mind: that long held E in the middle register that emerges out of silence and gradually draws the rest of the music into it so that it becomes, seemingly, a metaphor for the first life emerging from the sludge. That precious first cell regarded by God in order that it might *be*. I should not have allowed my finer feelings to become hijacked by cheap lust. Towards the end of that remarkable piece of music the cello is given a passage that sounds as what one might imagine first sounds to have been. The beginning of time. Perhaps, though, in mitigation of my feelings, the seed within us is always the first seed and we needs must scatter it – if only to the purer winds of gay love.

That something was amiss with this farmhouse, we both sensed on our approach. Outwardly, it looked like any other Italian farmhouse: a red-tiled roof, shuttered windows, window boxes packed with geraniums, ivy and lobelia. A few chickens pecked nervously in the gravel of the front yard. There was a small kitchen garden, reached through a rickety gate set in a low fence, with pumpkins, cucumbers and water melons.

I dismounted and hitched Monteverdi to a branch in the shade of a tall cypress. Callipo and I exchanged glances that betrayed our mutual anxiety. Or, rather, perhaps it was not so much anxiety as an apprehension of some huge sadness that infected the very air.

We entered the gate and walked up the path to the front door. There was no knocker, but a handbell on a flat stone had been placed there for the purpose. I shook it. Its jangle was uncomfortably loud, and in C sharp – a note I have always disliked. No answer. I was about to call out – I couldn't bear hearing that damn bell again, when a face appeared at a window on the second floor. It was a dark-haired boy of a beauty so exquisite I almost gasped aloud.

'We have come to see if we might obtain lodging for the

night,' I introduced. 'There are only two of us, and an old horse. It seems that the nearest village is over twenty miles away and as evening is drawing in, we did wonder . . .?'

The boy merely looked, not saying a word. His face was thin, with cheekbones so fine they might have been carved from bone china. He blinked steadily, and one's attention was drawn to the loveliest long eyelashes. His ruby lips were slightly parted and I envied the air that he so easily drew in between them!

'We will willingly pay!' added Callipo to my entreaty.

The boy's continued silence was becoming uncomfortable. In another situation the silence and his steady gaze would have been without question an invitation to sexual union; but here there was something different.

'If it's not convenient,' I said, 'perhaps we might simply be allowed a glass of water and a chance to replenish our bottle?'

No reply.

Then, from around the side of the building, came a woman. Her hair was grey and expression tired. Her skin was brown and leathery from long exposure to the sun. She looked to be in her sixties, but perhaps a hard life had aged her. She wore a heavy outdoor apron above a floral print dress. On her feet were muddy boots.

Recovering from the initial shock at seeing us, she glanced quickly up at the boy, then asked, 'What do you want here?'

'Perhaps lodging for the night?' I ventured cautiously. 'We would be willing to pay, only the nearest village is . . .'

'I know where the nearest village is!' she interrupted sharply. 'And you can go there! This is not a hotel!'

'I'm so sorry,' I apologised. There was no point arguing. I nodded to her and, of course, raised my head to nod farewell to the boy. A shame. It would have been pleasant to rest here in this solitude, and even more agreeable to get to know that boy a little better.

She watched us go back down the path. Then, when I was unhitching Monteverdi, she called, 'Is that your horse?'

'Of course!'

'You don't have a motor car?'

'We travel on horseback.'

'Then Pesaro is a long way. I didn't realise. Come back here!'

Callipo and I hesitated and exchanged glances.

'Well, come on!' she insisted. 'I'm not going to eat you.'

She led us into a pleasantly cool, dim kitchen. There was the thin, clean scent of fresh olives and onions. In the centre, on the red-tiled floor, stood a huge oak table, decorated with a bowl of oranges; a bunch of newly cut lilies lay waiting to be trimmed and arranged in a vase. Copper pans hung on one wall, another was occupied by a huge array of blue china plates. Shelves were crowded with tins, spices, jars of pasta. There hung a string of onions on the back of the door. In a corner stood a small shrine to the Virgin, complete with burning candle. On a cushion by the cooker a tabby cat lay sleeping.

'I mistook you for tourists,' the lady explained, washing her hands over the sink. 'Please, take a seat at the table. You'll have some refreshment.'

She set glasses before us and poured out home-made lemon juice from a decanter she took from the fridge. There was also a plate of spicy biscuits which we tucked into hungrily. When she had established her hospitality with this food and drink, she set the lilies clumsily into a porcelain jug and then joined us at table.

'No, as I say, I thought you were tourists, passing through in your car. We get them all the time. They come up here and knock on the door at all hours of the day and night. "What a pretty farmhouse! You do all this by yourselves? Have you ever considered selling?" They come from Rome or Milan or New York, and always with plenty of money. I hate them. But then I saw your horse, and knew you were genuine travellers, and one must always be hospitable to the true traveller. Where are you going?'

So we eased into conversation. We avoided going into too great detail as to the exact nature of our journeying, however. It was not so much that we felt a peasant woman would not understand, but a resurgence of that sense we had felt on initially approaching the farmhouse that all was not quite right here. There was a certain uneasiness of spirit.

Presently, I became aware of a quiet music being played somewhere in the house. The boy. Where was he?

'Excuse me, signora, but is that your son we can hear playing the lute?'

Her expression darkened, and she pursed her lips.

'My son,' she said, 'is a lunatic. He neither speaks nor smiles but sits all day playing melancholy songs on his lute.'

'He's a very accomplished player,' I observed. I recognised, with pleasure, the *Lachrymosa* of John Dowland that he was now playing. It was perfectly rendered. If he was indeed a lunatic, then he was one peculiarly blessed by God.

'I cannot tell that,' she replied. 'I myself am tone deaf. One note sounds much as another to me. To my ears music is either fast or slow. Fast music I tolerate because one can hope that the end will come more quickly. Slow music I loathe almost beyond endurance. The subtle shading of melody is lost to me.'

On hearing this, Callipo visibly shrank from the woman. I fancied I also heard him let out an involuntary hiss. More politely, and also to cover Callipo's lapse of etiquette, I leant forward. 'Oh, but that's sad!' I sympathised.

'Is it?' she challenged, quite harshly. Then, in a gentler tone, 'Perhaps so. Perhaps if I could hear music then that row the boy plays may not seem quite so terrible.'

I remembered the aggressive C sharp of the bell by the door, and wondered if this woman had a soul. Were it not for the fact of the loveliness of the boy's playing, I think that Callipo and I would have offered our thanks for her hospitality there and then and made a swift departure. The music, however, tied us with its gentle strings. I cannot bear to leave music. If the crazed Isabella, back at Castello Caccini, yearned for perpetual orgasm, my heart yearned for perpetual music. Tactfully, I changed the subject and accepted another glass of lemon.

In course of time, we agreed a fair payment for a night's lodging and supper and Signora Rufolo showed us to our room in an outbuilding: a pity, I had hoped to be led upstairs and gain the possibility of another glimpse of her lovely son.

The room was of a fair size, with whitewashed walls and a beamed ceiling. There were two single beds which Signora Rufolo set to covering with clean sheets. The only other item of furniture was a sort of trellis table beneath the window, supporting a long narrow box full of sprigs of thyme.

'Make yourselves comfortable,' she said, when she was done and had shown us all the facilities. 'Supper will be at seven. I shall ask Nicolo to look after your horse.'

Nicolo! What a lovely name, and how gracefully the tongue bounced when saying it!

We gave her our thanks and prepared to wash and change for the evening.

An hour later, I lay on my bed feeling spruce and refreshed. From where I lay I was able to gaze out of the open window to a view of rows of vines with grapes already full and further ripening in the heat of the late afternoon sunshine. Far in the distance, through a blue mist, one could discern a range of mountains. The silence was profound. Extremely tired, I was almost on the point of nodding off – how calm our spirits are when physical exertion fills our limbs with soft weight and the seeds of sleep begin sprouting in our minds – when I spied, walking slowly between the vines, Nicolo. The lute hung from a strap around his shoulder and he was idly strumming an aimless melody. My eyes drank the lovely image until he had passed out of sight.

When Callipo returned to the room from bathing, I said, 'It is a cruel fate of Nature to bring together such a boy as Nicolo with all his musical skills and a mother utterly unable to appreciate them.'

'It produces a conflict of spirit that impregnates the very air,' Callipo agreed.

'I hope we shall see something more of Nicolo before we leave here,' I said.

'You're in love with him!'

'No, I'm not!' I folded my hands behind my head and gazed up at the ceiling. 'But I should like to shower rose petals upon his naked body!'

Callipo lay down on his bed. 'And I should like to bathe him in ass's milk.' The statement was remarkable coming from my celibate Callipo. I was quite aroused.

'I would bathe him, dry him and scent him with soft perfume.'

'I would . . .'

A knock at the door interrupted our musings and Signora Rufolo entered without further preliminary. She stood a little awkwardly just inside the door. Clearly, there was something she wanted to say, but could not quite find the words. I tried to make her more at ease by commenting favourably on the room we were in, the view and her generous hospitality. She appeared not to hear what I was saying, but was preoccupied with other matters. Finally, she came right inside, shut the door firmly behind her and sat on the end of my bed, her hands folded in her lap.

'There are some things I perhaps should explain before we all gather for supper,' she said. 'All is not as it should be in this household . . .'

'Please go on,' I urged.

'It is about Nicolo.'

Our interest quickened.

'As I told you, he is quite mad. But that is not the whole story. The sorry truth is that I am responsible for his insanity. When he was a boy, growing up, he was like any other. He used to like playing with the lambs and making garlands for them, and dressing up his dolls and combing his hair for hours in the mirror. He was a normal little boy. He used to chat and sing and play – it was a Spanish guitar he had in those days, and he never played anything below allegro: blessed tempo! The house was filled with the sound of his innocent joy. But all that changed in his seventeenth year. His father and I – well, perhaps more his father than myself – wanted him to choose a bride. His father was not a well man (he is now buried beneath the vines) and he naturally

125

enough wanted to see an heir to the family farm before he died. Nicolo showed a marked reluctance to make his own choice from amongst the girls of the neighbourhood, so we took action ourselves and arranged a marriage with a pretty local girl from the nearby village. Such arrangements are not uncommon out here in the country. If you are townsfolk you must try to understand. Family blood and dynasty are important to us. I can trace my own family back to the thirteenth century: we were vinegrowers even back then: change happens only very slowly in our family. Although I did have a great-uncle who once went to Verona – but only for a day.'

Centuries of interbreeding, I thought to myself. No wonder Nicolo was mad; and his mother likewise seemed not entirely present in the known world.

'So this marriage,' she continued. 'The girl, Maria, came from a very respectable family. And she was still a virgin – all the more reason for us to act quickly. To introduce the boy and the girl, we threw a lavish party. Everyone was invited: all the vinegrowers from hereabouts, the local mayor, the priest, the high-ups of the local branch of the Comorra. It went perfectly. Everyone got along, and our boy and girl seemed to hit it off well with each other. That night, after all the guests had gone home, Roberto – that's my late husband – the priest, myself and the girl's father sat over a last bottle of good wine and set a date for the wedding. It was to be six months from that day. Why so long? Maria's father argued that it should be much sooner. He needed a strong son-in-law to help him with the next harvest, he said. But the priest was old-fashioned: he believed that girls and boys should have a long courtship. And seventeen is too young, he insisted. The boy at least should be eighteen. Stupid fool. What did he know about the ways of the world? Bless me, Father, for I have sinned!' She licked the tips of her fingers and quickly crossed herself with a glance to heaven. 'Father Crivelli is a good man, but he it was, I believe, who made the fatal mistake that was to lead to our downfall. So a date six months from then was set.

'The very next day, Maria's father was on the doorstep at dawn. He was flustered and uneasy, so Roberto and I invited him into the kitchen and placed a glass of wine before him. He clearly had something to say but did not quite know the way to go about saying it. Eventually, however, after a couple more glasses, he came out with it. It was to do with Maria – as we might have guessed. "You must understand," he said, "that our Maria is still a virgin. I swear it on the holy name! But she is a restless girl and very beautiful." To cut a long story short, he said that he believed that his daughter had no intention of remaining a virgin for another six months. The local village boys were already gathering around her like dogs around a bitch on heat and sooner rather than later she was going to succumb. In this part of the country, signori, you must understand that virginity is of the utmost importance. If a husband finds on his wedding night that another man has soiled his bride then the marriage will be instantly annulled.

'I was sanguine, however. "Once Nicolo and Maria begin their courtship, Nature will take its course," I said. "If she has an urgent need to experience the pleasures of the flesh, then let her do so with him – if he is to be her husband, it won't matter if he is the one to take her maidenhood. On a moonlit night amongst the vines, it will happen. He is as beautiful as she, neither will be able to resist the other."

' "But forgive me, mother," said Maria's papa, "if I point out that your Nicolo is perhaps rather backward in these matters. He is a long way behind other boys of his age." I protested. It was nonsense! Every boy goes at his own pace. "Nicolo is a sensitive boy," I said. "If he doesn't want to copulate in the pig-sty like his contemporaries (that's a famous place in this district for youthful indiscretions) but prefers to wait for a more romantic location – or even marriage itself – then it is not for us to force the issue."

'Alas, neither my husband nor Maria's father accepted my argument and they devised a plan to which I was forced to acquiesce. Nicolo was to be sent on an errand to Maria's house at a time when Maria would be by herself. Moreover, she was to be in on our plan (she had apparently already agreed to this with her father) and she would open the door to him in a seductive dress. Once inside: well, boy and girl . . .

'Perhaps you have guessed by now that it all went tragically wrong. The meeting was duly set up and Nicolo went to Maria's house. It was a Wednesday night, as I recall. He believed that he was to fetch a sack of grapeskins, which my husband dries and fashions into hats. Maria opened the door to him stark naked! Well, you can imagine the shock that it gave my poor Nicolo! He turned on his heels and ran all the way home. Some say they saw Maria pursuing him for part of the way; but I believe that to be wistful imagination on the part of lecherous men.

'Since that day, Nicolo has neither spoken nor smiled. And he abandoned the Spanish guitar for that horrible lute. The horror of seeing that naked girl turned him quite mad.'

We were shocked and much saddened by this terrible narrative: although we could readily understand Nicolo's reaction. Many must be the poor boys made crazy by the prospect of the forced heterosexual act.

'I had to tell you,' said the signora, 'in order that you might not make tactless remarks about marriage or girlfriends at our supper table. People in the past have come here and, not knowing our tragic history, have joshed Nicolo with the fact of his not having a female companion or wife at his age – he is nearly twenty-two, now – and it upsets him terribly. You see, I am certain that had we not forced the issue, Nature would have taken its course and Maria and Nicolo would now be man and wife. You are clearly men of the world. I ask only that you do not mention the world in his presence.'

'Believe me, signora,' I said, 'we will do no such thing.'

'God save you both!' she said. 'I feel easier in my mind, now.' She rose. 'Supper, then, at seven?'

'That will be fine,' I said.

'God save you!' she repeated, and left the room.

It was not long before exhaustion caught up with us and we both fell asleep.

I was awoken by the clatter of pans and the hiss of a tap. I lay for some time listening to the pleasant music of the kitchen. There was a scent of fresh herbs and peppers. Presently, I turned on my side. Callipo was sitting up on his bed reading *Orlando Furioso*. His expression was so earnest I could not hold back a giggle. He looked over at me with mock anger.

'Sorry!' I apologised languidly, and got up and walked over to the window. A pulsing disc of orange sun – it seemed almost to be dripping light – hung low over the vines. In the thick golden light swam (there was no other word for the languid, gracious movement) a large raven. This was the loveliest time, when objects seemed to possess at last their true colour which tended to be washed out of them in the fierce brightness of full day.

Beyond the vines I saw, for the first time, a river, and made a mental note to take a walk in that direction after supper. A swim! Perhaps there would be time for a swim before supper! I glanced at my watch. No, it was near seven already. Maybe later.

If we had imagined that, following Signora Rufolo's explanation of the singular situation and our full understanding of it, our meal would be a pleasant occasion, we were wrong. It was dire.

Oh, the food was marvellous. An antipasto of wild mushrooms and Parma ham, followed by pasta served with a rich sauce full of intriguing and ingenious flavour. The wine, likewise, was of the highest quality. There was nothing wrong with the food. The trouble came from the company: or, more precisely, one particular member of our company. Nicolo.

He entered the room a little after we had sat down. He was a vision in tight denims and a black sleeveless T-shirt that left a gap between it and his belt. Callipo and I gave him amiable greeting to which he did not respond. No matter. Taking into account the fact that he could not speak, we framed a number of questions that might be answered simply by nods or shakes of the head:

Have you had a pleasant day? It's been so hot! – that sort of thing. In response, all he did was glare. I, for one, was not entirely averse to his glare: it smouldered with fierce sexuality; but perhaps now was not quite the appropriate moment for such an expression. And a smile would have been lovely.

Finally, his mother spoke. 'Perhaps I did not explain sufficiently clearly. Because Nicolo cannot speak he demands that no one speak in his presence. We always conduct our mealtimes in silence. If you have no objection to continuing this custom?'

Oh, none! I widened my arms in a compliant gesture. Perfectly understandable. Callipo and I exchanged glances.

All silences are individual, no two silences are the same. Certain silences are intelligent, others are stupid, yet others have no meaning whatsoever. Silences can be awkward, sexual, joyful, sad: whatever. No silence, however, is quite so terrible as the silence of a mealtime. Conversation is as essential an accompaniment to food as is wine: one cannot imagine one without the other, eating cannot be done without some form of accompaniment. Trappist monks are put to their severest test at mealtimes. The point, perhaps, is that conversation, apart from being one of the pleasantest of human recreations, masks the sounds of eating and drinking. Human beings make the most appalling sounds whilst they are masticating and swallowing. One can hear the salivary juices swirling around the chewed gobbets of meat and vegetable and the mind conjures up a picture of the extraordinary vileness of the process. Eating is an obscene act. One is forced to consider the paradox that the insides of even the most beautiful boy are frankly repulsive: the workings of heart, liver, lungs and stomach are not for close consideration by the squeamish.

To counter oppressive thought I imagined making love to Nicolo whilst he lay naked on the table covered in pasta. I kept stealing furtive glances at him; and then, when I caught Callipo's eye, he smiled as if to say, Naughty boy!

Certain silences also have the power to arrest time (they share this in common with the poetry of Ariosto). The meal seemed endless.

Finally, Nicolo sat back in his chair, belched and abruptly left the room.

His mother listened with tilted head whilst he went upstairs. There was much banging and tramping. Then he came back down again. He had changed into a black jacket and baggy trousers and was barefoot. Over his shoulder he carried his lute. He walked through the kitchen and out of the door without so much as a wave or a parting smile.

'So!' said Signora Rufolo after the door had slammed. 'That's my Nicolo. And I feel it's all my fault. If I had not conspired in that plot to introduce him too early to love I'm sure he would have come to things in his own good time. Instead, what do I have but a dead husband and a surly madman for a son?' So saying, she burst into tears.

Callipo reached across the table and patted her hand. 'Don't worry, mother,' he said. 'Sometimes boys go through a difficult phase, but they usually grow out of it!' He sounded like a wise grandfather, and yet I don't suppose he himself was more than three or four years older than Nicolo.

Signora Rufolo wiped her eyes on a red napkin and shook her head. 'It is the punishment of the Lord,' she said. 'Would Mary have done such a thing to her sweet Jesus?'

'Perhaps her circumstances were somewhat different,' observed Callipo without a trace of ironic understatement.

Mind you, I have heard it said by the English that Italian men have a lot in common with Jesus Christ: they all think they are the son of God and firmly believe their mothers are virgins.

'Would you perhaps speak with him privately?' she asked Callipo. 'I can see that you have great wisdom and insight. Perhaps if you gave him counsel, it might help. He is not mad on account of a pathological reason. What damage comes about through trauma can surely be healed by the right counsel.'

'Surely your priest . . .?' protested Callipo.

'He has tried, but to no avail. Please, my friend! You are my last hope!'

It seemed to me that by asking Callipo to act as a psychotherapist she was betraying almost as much madness as her son. What could Callipo say to him, for heaven's sake?

Nevertheless, Callipo agreed to have a go.

After a few more words, we left the table.

'What on earth were you thinking of?' I asked, when we were alone in our room once more. 'You can't help that boy!'

'Maybe not!' he replied with a twinkle in his eye. 'But I shall enjoy trying! I have an idea of a few things that need to be said to him. We shall see!'

'Well, look, we need to be on the road again by tomorrow, so . . .'

'So I shall try my luck tonight. What did Signora Rufolo say? – that he spent these summer evenings sitting by the river bank? I shall go down there and sit beside him for a while. We'll have a little chat. That's all.'

'Can I come, too?'

'No, of course not. Certainly not. This will be a private consultation. Do you welcome visitors into the doctor's surgery to listen to your private matters?'

I had never been to a doctor's in my life; but I suppose I knew what he meant.

Accordingly, whilst I retired early to bed with only Callipo's well-thumbed soft leatherbound copy of *Orlando Furioso* to keep me company, Callipo set out to do his Herr Doctor Freud bit. I was not impressed. But I was tired. Within five minutes of my climbing between the sheets and opening the epic poem I had fallen asleep. My dreams were of knights, dragons and castles.

Sixteen

The next morning, Signora Rufolo, Callipo and I were taking our breakfast in the kitchen when we heard the faint sounds of music coming from upstairs. At first, I automatically imagined it to be Nicolo and his lute: but more careful listening proved the instrument to be a guitar. And there was another unusual detail: the music was a cheerful Allegretto by Fernando Sor. What had happened to the gloomy John Dowland? I looked at Callipo, but he was giving nothing away.

Presently, the music ended and Nicolo entered the room. He wore baggy white chinos, a striped Breton fisherman's top and a fancy red cravat around his neck. It was obviously pleasant to see him, but his sudden presence cast a cloud of grey silence.

Not for long, however!

'*Schiavo*, Mama!' he greeted. And also, he shook first Callipo's hand and then mine, and repeated, '*Schiavo!*' before sitting down.

Schiavo! Most Italians of my acquaintance were in the habit of saying the shortened, meaningless form of this word on meeting or leaving – *ciao* – but none, surely, would ever have used it in its archaic form like this? Quite literally it meant, 'I am your slave!'

Callipo caught Signora Rufolo's eye and gave a little shake of his head to indicate that she should not make any fuss.

'So, fellows, you are continuing your journey today?' He reached for the pot and poured himself a coffee.

'With great sorrow,' said Callipo.

'At least it looks as though you will be blest with another fine day!'

'Certainly!' said Callipo. 'We are looking forward to it.'

'And where are you headed?'

So began a perfectly ordinary, amiable conversation which under any other circumstances would have been quite unremarkable; but given the conditions up until this moment it was nothing less than astounding. What had wrought this change? Had it been Callipo? What on earth had he said to the boy to bring him out from his trauma? I longed to know; but of course nothing was going to be revealed at the breakfast table.

Under these changed circumstances, neither Nicolo nor his mother seemed inclined to allow us to leave. Signora Rufolo insisted that if we were to stay she could easily find honest wives for us both: 'I know two sisters, twins barely eighteen years old. Beautiful girls! They can sew and cook and sing, and come from a fertile family – any seed that you might sow in them would be sure to sprout into children.'

Nicolo, on the other hand, seemed to indicate by looks and smiles that, were we to stay, we might enjoy an experience of another kind.

But we had to leave. We had a long way still to go. Our parting was fond and familiar, with hugs, kisses and tears. When finally we detached ourselves, Nicolo and his mother stood at the garden gate and watched us progress slowly back down the rutted path towards the road. I was on Monteverdi, Callipo trudged beside me. Whenever one of us turned to wave yet another time, Nicolo and Signora Rufolo would shake the huge red flag they had dug out for the occasion.

★

It was not until several hours later that Callipo at last relented under pressure of my constant nagging and began to relate to me the story of Nicolo's transformation. We were on a quiet track winding through a wood. The hour was near midday and the sun hot: thus we were glad of the shade afforded by the trees. The birds were silent and the only sounds came from our close tramping and the trickling of water not far off. Flecks of light darted across us.

'So tell me!' I begged for the hundredth time. I had a shrewd idea as to what must have happened: they had had sex; but surely that in itself would not have served to effect the miraculous transformation of Nicolo's character? Unless Callipo's skills as a lover were superhuman? Once again I felt my desire for him growing: I had to fight it.

'We'll take a break for lunch when we come to the stream and then I'll tell you all about it!' he said. 'Honestly, Ramon, all you're interested in is gossip!'

'It's not gossip, it's story!'

'Story is merely an elevated form of gossip. Ask any writer. Ariosto, Dante, Pavese, Calvino – they're nothing but a bunch of tittle-tattling old queens and those who read them are merely voyeurs.'

'You said it!' He was the one who read books, not me. If ever I felt the urge to read something my usual practice was to settle down with a good score: perhaps Bach's B Minor Mass or, if in a lighter mood, a Haydn symphony.

He made no further comment.

So we came to where our path forded the brook. It was a pleasant spot with a broad, grassy bank and a spreading willow tree beneath which we might sit in shade. Monteverdi snorted his delight and immediately waded into the water and began drinking. Callipo and I settled ourselves comfortably and started on the provisions that Signora Rufolo had made for us: bread, cheese and olives, a bowl of strawberries, a bottle of wine.

'What more could one want from life?' asked Callipo after he

had eaten his fill and stretching himself out in the shade prepara-
tory to a postprandial nap.

'Don't you dare forget your promise!' I threw a strawberry at
his recumbent figure. He caught it in a deft, backhand movement.

'Nicolo!' he sighed. 'The lovely Nicolo!' This was indeed a
change from the Callipo I had known heretofore!

'You had sexual relations with him.'

'It wasn't as cold as that. Neither was it so straightforward.
Honestly, Ramon, I don't know where to begin.' He sat up and
folded his arms about his knees. 'The people in this part of Italy
are very strange. I mean, if you think about it, Nicolo's reaction
to seeing the naked body of his potential wife was pretty
extraordinary.'

'I'm not so sure,' I said. 'It sounded perfectly reasonable to me.
If Nicolo's temperament is what I think it is.' How I had matured
during these last few weeks in order to come out with an
observation such as that!

'Well, any of us might have run away; but would it really have
turned us bananas?'

'Not bananas, simply mute with horror and, thereafter, irrevo-
cably glum. Oh, come on, stop procrastinating! What's the story?'

'OK. Well, after I left you, I went down to the river, as I said
I would. It was quite broad, but with a gentle current. I noticed
Nicolo's lute resting on the bank beside his pile of clothes, so
guessed that he had gone for a swim. At first I could not see him;
but then there he was, some way upstream a floating head
amongst a jewel-scatter of last light. It was a warm evening, so I
stripped off and waded in myself. The water was as warm as the
air and the feel of it licking around my skin was quite sensuous:
all the more so as I sensed that this was the same water that, only
moments before, had lapped all round his naked body. Slowly I
swam towards him. At first I dared a backstroke; but then a
modesty overcame me, together with a spurt of common sense:
if the sight of Maria's nakedness had had such an effect could I be
so certain that my evident erection might not also frighten him?
Accordingly, I turned over and swam breaststroke.

'Nicolo, however, clearly did not want to greet me. As soon as he caught sight of me he began to swim further away. For some time, I gave unthreatening chase: simply following him, imagining the water sluicing over his brown naked skin, exploring every crack, every secret nook and cranny of him. Oh, how I envied that river!

'But after a time, this seemed silly. He was determined not to let me catch up with him and what did I propose to do if I should catch him? Grab him by the legs and fight with him? Take him by force? No. What good would that have been? Not that I wasn't, shall we say, a little tempted?

'I came to a rock with a large flat surface and hauled myself out. Sooner or later, Nicolo would have to come back down this way. I could bide my time quite pleasantly here in the evening sunshine. When he came back, I proposed to swim alongside him and, if he would not talk to me, then I would sing to him. Perhaps the *Ave Maria* by Caccini. Many is the boy I have seduced with the *Ave Maria* by Caccini. So I waited. I watched a luminous blue dragonfly skimming the surface of the water, creating ripples as it dipped and dipped. There was a kingfisher swooping after mosquitoes. From somewhere distant came the boom of a bittern. My erection, Ramon, was constant. My cock stood hard against my stomach seemingly as naturally hard a bone as my femur. I could do nothing about it, nothing would make it go away, not even thinking about the piano scores of Alkan. So from time to time I moistened my fingers with my tongue and gently rubbed them over the tip of the glans.

'Nothing happened for so long that I began to think that perhaps Nicolo had clambered out of the water and had made his way back along the bank towards his clothes. The more I thought of this, the more likely a scenario it seemed. I cursed myself heartily. Of course he would have done such a thing! Why take the risk of swimming past me if he knew he did not want to meet me? My next reaction, I freely admit, was to begin masturbating in a spirit of frustration and fury. In our fantasies we are free to admit to ourselves everything, so I had grabbed this

Nicolo by the hair and, as he lay on a moss-covered rock, was buggering him furiously as if riding a wild horse. His skin was chafing and he was crying with pleasure and pain . . . I had half closed my eyes the better to imagine all this; but it was a good thing that I had not shut out the world altogether; for, in the next moment, I saw Nicolo floating swiftly past me, out in midstream. You won't get away so easily! I thought, jumping in after him.

'Then I saw that all was not well with him. He was struggling desperately. A closer look at the water showed a tight knot of current where he was, markedly in contrast to the quieter stream closer to each bank. He was being swept away before my eyes! There was no use my trying to catch up with him without my also plunging into that deadly current. Accordingly, I headed straight for it. The first thing I noticed was how much colder it was. It took me in its icy grip and propelled me along at three times my usual fastest rate. Trees, bushes, roots, rocks flashed past me. And, in surreal slow motion, I saw also Nicolo's lute looking dry and calm and absurdly safe. The experience was terrifying. I had no control of my movement and feared that I would be smashed against a rock. But I am a strong swimmer, and presently I had established a control of sorts and was able, with strong, slow overarm strokes to increase my pace. So that, gradually, I came closer to the desperate Nicolo. When he caught sight of me he cried out, "The rapids!" And now I heard a monstrous thundering and saw, not far ahead, ominous white water. If I did not catch Nicolo he would be dashed to bits.

'I confess, Ramon, that at that time I all but lost hope. Nicolo was sure to die and, I think, in my despair I wanted to die alongside him. The loss of something ineffably lovely often causes in us a despair lacking in all balance and reason: the face we glimpse briefly in a passing train window can have the power to reduce us to a state of overwhelming *weltschmerz*. We live in a state of perpetual loss and lack of attainment. Even if we make love with the one whom we most adore, the feeling afterwards is often an empty one: we have spilt our seed so, like a flower, our purpose is spent, there is nothing more for us to do but wilt and die. True happiness lies only in listening to or playing music. Music is the one creation that goes on for ever and promises eternity.'

I could have done without all Callipo's philosophising. I suppose he had acquired the habit after being so long in the employ of Signor Cavallo. No doubt the good signor had told his servant to educate me along these lines at every opportunity.

'But, ultimately, instinct is stronger than despair,' Callipo continued. 'The instinct for survival. Despair is a refined, a civilised emotion – like gay love. Heterosexuality, the means to ensure the survival of one's blood and the species, is mere brute instinct: not worthy of consideration by the truly civilised.'

'Cut the parentheses, Callipo, you're starting to sound like Manuel de Falla: all vamp till ready without any ready!'

'Sorry. Anyway, all I could hear was the ever louder roar of the rapids, and the water was getting choppier all the time. But, when I could get a glimpse of Nicolo's head, I saw that I was closing in on him. Finally, I made a huge effort. I remember so clearly the exact moment when the tips of my fingers touched the side of one of his feet. Then he was gone again. But I persisted. In another few strokes I was almost level with his legs; a little more effort and we were side by side. I grabbed him. He did not struggle, perhaps because he was too exhausted, or perhaps because he was too full with the apprehension of death and already resigned to it. Strong as I am, and as able a lifesaver, I would have been of no use had there not been an overhanging tree up ahead. I steered us so that we crashed into its branches. And suddenly we were still. It was a curious sensation. Carefully, I inched towards the bank, using the tree as support. Soon we were away from the fierce current. Our feet found a hold on soft mud and the slower moving water was once again warm.

'On reaching the grassy bank, Nicolo was trembling and cold and unable to speak. I laid him gently down and massaged the water out of his lungs. He must have swallowed a litre at least: it was extraordinary to see so much choke out! When all this was done, I laid him on his back and allowed the sun to dry his body whilst I went to retrieve our clothes and his lute.

'When I returned shortly after, he had fallen asleep. Drops of water still glistened on his skin, so I thought it wise to wipe him with my shirt. He looked so frail and lovely at that time. His genitals were quite shrunken with all his effort and the cold. I covered them with my right hand: they felt much colder than the rest of his body; but, presently, they began to warm and emerge once again from the depths. It seemed wise to massage them back to life, to encourage the blood to flow through them once more lest they atrophy. Whilst I did this, he remained with his eyes closed although, clearly, his cock was obviously wakening. There appeared a lovely smile on his face.

'Then he opened his eyes, and sat up. "What are you doing?" "I saved your life," I said. I was also still naked, and I eased my body alongside him, allowing my warmth to complement his. "I have to do this, it's part of the necessary first aid." I leant over and kissed him. His first kiss was cold and unfeeling, the second a little better. With the third there was more than a touch of warmth. I held him to this last kiss, putting into it all that I knew about the art of kissing; and, as I did so, I continued to work his cock until I felt his body arching and his breathing coming in furious little gasps. It was obvious that he did not know what was happening. When he came his body was seized with a terrific convulsion and each spurt of jism was accompanied by a harsh cry. I have never seen so much come. His body was covered in it. Even when his cock stopped shooting, his body twitched with the effect of numerous aftershocks. It was not only his first time, as I learnt later, but his first sexual experience of any sort. He was shattered. One minute he had been near death, the next he was experiencing a first orgasm! What a time! He fell immediately into a profound sleep, from which he awoke five minutes later absolutely rested and believing that he had been unconscious for hours. So we talked. He told me about his life. About how he knew that he loathed the sight of naked women, but had not, up until that evening, realised there was any alternative or any other accepted standard of human beauty. He had known the mechanics of making love – he was, after all, a farm boy – but believed that because he found the idea of heterosexual love so repulsive and uninteresting then he would never in his life know sexual love: that was something for the bulls and the cows, the brutish village boys and their ugly girlfriends. He had his lute, what more could he possibly want? He thought the awesome loveliness of men as intangible as music or painting: something that appealed to all the senses bar touch.'

I was moved by Callipo's story and found it not so hard to believe as some might: after all, Nicolo's experience was not a million miles from my own, although my lasting virginity was on account of a passion that simply put everything else in the shade.

'Poor Nicolo!' I said, without really meaning it.

'Oh, not so poor! We made love half a dozen times after that, and still he showed no signs of flagging.'

'No wonder he came to life so cheerfully, this morning! Not such a miracle, after all.'

'Life itself is a miracle,' said Callipo. 'The joy of making love is a miracle. The sheer extraordinariness that we, as individuals, should exist is miraculous.'

'And music! Music, too!' I said eagerly. 'Surely that's the greatest miracle of all!'

'No,' he said. 'Music is simply the breath of God.'

And with that he stretched out, arranged his jacket for a pillow, and fell asleep in the shade.

Seventeen

L ater that day, whilst we were trekking along a quiet, dusty road that led through a landscape of rolling hills, fields, stone walls and cypress trees, I noticed that Callipo had become unusually quiet. Thinking that this might be because I had been hogging Monteverdi for too long, and that the time was overdue when Callipo should be granted his turn, I offered to swap places. He declined.

'What is it, Callipo? What's wrong?'

'Nothing. I'm just tired, is all.'

'Then let's swap places!'

'No! How many times do I have to tell you, for heaven's sake?' he snapped.

I said nothing. Silence will often draw out truth where probing questions fail. I was not wrong.

We were about half a mile further down the road and passing a small lake delicately patterned with pink waterlilies, when Callipo said, 'I'm sorry, Ramon. It is not your fault. Only . . . only the truth is there is no sadness quite so deep as that of having to leave your lover behind.'

'You fell in love with Nicolo? That's not so terrible. Look, we can always go back . . . You can go back by yourself, if you want.

If you're really in love, I'll carry on by myself. Forget Signor Cavallo's orders: I can get along by myself. Honestly, Callipo. There's not enough love in the world. It's our duty to propagate it whenever we come across it.'

He shook his head. 'It's not like that. It's more complicated. Sure, I fell in love with Nicolo; but it was a brief love, a love of the moment: that kind of love that we gays are best at. It's a good thing because it exists not only for itself but serves to inform our natures that love may be found everywhere and in all places. It's the kind of love that keeps most gays out of the armies of the world, for one thing: how can you shoot or drop bombs on boys with whom in normal circumstances you would be happy to share the most intimate moments of passion? It's a good form of love, but we usually know, instinctively, that it is not lasting: and yet our spirits long for it to last for ever and so, after the exhilaration and joy have worn off, a grey sadness seeps into our very bones.'

'Oh, Callipo!' I tugged at the reins and brought Monteverdi to a halt. 'Look, go back.'

'No. You can never go back.'

He continued tramping onwards. I watched him for a time before giving Monteverdi his familiar two pats to get him moving again. I knew that nothing more could be said about the matter, and it was best forgotten. The moment was as brief and as concentrated as a piano piece by Webern; and, like Webern, it would haunt my subconscious for ever.

Distant music thickened the evening breeze. Scraps of melody appeared on the air, now clear, now indistinct according to the direction of the wind. It was Verdi, and played by one of those braying town bands who make up with enthusiasm whatever they might lack in skill.

There is nothing like Verdi to chase away feelings of gloom. I felt my spirits rise and, judging by the lighter spring in his step, I knew that Callipo's melancholy was being justly banished. Away with melancholy! It serves to deepen our understanding of certain moments and conditions, but we must never allow it to inhabit us for too long because then it establishes a hold over us that it does not deserve. It can become an addiction: I know, because my own father was thus inclined and, during the last years of his life refused to listen to any music lest it rob him of his awful fix.

We rounded a corner, and there in the valley below was the small village of Pizzo which Callipo had earlier decreed was to be our resting place for the night. Red rooftops amongst cypress trees beneath the thin blue sky of early evening. A black cloud of starlings swooped and curled in perfect formation over the village, twisting and turning like wreaths of smoke.

The road down to the village was full of potholes. Monteverdi was naturally cautious and reluctant to continue, so I dismounted and led him by the reins. It was good to walk. In addition to the music we now found ourselves surrounded by the low drone of bees. There must have been a hundred hives in the adjoining field. Bees are amongst those creatures who, by their intelligence and doggedness of purpose help more than most to bind the world to itself and seem to make sense of things. Apart from the bees, the fields had an aimless quality about them. The grass was long. There were a few rows of vines, but these looked straggly and untended: they certainly had not been pruned for a couple of seasons. And now a closer look at the hives revealed many teetering on rotten struts and missing planks of wood. A goat, tethered to a stake, had worn away the grass within a circumference bounded by the length of its lead, and lay listlessly with its head resting on the ground. It watched us as we passed; but, unlike most goats of my acquaintance, did not bound up to greet us.

The music stopped abruptly midway through the fifty-third bar of the overture to *La forza del destino*. I shuddered. Ordinarily, I might have assumed that this was a rehearsal and the conductor had brought things to a halt in order to have a word with the second flute, who was more than a little off the beat; but, combined with the destitution around us, the sudden cessation of music took on a more ominous tone.

We passed an empty farmhouse that stood isolated in a large, rambling and overgrown garden. Shutters barely hung on rusted hinges, glass was broken in the windows, the front door stood half open, broken tiles on the roof exposed rotting rafters like the bones of a corpse.

If we were no longer melancholy, we were certainly apprehensive. Perhaps even a little afraid.

I stopped. 'Do you think we should turn back?'

'No,' said Callipo. 'We can't. We need lodging for the night, and the next village is twenty miles away. Monteverdi is dead beat, and so am I. We must rest. There was music, just now. Things can't be quite so bad as perhaps we imagine. Let's press on.'

An oily black crow perched on the low signpost that read PIZZO by the side of the road. Bindweed wound its way up the post, almost obscuring the name. As we passed, the bird dipped its beak and shat drops of vile green excreta. Its eyes were glistening black stones.

The main street was deserted and silent; but, as we made our way up the cobbled street – Monteverdi's shoes clacking and sending off sparks – we sensed eyes watching us. We came to the square. A circular wooden bench surrounded a fountain which trickled water. There was also a horse trough. Monteverdi made straight for this, whilst Callipo and I sat down on the bench. Callipo took off his boots and fanned himself with his broad-brimmed hat.

'Well,' he said. 'We're here. And there was music.'

But where was it now? I remembered how, when the first blessed sound reached us up there on the road, I had fondly imagined to come upon a town band playing here in this square, with groups of people sitting around in cafés and bars, or perhaps simply lounging in doorways or hanging out of windows, listening. Children playing marbles, loving the sound and the security that the music offered without being intellectually aware of any of it beyond its simple melodies. Instead, here was a town with neither music nor people.

Out of the corner of my eye I thought I saw a slight movement behind an open window on the second storey of one of the surrounding buildings. Poor-looking properties, these were, a few glass-fronted shops with CLOSED signs in the doors, the rest houses: all peeling paint on the window frames and moss growing up the walls. I regarded a few blades of grass growing in a crack on a front step, whilst all the while keeping that open window in the circumference of my vision.

'Don't look up,' I told Callipo, 'but I think we're being watched.'

'I know,' he said, looking the other way. 'It's an old woman with a monkey on her shoulder. I can see her reflected in the window of the house opposite.'

'Do you think we should go and knock on her door?'

'Not yet. She's obviously suspicious of us and it might be better to wait to see if she makes an initial approach.'

'Do you suppose she's a serial killer, and has wiped out the entire village?'

'I'm absolutely certain of it. I think the monkey is the evil power behind her actions.'

I began to whistle the plaintive melody from *La forza del destino*. It is a curious, winding little tune redolent of mystery and the attraction of the unknown. It seems to fuse together the music of both West and East without losing its essential Italian character. The melody has a come-hither quality: a watcher regards and then begins to follow. It had, after all, lured us down to this little village in the first place. Would it now tempt the old dame out of her secret hiding place?

'Good afternoon, travellers!'

There!

She stood in her window, hands resting firmly on the sill. She was a sturdy-looking woman of great age, her face criss-crossed with lines as though her skin were made of crumpled paper. Her grey hair was done up in two buns and, on the shoulder of her velvet dress, the monkey, wearing a red fedora, sat blinking and wringing its tiny hands.

'Good afternoon!' Callipo rose swiftly and replaced his hat in order that he might remove it again in an extravagant gesture linked to a bow.

I quickly followed suit.

'What brings you here?' she asked.

'We are lovers of Art and life,' said Callipo, 'journeying across the countryside, and we thought we heard your town band playing Verdi. Naturally, our souls drank in the sound and we were unable to resist a diversion from our set route. We had hoped to find a throng of fellow musicians and . . .'

'You are musicians?' she interrupted.

The monkey abruptly changed his position, jerked his head forward and regarded us through narrowed eyes.

'But of course!'

She held a finger to her lips. 'Wait one moment!' She disappeared from the window. Presently, after much rattling of chains and sliding of bolts, she appeared in the doorway below.

Callipo and I had not moved and were still standing at some distance away. This seemed to exasperate her, 'Well, come on!' she said, beckoning furiously. 'Come in!'

Were we to have our throats cut and our livers and lights fed to a monstrous regiment of monkey princes? There was no turning back, however. We were about to discover the mystery of the melancholy village.

We entered a dark hallway and the crone led us up a narrow flight of creaking wooden stairs. There was a smell of monkey. The peeling wallpaper was of harps and flutes, and on it were stuck framed photographs of various besuited worthies frozen into permanent paralysis in the photographic studios of sixty or seventy years ago.

Her small living room was also dark, and filled with heavy furniture. A sofa and armchairs, covered in blue velvet and full of cushions, looked wonderfully comfortable and inviting after all my heavy riding. Softness: what did that feel like? A mahogany sideboard was scattered with numerous small objects and framed photographs. There was also a tiny harpsichord – or perhaps it might be better described as a spinet. It was covered with a cloth of intricate pattern featuring parrots and monkeys in a lush tropic forest, and the sides were painted with similar features. Every inch of wall space was taken up with pictures. Hanging from the ceiling was a cage containing a parrot. She introduced him straight away. 'This is Frescobaldi. He's dead. And here on my shoulder is Buxtehude. My name is Signora Scala. Please. Sit down.'

On a small table sat a gramophone connected to two gigantic loudspeakers on the floor. I had thought that only rap artists ever possessed such speakers: they looked incongruous in this room.

Signora Scala fetched us something to drink together with a bowl of hazelnuts. I was starving and could have bolted the nuts down in a matter of minutes; but this was clearly a decorous apartment, if a little poor, and I politely helped myself to one small nut at a time. Buxtehude scrambled off his mistress's shoulder and made his way to sit at the spinet on a high stool and played a few cautious notes with a delicacy and intelligence of feeling surprising for a monkey. There was no melody, but the note progression was an interesting one which suggested something more than mere fragmentation. I was reminded of the spare caution in certain of the music of Gyorgy Kurtag. Frail, delicate spikes of music accompanied our rather lumpish human sounds.

When we were settled and the few conversational formalities had been completed, I naturally introduced the topic of music.

Signora Scala visibly stiffened before she relaxed into a cautious smile.

'I play,' she indicated the spinet with a small turn of her hand, 'as you might have guessed. And Buxtehude: he enjoys it too. Alas!' She set her glass of mint tea on to a low table. 'We are in a minority in the village of Pizzo.' She bowed her head and regarded her old hands entwined on her lap.

I looked at Callipo. *No*, he shook his head. *Don't interrogate. If she wants to say something, she will.*

There was a long silence.

Then Signora Scala said, 'No doubt you noticed that all is not well with this village.'

148

'It seems a little poor,' said Callipo, 'but many villages are poor . . .'

'No, we are not poor! Or we should not be. The soil is fertile, the climate wonderful. We used to grow the finest vines, the best sunflowers, glorious maize. Our bees produced the best honey in the region from the finest blossom. If you had passed this way only two years ago you would have found the happiest little village in all Italy. Through my window I could hear the happy singing of the children in the junior school down the road, and just down there, in the square, our band used to play every Sunday afternoon and during the festivals and sometimes just spontaneously the musicians would gather on any summer's evening and play simply for the joy of it. Not any more. This, my friends – and I tell you this because you are musicians and can therefore take you into my intimate confidence – is a town where the music has died. And where the music dies everything else gradually collapses also. Music, you see, is the lifeblood of any society. It is what keeps us human beings going. The slaves in America – what would have become of them without their spirituals? The sailors on their rough voyages, the workers in the factories, the sad, the dying, the lonely: all need music to sustain them through the darkest moments. Music is the one thing that can transform. And the lack of it brings destruction.'

She became silent, biting her lower lip and fighting back tears. I leant forward and, kneeling before her, took hold of her hand. She looked up. Tears were budding in the corners of her kind old eyes and my heart felt full to bursting. I knew from what she had said that she, myself and Callipo all shared one philosophy. We were soulmates. Buxtehude continued to play his vague, scattered music.

'So what happened?' I whispered. 'What happened to the music and to the life of this village? Callipo and I, we heard music when we were on the road . . .' Had this perhaps been from a ghostly band?

She pulled away from me and averting her head blew her nose. I returned to my seat. Callipo patted my arm. When it seemed as though she could not bring herself to say anything further, I said, 'Well, at least you have your gramophone. It may not be live music, but . . .'

She interrupted me as if not hearing. 'One man,' she said. 'One man has brought us to this. Signor Malignato.' She spoke the name as if she were chewing a sour lemon. 'It is all his doing. Signor Malignato is the town mayor and he has issued a decree banning all music. Transgressors are fined or locked in the town hall dungeon.'

This was terrible! I didn't want to offend Signora Scala or her fellow townsfolk but hadn't news of democracy reached this part of Italy yet? This was, after all, 1998, not 1398. But power is a curious thing and one of the great mysteries of human existence is why so many people are happy to accept the word of a tyrant. Perhaps it is due to the desire of so many to relinquish responsibility. Let someone else shoulder all the burden and if that should mean less freedom, then so be it: it is a price worth paying. Musicians, however, are in the forefront of freedom. We create freedom each time we play. Therefore, I was not surprised to hear Signora Scala then relate how all the members of the band had been locked in the dungeons until they had been obliged to sign documents stating their willingness to abandon their instruments.

'How could they do otherwise?' she said. 'They all had friends and families who needed them. You cannot feed your family on principles. The music teacher at our little school, Signorina Bellini, refused the edict and was fined so heavily that she had to sell her flute in order to keep body and soul together.'

'You tell a sad story,' said Callipo.

'I try not to be sad. I am defiant. That music you heard on the road: that was me. When I can I play my gramophone as loud as I can, and turn the speakers towards the open window. I have recordings of the town band stretching back to 1932. But when he hears my music, Signor Malignato orders the electricity supply to be cut off. He would imprison me, if he could, but I am old and infirm and he fears that if I were to die in jail it might reflect badly on him.'

'The man's a maniac!' I said. 'Why is he like this?'

'He used not to be. When he was first elected he used to sing tenor in our small oratorio and opera productions. He was a wonderful Rudolfo and when he sang Nero in *L'incoronazione di Poppea*, there was not a dry eye in the town hall.'

'"*Pur ti miro pur ti stringo . . .*"' Callipo sang the opening of Poppea and Nero's final sad aria with delicate softness yet strength.

'"*Pur ti godo pur t'annado . . .*"' Signora Scala picked up the melody.

They fell silent. Buxtehude continued to pick out his sharp, hesitant notes on the spinet.

'So what happened?' I asked eventually.

She shook her head. 'No one knows. But the change in him came almost overnight. One Sunday night he was treating us all to arias from *I Puritani* in the square, accompanied with exquisite charm by a young man friend of his on the harp; and the next morning we see posted up a notice: A SPECIAL EDICT!! on every wall and tree. Music was banned from that moment.'

'He can't have that power!' I said confidently. 'Surely the police must refuse to carry out his orders. It's impossible!'

'Sadly not. There is legislation, applicable only to this district, that invests in the mayor of each town or village almost unlimited power. It dates back to the time of Garibaldi when he and his troops were suffering major setbacks but were given invaluable assistance by the mayors and councillors of this region. As personal favours he gave them the legal backing to do almost anything they wanted. Oh, such a thing was necessary at the time when insurgency and counter-insurgency and goodness knows what were trying problems: mayors needed to have the right to arrest, execute, fine or imprison at will. But an anomaly in the legal documentation meant that, although Garibaldi had intended this power only to remain in the hands of a small number of named persons for a limited period, in reality the power has stayed through generations. The police are obliged to follow orders, they can do nothing else.'

Callipo did not appear to be listening. 'But why,' he said, 'did your mayor change in this way so suddenly? The legislation of which you speak does not surprise me, there are many such laws in obscure parts of our country; but the metamorphosis of a person's nature: that is far more intriguing and mysterious. How long is it since you have suffered in this way?'

'Had you passed this way last spring, you would have found nothing amiss. Indeed, as musicians, you would have been highly honoured. Pizzo used to be known as Pizzicato in the neighbouring villages.' She laughed shyly at the small joke which was suggestive of an infinite refinement of feeling and a fundamental good-naturedness that is all but non-existent in our metropolitan centres. 'It is just over a year now since Signor Malignato's character changed.'

'Where does he live?' asked Callipo.

'In an apartment above the town hall, but . . .'

'My friend and I will pay him a visit and . . .'

'. . . you cannot see him. He receives no visitors. He has become a recluse.'

'Signora, before I became manservant to Signor Ernesto Cavallo, of whom you may have heard . . .'

'The cellist? Oh, my gracious!' She sank back and pressed a beringed hand to her heart. 'Great Signor, I had no idea, I . . .?'

'No, please, it is nothing. What I mean to say is that before I was in Signor Cavallo's employ I was in the diplomatic service. I used to accompany our ambassador and Ministers of State everywhere on their travels, and I got many of them out of many a tight fix. Signor Andreotti himself once said that were it not for my services Italy would have become embroiled in the Ethiopian civil war.'

'Gracious!' Signora Scala raised her eyebrows.

I had the notion that Callipo was offering a rather free interpretation of truth. Whilst he detailed certain moments of his personal history to the possibly gullible signora, I stared at

Buxtehude. He was a very strange monkey. In addition to the fedora, he also wore a red waistcoat which was decorated with a treble clef on the right-hand pocket and a bass clef on the left. From his left ear hung a ring in the shape of a harp. And his concentration on his playing was absolute. One had no choice but to conclude that the monkey had chosen this life for himself out of his own free will. Here was not a creature who would be more at home in the jungles of Brazil: Buxtehude was as fully civilised a being as, say, Carl Philipp Emanuel Bach.

My mind had led me to an idle consideration of Villa Lobos, when suddenly Callipo slapped his knees forcibly and said, 'So we must go! Are you up to it, Ramon?'

'To what?' I asked.

Callipo made a gesture to Signora Scala which seemed to indicate *These cellists!* 'We pay a visit to our friend Mayor Malignato, and get to the bottom of this mystery once and for all!'

'Er, sure. Of course, Callipo.'

'No!' said Signora Scala. 'First of all you must allow me to give you some supper. You have been travelling long distances – I can see from your dust and the state of your clothes. I have a spare room and you may stay awhile. Please. Freshen up, change your clothes, have some supper and a night's rest. Signor Malignato can wait another day before you see him. First: rest. I will not hear of anything less. And there is also, of course, your poor horse to consider. I shall send for a boy to take him to the local stables.'

That night, following supper, we made a small concert. Callipo alternately sang or strummed a lute, I played a viol that Signora Scala said had belonged to her great-great-grandfather, and she herself accompanied us on the spinet. The music was curious. No matter what the markings, we were obliged to play everything with the dynamic *piano*, lest it be heard outside. The most stirring melodies, the most rousing songs: we played them all as softly as possible. The effect was curious, and the novel rendition gave a fresh interpretation to many a familiar piece. Most delightful of all was 'Summer' from Antonio Vivaldi's *Four Seasons*. This music, with its well-known and one would have thought inescapable and dramatic dynamic markings, sounded like something entirely other under the strange circumstances of that night. Although Signora Scala, given the limitations of her spinet, could only ever play at *piano*, Callipo and I employed all our musicianship to wander the dynamic range between *piano* (p), to *pianissimo* (pp) to pppp, and even ppppp.

It was a pleasant evening, and there was copious wine.

Towards midnight, Buxtehude, who had been listening to us with evident delight, took himself off to bed: a violin case done up as a cosy crib complete with a pillow, blankets and red curtains. Seeing him do this, Signora Scala indicated that it was time for us also to retire. Callipo and I were shown to a spare room with ready-made-up single beds.

'My mother always taught me to have beds ready for travellers,' Signora Scala explained. 'You see, she was very devout and used to say that one never knew when Christ might come visiting in disguise. Sleep well, dear boys. If you were our Saviour and John the Baptist you could hardly have given me greater pleasure than that bestowed upon me this night. If I should not wake in the morning, I shall be preparing a place for you in paradise.'

Humbled by the generosity of the old lady's spirit we said our prayers and prepared for bed.

The day that had begun so long ago with our leave-taking of Nicolo and his mama was at last drawing to a close.

For some time, Callipo sat propped on his pillows reading *Orlando Furioso*. I, who had not brought anything to read on the journey, chose a volume from a sagging bookcase close to my bed: *The Faerie Queene* by Edmund Spenser. My knowledge of English was never that great, and my knowledge of ancient English even less, but I enjoyed picking out what story I could, and the rhythm and sound of the poetry lulled me gently to sleep. I was becoming a reader. How curious!

Deep in the night, I awoke. Some sound had touched the sides of my sleep, nudging me into semi-consciousness. Gradually, I understood the sound to be that of a harp; but not one played by human hands. This was an aeolian harp, its notes formed by the breeze. Faint and distant, it was coming from whence I knew not. The music seemed to suggest that Signora Scala was not the only one in active opposition to Mayor Malignato: she had the gods themselves on her side.

Eighteen

Signora Scala provided us with a fine breakfast of peaches, grapes and yogurt washed down with the purest water I have ever tasted.

'I still tend my own patch of land,' she explained, 'even if my neighbours no longer have the heart to care for theirs. My spinet has kept me going, you see. A spinet you can play under the harshest of regimes, but the rest of us here are trumpeters or fife players or drummers, and what can they do? We pass each other in the street and some of them do not even have the spirit to offer me a greeting.'

We were refreshed by the time Callipo had decided it was appropriate to set out and seek Mayor Malignato, but, speaking for myself, not without a modicum of trepidation.

I was astonished to find that the town hall, where Mayor Malignato both lived and worked, was a stone's throw from Signora Scala's house: just across the square. Hadn't we taken a huge risk in giving that concert, the night before? But the signora poo-pooed my fears: '*Pianissimo* he does not hear. He is a coarse man and lacks the sensitivity to respond to anything below *mezzo forte*. We were always going to be safe: your expert musicianship – and by goodness you boys can play! – guaranteed that.'

It is common knowledge that one gay man can recognise another at a hundred paces. As soon as we set eyes on Mayor Malignato we knew that here was one of our kind; and, despite his reputation, it made us feel more at ease.

We had entered the town hall and progressed along tiled floors through wood-panelled corridors without any guidance from any form of Reception. There was a desk at the entrance, but it was unmanned.

When knocking, followed by loud knocking, followed by banging failed to produce any response from inside, Callipo simply tried the door handle and entered cautiously, me close behind.

It was a dark room. Tiny spots of light from outside pierced through the heavy curtains at the windows, but anything more exuberant was firmly barred.

Mayor Malignato sat in a pool of vile yellow light that was vomited from a hideous, twisted desk lamp that reared cobra-like above his desk. He was bent low over a pile of papers: it almost seemed as if the lamp were holding him transfixed in its evil power. Close at hand was an ancient typewriter. I was not surprised: anything so modern as a computer would have seemed out of place in this village.

The mayor looked up, startled. We were later to discover that it was not the sound of the door's opening, nor yet Callipo's soft greeting that had roused him, but rather the vibrations caused by our feet on the parquet floor. He had a round face, pitted like the surface of the moon. Perhaps our perspicacity as to his sexuality was not so surprising considering the look that he gave Callipo. My friend was wearing tight-fitting jeans and a calico shirt with a fetching red cravat. One just knew that the Mayor had stripped him down to only the cravat in a matter of mental moments. Lust at first sight is not such a hard phenomenon to detect.

'Please excuse us for intruding upon you like this,' said Callipo. 'We knocked, but you did not hear. And there was no clerk who might have introduced us.'

Mayor Malignato turned down the corners of his lips in an expression of utter distaste. He wrote something on a notepad and turned it round on the desk so that we could read:

SPEECH IS REPULSIVE TO ME. WRITE WHAT YOU MUST SAY, AND BE QUICK. I AM A BUSY MAN!

Callipo made a sign requesting that we might sit down and, when the request was granted, fetched two hard-backed chairs from a corner of the room and placed them on the opposite side of the desk to the mayor. I think Callipo was assuming that the mere fact of our presence was comfortable on the old man's eye and that his impatient protestations could be safely ignored for the immediate future.

Callipo wrote: WE HAVE BEEN SENT HERE ON A MISSION BY THE PAPAL NUNCIO.

Mayor Malignato returned: WHAT THE FUCK ARE YOU TALK-ING ABOUT?

Callipo: WORD HAS REACHED ROME THAT THE VILLAGE OF PIZZO IS A VILLAGE IN SOME DISTRESS.

WORD CAN FUCKING WELL UNREACH ROME!

THE POPE HIMSELF

Here, Signor Malignato snatched the pad from Callipo's hands. He wrote, YOU DON'T LOOK LIKE ENVOYS FROM THE POPE YOU LOOK LIKE A COUPLE OF CHEAP RENT BOYS FROM CALA-BRIA WHAT ARE YOUR NAMES? WHAT'S THE NAME OF THE NUNCIO!

CALLIPO AND RAMON.

CALLIPO?? WHAT SORT OF NAME'S THAT? YOU'RE JUST A CHEAP CLOWN GO BACK TO THE CIRCUS HANG AROUND THE BACK OF THE TENTS AND SEE WHO YOU CAN PICK UP GET OUT OF HERE YOU CHEAP SLUTS GO ON GET OUT!!!!!

BUT WE'VE ONLY JUST ARRIVED CAN'T WE PUT OUR CASE?

YOU CAN PUT YOUR COCKS UP A TIGER'S ARSE! GO ON GET

OUT OF HERE AND DON'T YOU EVER DARE COME BACK I'VE
FINISHED WITH THE LOT OF YOU!

'But!' Callipo offered, when it was clear that Mayor Malignato
was not going to return the pad for further delightful discourse.

Mayor Malignato stood up in order to demonstrate by practical
example what he hoped we might also do. There was not much
alternative. We hesitated for an instant, but when the mayor
began to growl like the black bear he most resembled we knew
it was time to be on our way.

At the door, Callipo turned and said, 'We shall return. That I
promise.'

His words, naturally, fell on deaf ears.

We were making our way back along the corridor, when one
of the unmarked side doors suddenly opened and a moustachioed
man of middle age whispered, 'Pssst!' Despite having read the
word before in detective novels, this was the first time I had
come across it in real life. It was a fascinating sound and reminded
me of a moment in *Sequenza Three* by our great contemporary
Luciano Berio; but I digress. The man was of medium build and
looked rather fetching in black trousers, red shirt and black
waistcoat. He wore a tie patterned with black cats playing white
pianos. This last part of his attire was a terrible mistake: like the
music of George Gershwin. Without another word the man
beckoned us into his room: a rather banal office with square
furniture, leather chairs and pot plants. There was an air of
normality about the place, however, which was reassuring.

'Please, take a seat!' the fellow offered. 'My name is Luigi
Bassano and I have been watching you ever since you entered
our humble village last evening. My younger cousin, Claudio, is
a stable boy here and he it is who is taking care of your horse.'
He sat down behind his desk, stretched his legs and crossed them
at the ankles and placed his folded hands beneath his chin in a
gesture of thoughtfulness. 'I must say first of all that I know some
things about you. I happened to be passing Signora Scala's house
late last night and I heard the music. Such sounds we have not
heard in the village for so long! I sat on the pavement hard against

the wall and listened for as long as you played. And when you had ceased to play I stayed on for some time feeling the presence of the spirit of the music as it lingered in the walls and in the air. You are true musicians!'

'And you are a true listener!' replied Callipo, paying a high compliment. Anybody can *hear* music, few are able actually to listen.

'You will have heard the story of the tragedy of our village from Signora Scala?'

'Of course,' said Callipo.

'Sadly,' I added. I had become conscious, during our intercourse with Mayor Malignato and, indeed, during our time with Signora Scala, that Callipo tended to take the lead in most conversation and I resolved to right the balance a little. Although, of course, I lacked his wisdom and experience I did feel that little by little I was becoming more mature and was gaining a degree of perspicacity in some matters that I had entirely lacked before the time of my first meeting Signor Cavallo.

Luigi said, 'And may I guess the purpose of your visit to our mayor? Such musicians as yourselves, I feel, would do your best to ease our terrible situation.'

'Correct!' said Callipo.

'Then I must apprise you of a little background information that I alone know. It has not been possible for me to divulge this to others – for reasons that will soon become clear – but I can tell that you both have the wisdom to understand the situation in all its roundness. Mayor Malignato has become stone deaf. It happened last year. You see ... I should perhaps explain that I am his private secretary and have access to all his papers, and it so happened that I chanced to read his diary one afternoon when I came across it lying open on his desk after he had gone home. I would not normally have read such a document; but I think that when people leave things lying open their subconscious, at least, is requesting that certain of their innermost thoughts are shared with others. To shorten the narrative, Mayor Malignato contracted syphilis from a Calabrian lion tamer who passed through

Pizzo with his circus some eighteen months ago.' Luigi was silent a moment and his eyes glazed over, apparently remembering the occasion with delight. 'That circus was an event such as few people can ever witness. The highlight came when the lion tamer – a dark youth with wild hair and Arabic appearance – wrestled naked with a tiger. Of course, the beast had had its claws clipped and was no doubt toothless; but there was no doubting its strength. It seemed to those of us watching that we were witnesses to the very struggle between brute barbarism and civilisation. Everything depended on the outcome of this struggle. The entire tent was in darkness, the only illumination being a spotlight fixed on the fight. There were no words, no music, only the roaring of both the man and the beast. It was a fair duel, boy and tiger were evenly matched. In the end, after a contest of epic length, the tiger was subdued: it simply lay exhausted on the sawdust. For long minutes the boy appeared also defeated and he lay still atop the beast. No one dared approach. Finally, the boy rose, picked up a green and yellow flag and held it high. The applause was tumultuous. There was not a person in the whole of Pizzo who had not fallen in love with that boy; but, speaking for myself, it seemed there was something unapproachable about him. He was too strong, too handsome, too sturdy for any of us even to imagine making love with him. Mayor Malignato, however, was always a man of great ambition. I read in his diary that he met the boy, later, behind the tent and they had sexual congress. His earache began a week later and, as it worsened, he diagnosed himself as suffering from syphilis. And there you have the whole dreadful story. Mayor goes deaf, Mayor can no longer hear music – a passion for him even greater than sex – Mayor orders music to be banned from the entire area over which he has jurisdiction.'

'But syphilis is so easily treated, these days!' said Callipo. 'A few shots of penicillin and . . .'

'Mayor Malignato will not go near a doctor. It's a phobia he has had from when, as a child, he was visited by a doctor who insisted on playing the ukulele and thereby seduced his mother who subsequently left home, husband and seven children.'

We nodded in perfect understanding.

'I would have injected him in his sleep,' I said.

'Or ground the antibiotic into his soup,' said Callipo, much more sensibly.

Luigi squeezed his mouth and raised his eyebrows in a gesture that I have never understood and probably never will understand.

'It's too late now to do anything,' he said.

'And I'm afraid there's nothing that we can do,' sighed Callipo. 'When are the next mayoral elections?'

'Mayor Malignato is mayor for life. Signora Scala may have told you of Garibaldi's edicts?'

'Then move out of town!' Callipo suggested. 'Go now, whilst you are still young and still have your strength. Go to Calabria! Go anywhere, but don't for pity's sake stay in this slough of despond!'

I suppose Callipo meant well, but nevertheless Luigi burst into tears at these words and the time before we left was spent in comforting him.

It was with a heavy sense of failure that later that day we stood beneath the oak tree in the square and prepared our leave-taking. Whilst Callipo filed Monteverdi's shoes, I hitched up his saddle. He was a placid creature and did not mind in the least all the attentions he was receiving which, for a lesser spirit, would have proved irritating in the extreme. Close by, Signora Scala, with Buxtehude on her shoulder, stood watching us and I knew that we were being observed also by Luigi from a window in the town hall. Signora Scala had wanted us to stay another night. She wanted another concert; but Callipo believed that one should never try to repeat perfection: it is always slightly tainted the second time around. For myself I don't entirely agree with this; but a philosophy is a philosophy and as such impervious to argument and reason.

In my heart, I suppose I was glad to be leaving. Pizzo was a prison: as a visitor one can help the inmates, but one can do no good by staying overlong.

Suddenly, the quiet afternoon air was shattered by a low moan. So appalling was the sound that Callipo and I froze. Signora Scala and Buxtehude were, however, completely unfazed.

'It's only Mayor Malignato,' she explained. 'He often has these moments. You get used to it.'

It would be uncharitable to attribute any *schadenfreude* to the sweet dame, but at the same time one could not help but notice a certain air of satisfaction in her tone and manner as she spoke these words.

Our farewells said (with more than a touch of the tone of the valedictory *abschied* from Mahler's *Das Lied von der Erde*), we followed the same path away from the village as we had taken on entering: it was the quickest way back to the main road.

We passed the dilapidated vines, the neglected gardens and the collapsing beehives. Callipo, riding Monteverdi, talked about the metaphoric significance of the beat in music: no matter how diverse or complex the rhythm of any particular piece, the innate inner beat was always steady. If only we, as individuals, could go through life with that steadiness of purpose and observation!

I agreed, and was making a point about the final three bars of *Les Noces* when I became aware that Callipo and Monteverdi were no longer beside me. I turned round. They had stopped some distance back.

'What's up?' I called.

Callipo was staring at the beehives. OK, so bees appeared to operate randomly but really all their actions followed a highly mathematical pattern! Big deal, Callipo! Come on, make your philosophical point and I can nod sagely and we can get on our way.

'The bees!' he said.

Yes. I know the bees.

What came next, however, was a wholly unexpected line of reasoning.

'What do they produce?' he asked.

'Honey.'

Honey. Perhaps he was thinking back to our fantasies concerning Nicolo. Perhaps he had suddenly realised himself to be in more permanent love and was going to announce that he must return to the boy. Ah, well, I could carry on alone. The only sounds were of the humming of the bees and the gentle wind as it flowed over the long grass.

'Beeswax,' he said.

A year ago, I would have thought the observation unremarkable; now, however, I wondered if he were proposing to make a wax dildo. It occurred to me that it would be agreeable to have such an object lodged in one's arse whilst riding. But Callipo's reasoning was following an entirely different track.

'I don't believe Mayor Malignato has syphilis,' he said. 'The symptoms just don't sound right to me. Did you not notice the swellings just beneath his ears? And the fact that he has no teeth – if you don't chew properly the wax will build up. And the periods of pain he has: I'm no doctor, but I think that all this indicates that his ears are full of wax. Forget the Calabrian lion-tamer, this is something quite different! Come on, Ramon, we're going back!'

It was curious to re-enter the village. Despite the brevity of our stay, the place seemed extraordinarily familiar, almost like a place where one has lived for a period of years. There was the old oak tree, there Monteverdi's water trough, Signora Scala's house, the town hall. And the silence had a familiar quality.

Without preamble, Callipo slid neatly off Monteverdi, unhitched a saddle bag and stormed into the town hall. I followed close behind. Luigi Bassano, who must have spent all his time gazing out the window had obviously seen our approach and was in the corridor to meet us.

'What is it? Brigands?' he asked. It was an old-fashioned turn of phrase in an old-fashioned sort of place from an old-fashioned sort of person. I was quite charmed and felt an urge to hug him: such people give continuity to our lives and a sense of belonging to a time and to a history.

'Boil some water!' Callipo ordered.

'Holy mother! Are you going to have a baby?' he asked me.

'Do as I say!' insisted Callipo, striding on towards the mayor's office.

Callipo entered Mayor Malignato's room following the briefest of knocks. Mayor Malignato was discovered rolling on the floor with his head in a paper bag.

'We're not a moment too soon!' Callipo produced a contraption of tubes, funnels and rubber bulbs from his bag. Its function was obvious. Trust Callipo not to travel without this particular source of pleasure!

'Do I have to stay?' I asked.

'Of course! I need your help!'

'What would be the good of giving him an enema?'

'Don't be so stupid!' he snapped. 'I'm going to use this to syringe his ears. Now take off that bag and hold him steady whilst I put in a few drops of oil to loosen things up a bit.'

Had Mayor Malignato not been in such an extreme of distress, I doubt whether he would have consented to our operating on him; but such was his pain he was beyond caring. The drops went in easily enough; then, after Luigi had come with the water, Callipo inserted a little into each ear with a pipette. He bunged up each ear with cotton wool and announced that now we must wait for an hour or so whilst the wax loosened up. Mayor Malignato simply lay still on the floor and growled softly.

'I've never seen him as bad as this,' said Luigi.

'Looks like we're just in time,' said Callipo. 'If wax is left too long untreated it can burst through the ear tubes and block the major vessels leading to the brain. Eventually he would have become a madman and would have had to be committed.'

'He was on that route already,' said Luigi. 'As you perhaps know. And taking us with him.'

During the time of waiting that followed, Callipo stayed in the room with the mayor and played a game of patience, whilst Luigi and I – who had been exchanging glances – went to his office and had a delightful act of sex culminating with him buggering me across his desk. The pain as each thrust forced me against the edge of the desk contrasted with the ecstasy as the tip of his cock slammed on to my prostate. It was all very pleasant and afterwards we took a shower together in an adjoining bathroom and he showed me the rubber duck that, he said, he always inserted in his arse before council meetings that looked set to be exquisitely boring. It was a coincidence that I had had a similar thought concerning beeswax dildos not so long before. I have often found such coincidences appearing in life. In this manner, he went on to say, he could give himself an erotic charge simply by crossing his legs. He knew of several barristers and politicians who used similar devices; and went on to name one especially well-known national politician who never gave a public speech without wearing a battery-operated dildo in the shape of a weasel. I wish I could name that man here, but, of course, I must refrain from doing so. Suffice to say that since hearing that information I have never again looked on any politician with quite the same eyes.

We returned to the mayor's room to find the situation much as before: Callipo turning cards, Malignato writhing on the carpet deliriously muttering about popes and flutes. Callipo looked at his watch and asked Luigi for more hot water.

The operation was not a difficult one, although it needed all three of us to hold the mayor steady and pump the warm water into his ears. I recalled Signor Cavallo saying to me once that the greatest pleasures in life involve some form of excretion from the body: pissing, shitting, the squeezing of a pus-filled boil, sexual ejaculation – and the mayor certainly cried out with the pain and joy of ejaculation.

When finally the business was done we were all exhausted; but none more so than the mayor who lay gasping and shuddering like a fish out of water. We sat on the floor, none of us daring to move until we heard an almost imperceptible sound. Sighing or singing we could not be certain at first until, eventually, one detected a frail tenor voice reaching for certain sounds that were more than mere sounds: they were notes in music.

'*Pur ti miro pur ti stringo*

166

'pur ti godo pur t'annado . . .'

It was the mayor. And this aria was becoming something of an *idée fixe* in our lives.

'Piu non pero piu non moro
'o mia vita o mio tesoro.'

Let me gaze on you, let me enjoy you,
let me embrace you, let me enfold you.
No more strife, no more death,
O my life, O my treasure!

Music returned that day to the once sad village of Pizzo. That night there was an impromptu festival to celebrate. The town band played, fireworks were set off, children, adults and old people danced in the streets. Mayor Malignato sang arias from Bellini, Verdi and Donizetti. And there was a small ceremony to confer on us the Freedom of the Village of Pizzo: which meant, loosely, that we could have our pick of any boy or girl. Not that we needed any such award to take such advantage because the youth of the village would not leave us alone.

So Callipo and I, after contributing to the musical side of things with several duets (myself on the viol, Callipo singing), chanced to find separate companions who urged us to spend the night in different parts of town. I found myself again with Luigi in his tiny room which he rented from an ancient widow in a narrow backstreet; Callipo spent the night in a barn with the stable boy who had been tending Monteverdi.

The next day, at dawn, by mutual unspoken consent we met again in the main square and left the village quietly. We didn't want to make any fuss. We had done good things and that was enough.

Nineteen

The next day found us close to our destination. There was little sign, however, of the loveliest city in the world in the approaches. We travelled along noisy, dusty roads through bland grey suburbs and acres of wasteland. A constant wind – the sirocco – was blowing and our eyes were constantly watering and sore as if filled with tiny shards of glass. The landscape was bleak and depressing and we were tired unto death. Occasionally we exchanged a few words but conversation had long since died between us.

The traffic grew heavier. It was coming up to the rush hour. A light drizzle began to fall. I felt us to be stupid and out of place: travellers from another age progressing along streets now busy with shops, cars and pedestrians. Cars hooted at us, a flock of boys on Lambrettas whistled and shouted, 'Hey, ride him, cow-boys!' The rain had a peculiar quality of softness, like fur, and, although we wore long waterproof red capes and yellow sou'westers, one felt that the damp gradually penetrated to one's very bones.

Callipo knew of lodgings near the Mestre railway station. Here, in a tiny back street *pension* we spent the night. Monteverdi was stabled nearby and, Callipo said, here he would stay whilst we went on to Venice by ourselves on the morrow.

That morning dawned clear and bright. Rested and following a good breakfast, we walked down to the Lido in good heart. The only way to approach Venice was by sea, Callipo said.

We joined the throng of tourists and caught a water bus.

And there was the city, at last, rising up out of the water like a vision appearing in the sky. It seemed to float on dreamy reflections of churches, palaces and villas, all in one colour of mellow stone. I sat amongst the tourists and their snapping cameras and babble of half a dozen languages and felt . . . horror. The beauty was just too overwhelming. How could such things be? How could they ever remain on this earth? The tangible beauty of man is a fragile thing.

Once we landed, however, I felt easier. There was a smell of sewage, a rat darted across the landing quay, the captain of our vaporetto swore when we crashed too heavily against the dock; and an exquisitely beautiful youth who had clearly been drinking the night before vomited an appallingly yellow and violet bile over the side of the boat: life was played here at an ugly human level, after all, and somehow that was reassuring because one need no longer fear destruction.

Callipo knew where we were going, but he refused to tell me. He led me through a maze of back streets: children squatting to play marbles and talking in that thick Venetian accent that makes the speakers sound as though their mouths are filled with sticky toffee; an old lady in an upper floor apartment hanging out her washing on a string suspended across the road; crossing St Mark's Square and the pigeons flying up before us like dust, one bird an angel for an instant as its straining wings became gilded with golden sun; cats peering round corners, intent on the jerky movements of flies or rats; the sound of a string quartet; a children's choir rehearsing Palestrina in a school; old bridges over narrow canals. We went through a passageway that was so narrow we almost had to turn sideways in order to move along, and came to a lovely small square bathed in soft sunlight and quite deserted. Here was an old villa, with peeling yellow paint and dilapidated shutters. Callipo led the way up a flight of stone steps (moss growing in every available gap) and knocked on the wide front door.

'Where are we?' I asked.

He merely looked at me as though he had not heard.

Some instinct made me look up – I had felt as though we were being watched, but there was no sign of movement. It was a tall building of several storeys and must originally have been a palazzo. Now remained only traces of a former grandeur: faint traces of a coat-of-arms on the door, elaborately patterned stained glass in some of the windows – most contained only plain glass.

After an age, during which Callipo simply ignored my suggestions to knock again, the door was eventually opened by a young boy. He was charming, in that lovely bloom and springtime of manhood when, if ever angels be for God's good purposes enthroned in mortal forms, they may be supposed to abide in such as his. He was not past seventeen and cast in so exquisite a mould, so mild and gentle, so pure and beautiful that earth seemed not his element, nor its rough creatures his fit companions. The very intelligence that shone in his deep black eyes and was stamped upon his noble head seemed scarcely of his age or of the world. He was dressed all in blue silk and his long black hair trailed over the shoulders of his loose-fitting blouse. It was an honour simply to be in his presence, let alone also have the thrill of breathing the air that might, only moments before, have dwelt in his sacred lungs. Only in Venice could such a boy be found.

I was so enraptured that I scarce noticed the conversation the boy was having with Callipo until I heard my name mentioned. The boy's eyes met my own and, in that one moment, I knew a platonic love of such intensity I could have fallen to my knees and wept. Later, much later, I was able to equate the experience with hearing the first bars of the *Pie Jesu* from Fauré's *Requiem* sung in an empty English cathedral at dusk on a summer's evening.

'Tonio will look after you,' Callipo was saying. 'You're on your own now.'

He held out his hand.

'What's this?' Now I was utterly confused.

'This is where we take leave of each other for a while. I have been instructed to tell you that you do not have to stay to complete this journey, you can turn back now.'

'But of course I don't want to turn back!'

'Then go in with Tonio.'

'And what about you?'

'I have another appointment elsewhere in the city. Goodbye, Ramon. I shall return for you.'

'But when?'

'Afterwards.'

And with this word he literally grabbed my right hand and shook it. Then, with a bow to Tonio, he took two paces backwards, turned and hurried down the remaining steps.

'Welcome to the Villa Scarlatti!' said Tonio, indicating with a generous sweep of his arm that I should enter.

And so I stepped forward alone and began on the final and most extraordinary stage of my initiation into the world and into an understanding of the very nature of Art.

Twenty

Tonio smiled sweetly at me and led the way across a wide, black-and-white tiled hallway. My boots clacked loudly; but, wearing soft, pointed slippers in the Renaissance style, Tonio's step was silent. His walk was elegant. I felt gauche in his presence, a clumsy inhabitant of space. If the outside of the villa was run-down, the inside could not have presented a greater contrast. Above us hung a chandelier that seemed to smash the light that poured in from high windows and send it glittering and spilling in all directions.

We climbed a carved oak staircase carpeted in Prussian blue with a repeated fleur-de-lys pattern. There were portraits on the wall beside the stairs: serious-looking men in Renaissance costume whose eyes seemed to follow my every movement.

Walking along a blue-carpeted corridor, I attempted to engage Tonio in conversation. Where were we? What was this place? Who was I to meet? But to all these questions he simply shook his head and replied softly that he was under instructions to divulge nothing.

'I am very junior, signor, merely an apprentice.'

'Do you like music?'

'I would not be here, signor, if I did not. I am an organ scholar at San Marco.'

'That's splendid! I . . .'

But he had stopped before a certain door and, indicating that our time for conversation was at an end, he tapped a brief, complex rhythm that, despite my natural ability to pick up such things, I could not have repeated.

A sound very like a grunt came from inside, and Tonio pushed open the door.

The room was large and saturated in light that came flooding in from a bank of windows that made up one side. Each window consisted of numerous tiny panes: most were plain, but a few were of coloured glass and yet others bore intricate patterns. Through the windows one saw a view of canals, palazzi and churches; and, as always with Venice, one could not initially be certain that one was not seeing a fantastically marvellous picture rather than something that actually existed. The carpet in this room was woven with a map of the world, each continent illustrated with appropriate creatures, peoples and landscape; the vivid blue seas were alive with dolphins, fishes and islands. There was scarcely any furniture that I could make out at first glance, but at one end of the room on a large throne an old, plump man, dressed in purple robes, sat with his chin propped on his hand and his feet resting on a stool. He appeared deep in thought. By his side slept a leopard cub.

Tonio led me towards this man; and, when Tonio bowed, I imitated his movement.

With an almost imperceptible flick of his fingers, the man dismissed the boy. I watched Tonio take up a position in a corner of the room at a solitaire table. He quickly became utterly absorbed.

For a long time the man did not speak. There was no sound in the room save the sound of water lapping outside and the heavy breathing of the baby leopard. I noticed that the man's fingers were stuck with rings of jet, emerald, gold and ruby. Above his robes he wore an embroidered waistcoat and on his feet he had black slippers. His face was heavily lined and his hair grey.

Finally, after a vast intake of breath, he spoke:

'Maestro Cavallo tells me you want to be a musician.'

'Yes, signor.'

He did not look at me, but gazed out of the window. When he next spoke, I could not be entirely certain whether he was actually addressing me or merely talking to himself.

'Jacopo Peri, by the time he was twenty-one, had already written half a dozen operas. All now lost.'

I gazed at the clear blue of the Pacific beneath my feet and was ashamed of my dusty shoes.

'So,' continued the man. 'What can you do?'

I looked up and saw that, at last, he was regarding me. His gaze was steady and unnerving. It seemed that not only was he able to read my thoughts, but that also, by simply looking, he could know me utterly.

'I, I play the violoncello.'

He sighed, as though unutterably bored. Perhaps Maestro Cavallo sent him aspiring young musicians every week.

'And what is the violoncello?'

I was flustered, and blushed. 'It's . . .'

He interrupted. 'Do you think the world would have benefited had Piccinni in fact murdered Gluck?'

I wanted the Pacific to swallow me up. I hadn't a clue what to say.

The man began to lick and suck his fingers lasciviously, like so many cocks at an orgy.

Finally, when it became apparent he was willing to wait for ever for an answer, I said, 'The world would have lost some fine operas.'

It was a pat, pathetic observation and he yawned. Oh, fuck it! I was fed up of this! I wanted to go back home, get back to my cello and forget all this nonsense about being a 'great' performer. So what? Let me be a teacher or a player on the first desk in a municipal orchestra.

Gazing out of the window the man said, abstractedly, 'The greatest musicians must sacrifice everything for their Art. What do the names Gualberto, Senesino, Farinelli mean to you?' Suddenly he was looking at me again with those appallingly piercing eyes.

Oh, no! No way! I felt my testicles shrivel automatically. No. There were limits, and if this was part of Maestro Cavallo's plan I wanted none of it. The man's gaze was steady, his eyes boring through mine and into my innermost soul. I felt a first apprehension of terror and a cold sea water sped through my veins.

'Well?' He was waiting for an answer.

I looked over at Tonio and it suddenly struck me that although he was plainly in late adolescence his face was hairless and his voice pure and unbroken.

I swallowed nervously and licked my lips before answering, 'They were all castrati, signor.'

'They sacrificed everything, did they not?'

'Perhaps the times were different, signor.'

'Music is an Art beyond Time, beyond temporary morality or social convention. Have you ever heard a castrato sing?'

'No.' Of course not.

'There is no sound on earth quite like it. One might describe it as a *hard innocence*: the voice of an angel knowing everything and yet utterly at peace, utterly at a place of understanding and wisdom. No female alto, no boy treble can truly interpret certain of the roles of Monteverdi, Cavalli or Allessandro Scarlatti. It can't be done. The music is as lost to us as if the original scores had all been destroyed.'

'Forgive me, signor, but I think the practice of castration, the tearing open of a boy's scrotum in order to cut out the testes, was a barbaric and abhorrent practice. Frequently it resulted in infection and death and, besides, no man has the right to dictate the course of another's life in such a manifestly brutal way.'

From his waistcoat pocket he produced a letter which he carefully unfolded and examined.

'Maestro Cavallo told me solemnly that you believed music was the manifest expression of God's benevolence on earth.'

'I don't dispute that, but . . .'

'But you believe that God cares more for temporal convenience than for what is eternal?'

'I won't be castrated!'

At this he raised his eyebrows. A shudder passed through him, and then another and another. It was as if he were trying to suppress a bubbling of water inside his body. He looked around the room, at me, at Tonio, out of the window. Then he began to wheeze and splutter before finally erupting into howls of giggling.

I blushed and took refuge once more in gazing at the ocean beneath my feet. A surreptitious glance at Tonio revealed that he was regarding me also, albeit with a better-disguised amusement.

The man finally subsided, although secondary shudders continued to convulse his body like the aftershocks of an earthquake. He mopped his face and neck with a glowing white handkerchief.

'Yes,' he said. 'We are so crazed with adoration of music that we castrate cellists now! A Musical Offering! Heh-heh-heh! No, my dear, your balls can stay where they are! I was merely talking metaphorically, shall we say? Trying to find out the lengths you might be prepared to go for the sake of your Art.' The smile washed from his face leaving a severe countenance that looked as though it had never ever known laughter. 'I confess, however, I am disappointed to discover so soon that you have your limits.'

'I am human, signor. Perhaps the acknowledgement of the frailty and failing that that entails will serve to make me a better interpreter of music. Music may be the voice of God, but it is the voice of God heard through the ears of men and, therefore, must be inherently imperfect. Only in death will we at last hear what was meant to be heard.'

'Prettily said.' He suddenly leant forward and in a harsh voice hissed, 'Do you know who I am?'

The fear swirled back in. I trembled.

'No, signor, I do not.'

'My name is Francesco Morlacchi. You may have heard of my great ancestor and namesake?'

'Who composed the cantata for Napoleon's coronation as King of Italy in Milan in 1805?'

I had clearly pleased him with this piece of otherwise quite worthless knowledge. Morlacchi was a composer of utter insignificance. In my estimation only Giacomo Puccini ranked beneath him.

Signor Morlacchi continued, 'I preside here as head of an academy. We are dedicated to excellence in poetry and music. Alas, the art of poetry is all but dead now in Europe and has been so for the past two hundred years, although people tell me there have been exceptions. Music, however, survives, as do those who can interpret it most excellently. If I were to commence a roll-call of some of the names who have passed through these doors in the past three hundred years you would recognise the best and most famous musicians the world has ever known.'

If this indeed was a music academy it was strangely quiet. I remembered that the place of my studies back in Madrid was always abuzz with the sounds of scales and melodies and tunings-up. There was nothing here.

'No,' said Signor Morlacchi, indeed reading my thoughts as I had suspected him of being able to do, 'this is not a place where students come to practise. The students who come here do not come to learn technical or interpretational expertise in that manner. Although, naturally, there is that side to our curriculum. Do you know, by the way, what your honour will be if you should stay the course? – although, frankly, I feel that judging by what you have already said you will not complete this course.'

'The silver mandala?' I whispered.

'Precisely. I believe, however, that Maestro Cavallo has already taken you through some of the preliminaries?' He looked down again at the letter in his hand.

'If such they were?' I shrugged. 'I didn't know quite at the time, but . . .'

'Oh, yes! Some of the young men who come here, you see,

are quite without any experience – much as you were when you first appeared at Maestro Cavallo's door. Cavallo has told me everything.' He fell silent again as he read the letter carefully.

A large blue butterfly fluttered across the room; and, seeing it, I began to notice others. There must have been a dozen or more. How had I failed to spot them before? They were everywhere. And now also I saw that the room was hung with many fine paintings: still lives, memento mori, landscapes, portraits. A low growl came from the sleeping leopard cub and it snatched its claw at something in its dream. Looking about the room, my glance kept returning to Tonio, still intent on his game of solitaire. Was he really a castrato? I had to find out, but how on earth could I do it tactfully? And something told me that here was a boy beyond seduction. As lovely as he was, I could not imagine making love with him. He seemed to possess a transcendent quality that put him above the mundane passions of sexual experience.

'The Maestro tells me that you have a special affection for the cello suites of J.S. Bach?'

'I would love to be given an instrument here so that I might play them again. It has been so long since I played, Signor. Maestro Cavallo said that I must not, and yet I miss music with an ache that is almost tangible.'

'Of course. And so imagine the joy with which you will eventually return to them. The music will be new. Those who have practised every day of their lives since they were six years old have many skills; but they can never play Bach as though reading him for the first time. Their interpretations will be jaded, no matter how good they might be at disguising that fact. Maestro Cavallo knows what he is doing. Your pilgrimage took you to the right man. Tell me why.'

'Why I sought out Maestro Cavallo? But surely he is accepted as the greatest living musician? I don't understand your question. It's obvious why!'

'No. Think again. When was your moment of epiphany? –

178

when you knew for certain that what you must do was seek him out?'

I shook my head. 'All my life I've wanted to meet him!'

'When you were a baby? When you were a toddler?'

'No,' I admitted. Then, after careful thought, 'I was eleven years old and I heard for the first time the Double Concerto of Johannes Brahms. When Maestro Cavallo's cello played the first subject of the second movement a space opened in my heart and I knew that as long as such interpretations of such music existed then I would always be free no matter my personal circumstances. I remember thinking clearly that even were I to be imprisoned or sent into exile, blind, crippled or even become deaf the memory of this music would remain for ever with me and my mind would be free no matter what temporary trapments my body might endure. Does that answer your question?'

'Tonio will take you to your room.'

'One moment please!' I held up my hands. 'You haven't really explained what this place is or what is going to be expected of me. What is the name of this academy? How long must I remain? What will I be expected to do?'

'Tonio will take you to your room. You are free to leave. You are not free to ask questions.'

I turned. Tonio was waiting by my side and he flashed me a sweet smile. I had no option but to obey.

Twenty-One

When Tonio brought me once more before Signor Morlacchi it was as if the old man had not moved in all the time that I had been away. There he sat on his throne in the same room with the same carpet featuring a map of the world and its wonders. This time, Tonio brought up a chair for me before retiring once more to his solitaire table in the corner. The leopard cub remained asleep at Signor Morlacchi's feet. Was it real, or perhaps some kind of mechanical toy? Whilst waiting for the signor to speak, I looked at the creature surreptitiously from time to time until I was satisfied I could see a steady breathing coupled with a delicate shivering of nerves such as only could have come from something alive.

The view of the city from the windows was breathtakingly lovely. It was the hour of gold, when the sun sinks back into the sea and the very air seems drunk with an excess of light. I saw the silhouette of a figure punting a gondola and it was as if he were made of charcoal. Every moment is doomed to remain for ever in the past. That is the curse of Venice: a city constructed for regret.

'So!' the old man said eventually. He tilted his head and scratched his scalp, then examined his fingers as if to ascertain whether he had captured any fleas. He chewed his tongue thoughtfully. He was plainly in no very great hurry this evening. 'You have been with us several days, now. Mm?' he grunted, narrowing his eyes at me when I did not immediately respond.

'Yes, signor.'

'And according to my reports you have submitted to everything without protest or hesitation.'

'Of course, signor.'

'That is an essential quality that every great artist must have. A willingness to be open, a willingness to submit. The artist must absorb everything in order to be able to give birth to everything. When you embark on a Bach suite you are remaking the world.'

'Yes, signor.'

Maestro Cavallo had told me much the same sort of thing. Only now, however, was I beginning to understand the truth of it. I longed for my cello! Maestro Cavallo had said that once here I would be supplied with an instrument; but this had not so far happened. The sound that I knew I could produce now would bear no relation to my uninformed, childlike interpretations of just a few months ago!

'What is the purpose of your life?' he suddenly asked, not taking his eyes from close regard of the leopard cub.

'To realise music,' I said promptly.

'A true musician,' he said, slowly, 'must be prepared to sacrifice everything in order to achieve that realisation of which you just now rightly spoke.'

'You have told me so.'

'Everything. Nothing must stand in the way. You have shed all inhibitions in your mind concerning your own body. This is good. That is the area that Maestro Cavallo told us we must work on. Each person who comes to this academy goes through a different form of initiation tailored to his particular needs. One boy might have to submit to enforced celibacy and a strict regime of yoga. Another might be required simply to remain silent for a year. Only once in the academy's five-hundred-year history has it ever been necessary to remove the sight from one of our students. But that was an extreme case. He was an organ player in the eighteenth century, and went on to very great things. You would know his name if I divulged it; but, alas, that is something we are never permitted to do here. This is a secret organisation and anonymity is essential. How could we carry on otherwise? The state would close us down in a moment.

'Would you concede to blindness?'

I had to think long and hard about that one. Finally, I said, 'I think if Maestro Cavallo instructed me that that would be the correct way forward, then I would give it true consideration and might well accept. I trust him utterly.'

'Well spoken. So you do agree that Art must be placed above all petty considerations? It is its own morality. It is never relative, it cannot be set alongside the temporal laws of Church or State.'

'I am a Roman Catholic, signor, and cannot necessarily accept that the laws of the Church are temporal; but nevertheless I agree with your statement.'

A bee entered at the window and hovered around the head of the sleeping cub. In a charming movement, the baby creature wrinkled its nose and snatched its paw in the air without, however, waking.

Signor Morlacchi sighed heavily, chewed his tongue and studied his fingers.

After an age, he said, 'Words are easy. They slip from the tongue and decorate idle moments. There can never be truth in them because they are always informed by the subjectivity of a particular speaker. Music, performed by one who has renounced self, is the only truthful Art. And now, soon, we shall see if you are capable of reaching the heights.'

He did not dismiss me, then, but simply ignored me: first gazing abstractedly out of the window, then settling to work on his nails with a tiny gold file. I could say nothing, but kept glancing over towards Tonio, waiting for a sign perhaps from him.

In the end, Tonio looked up from his game and, perceiving

the situation, came over to me, took me by the arm and led me out of the room as though I were a simpleton.

Later that day, I was sitting in my room at the desk, writing a letter to my mother, when there came a knock at the door. Without waiting for a response from me, the door opened and in walked an old, white-haired man wearing a formal dark suit and carrying a cello. My heart began to pound and my mouth went dry. A cello! At last! I gave an amiable greeting, naturally; but the old man seemed to be unaware of my presence. He sat down on one of the red-covered chairs and began to play.

The music was baroque, of a Byzantine glory and complexity; but I was unable to identify it. It was glorious, and I drank in the sound gratefully in the manner of a parched man in a desert.

As I listened, certain subtleties of sound and technique were revealed. The old man was a remarkable player. The music had a quality of freshness and verve, combining a sense of newness – it might have been composed only the day before – with an appreciation of all history. In short, the piece itself and the performance of that piece was a moment of epiphany. Shadows, that I had not even known existed, lifted from me and it seemed that I stepped out into a new world of clarity and light. Through the mere act of listening I understood a little better. And became more free. For some reason, I recalled my uncle, a sweet-natured man wrongfully imprisoned in a Levantine jail for nearly twenty years. On his release and his return to our village he was not the broken man one might have expected. A fanatical adherent of Wagner he had, he said, spent his time playing and replaying *Der Ring des Nibelungen* in his mind. With this music speaking to him constantly of an outside world he had never felt himself to be imprisoned. Freedom is a state of mind.

When the old man finished playing, we both sat and said nothing. Any congratulations or expressions of joy on my part would have reduced the moment to banality. On some occasions one must observe respectful – and meaningful – silence.

He played another piece. This sounded very like a Moldavian

folk melody: it had a dying fall and seemed to evoke long-ago images of children playing amongst apple blossom and calling to each other through a frail mist of morning sunlight. I was moved to tears.

The man stayed with me for a couple of hours. During that time neither of us said a word. The music he played was all unknown to me and yet, somehow, I could at least categorise each piece according to possible historical period or geographical location.

Just before he left the man looked at me for the first time. I smiled and nodded, but still he gave no sign of mutual recognition. He loosened the strings on his bow, picked up his instrument and exited the room as silently as he had entered.

'Who was the cello player?' I asked Tonio, when the boy brought me my supper that night. 'He plays in a style such as I have never heard.'

'That's Antonio Crivelli,' said Tonio, spreading a white cloth on the small table and setting out the cutlery and plates. 'He's quite something, eh? Deaf, dumb and blind, but you wouldn't know it!'

'Not at all!' I exclaimed, astounded. 'He seemed to know where everything was without bumping into anything. And if he was deaf – which I frankly doubt – his intonation was uncannily perfect.'

'He does everything by the interpretation of vibration. The vibration he feels as his feet move across a floor tells him where objects are located. And the quality of vibration when he plays tells him if his notes are in tune or not. People he senses by their body heat. He has a lot he can teach you, if you are prepared to learn.'

'But of course!'

'He'll come again tomorrow. Now.' Tonio unloaded dishes from the trolley and lifted lids to reveal pasta and wild mushrooms in a fragrant sauce together with a bowl of sugar snap peas and another of spinach. There was a decanter of water from the Italian Alps and a bottle of 1976 Graves. 'Eat.'

'Won't you join me?' I offered, pulling up a chair. There was plenty for both of us.

'Thank you!' He bowed sweetly, and sat opposite.

I had not expected him to accept my offer and was delighted to have his company.

The meal was leisurely and, in the ensuing hours, we talked of music, philosophy and God. For one so young, he had an astounding range of understanding and appreciation of the liberal arts. But, whilst all this was interesting, I was more curious to know his story. How came he to be at the academy and what, exactly, was he doing there? It seemed a subject that he was unwilling to dwell on. Several times he deflected my more personal questions: politely, but effectively. In the end, however, perhaps on account of the wine, he became freer in his discourse and, when I asked the direct question, 'When did you first come here?' he pushed his chair back from the table, settled into a more comfortable position and began his tale.

'I was born on a small, remote island in the Pacific. My mother was a missionary doctor, my father a captain of a cargo ship that one day delivered a crate of Bibles and tracts to the island. The boat remained offshore for one night only. On that night I was conceived. My mother never saw my father again. She did not mind. She was, as she confided in her diary, "A field needing to be sown." Her sensible interpretation of the holy book enabled her to realise that her one act of almost anonymous passion was not a sin. It gave her pleasure, fulfilled a deep need and enabled me to make the journey from heaven to earth.

'For ten years I knew only joy. I swam in the sea, played with the island children, learnt to sing the harmonies of the Pacific, played the flute; and, eventually, came to assist my mother in certain surgical operations: my fingers were slim and nimble and, although young, I quickly picked up the principles of tying internal sutures and sawing through bone. Perhaps that sounds unusual but, when you are ten thousand miles from the nearest hospital with sophisticated instruments, you cannot expect every person in an operating theatre to be fully trained. I was good at the work and the native people called me *e lavala piarao* which, being translated means the Little Doctor.

'Paradise, however, cannot last. My mother died when I was eleven years old, poisoned by a venomous fish which dug its spikes into her right foot when she was stepping into the ocean for a swim following a long day at the hospital. I shall never forget how they brought her to me when she was already delirious. I amputated her foot straightaway, but I was too late: the poison was already speeding towards her heart.

'I believe, Signor Ramon, in fate. What is written, is written. My mother's death was part of God's destiny for me. So, after a period of natural intense grief, I was ready to take on the challenge of my life alone. I did not want to remain on the island and felt I needed to make a clean break. Accordingly, I took the next passing ship and asked the captain to let me disembark at the first European port of call. That port was Venice. For some time I lived rough in this city, earning my living by busking on the flute. It so happened that one day my playing was heard by Signor Morlacchi and he was so kind as to admit me to this academy. I continue to study the flute here, but perhaps my main function is as a factotum. It is work that I enjoy because it is in the service of music. Which is to say the service of God.'

I was fairly dazed by Tonio's weird history; but he was clearly telling the truth.

When he was finished, we both gazed out of the large windows at the city which, now lit up, resembled a fantastic oil painting with degrees of light and thick shade, but no clearly defined lines. The lights seemed sprinkled haphazardly in the manner of Whistler. The effect was one of stupendous unreality.

'What is going to happen to me here?' I asked in a soft voice, after a while.

'Signor Crivelli will come again.'

'Yes, but after that?'

'He will continue to come to you. Perhaps for days. Perhaps weeks. If you are lucky, you may get a chance to play yourself.'

'Really?' I sat forward eagerly.

'Possibly. But don't hope too much. Your listening and under-standing is what Signor Morlacchi is striving above all to achieve.'

I sat back again.

'And then I go back home?'

'No. There is the final test. Of course, you can go home at any time, but . . .'

'But what is this "final test"?'

'Something truly terrible,' he said.

'But what is it?'

'I cannot say!'

'You must!'

'No.'

And with that he pushed his chair back and stood up. He was wearing a white silk shirt with a high collar in the Japanese style, and black silk pyjama bottoms. With graceful movements he loosened his clothes and they slipped easily from his skin. His body was smooth, apart from the tangle of hairs about his genitals (which clearly showed no signs of castration!) and his cock was stiffening by gradual but sure degrees.

Tonio pulled me to my feet and pressed himself against me; or, rather, insinuated himself against me like a snake: I felt wrapped in his voluptuousness. We kissed deeply, open mouth against open mouth, breath pressing into breath, tongue upon tongue. He let out faint gasps of joy as he rhythmically thrust his cock against me, and my hand explored the crack of his arse.

Carefully, Tonio eased my shirt off my shoulders and down my back so that it remained hanging on to the waistband of my trousers. He undid my belt, then the buttons of my trousers. The moist tip of my glans penis was emerging from the hem of my briefs.

To pull down my trousers and briefs, Tonio knelt before me. I felt his warm breath and light touch of lips and tongue on my genitals as I allowed him to remove my clothes. At last, I stood naked and ran my fingers through his lovely hair whilst he gave me fellatio with the skill that only a flute player practised in the art of flutter tongue can truly possess. Whilst his tongue worked on my cock, his slim fingers were caressing my arse, teasing and relaxing it. I knew what he was wanting and, when I felt ready, turned and bent over the table – scattering the dishes carelessly. The sound of breaking glass and china only added to the erotic thrill.

Tonio's tongue, at first slowly licking in circular movements around the edge of my rectum and then gradually focusing more and more on my sphincter with ever increasing flickerings, had me literally mewing with pleasure. I pressed my head hard against the table-top, grateful for the pain, and I squeezed a knife in my hand relishing the sight of blood.

When Tonio's cock entered me I was all too ready. He slid in easily and deeply. My reaction was of relief and joy combined. Now began a slow, rhythmic fucking. The sound of his flesh slapping against mine, the rocking of the table, his groans and occasional high-pitched cries. After a time, his hand reached for my cock and wanked it between thumb and four fingers. The sweat poured off my body.

I was on the point of ejaculation when he pulled out, turned me over and, with the barest touch of his hand on his cock, came over my legs and chest with one spurt of jism after another. I came moments later and, thus spent, we collapsed to the floor and hugged and kissed one another affectionately for a long time.

Twenty-Two

My room was magnificent. It seemed like the retiring chamber of a seventeenth-century Venetian prince. A large double bed was the dominating piece of furniture. It was covered with a spread depicting part of the ceiling of the Sistine Chapel, and its headboard was a mirror framed in a pattern of harps and flutes. On the walls were painted *trompe l'oeil* figures of naked youths clutching musical instruments and accompanied by dogs, some were leaning against tree stumps, others appeared to be floating amongst cloud. There were various red-covered chairs and a chaise longue all constructed in different degrees of discomfort. The wood-panelled floor was carpeted with an assortment of Belushi rugs. A set of French windows opened out to a balcony overlooking the city. Pools of water-reflected light filled the room giving a sense of timeless tranquillity.

Tonio showed me the en-suite bathroom – a huge tub raised on metal claws, mirrored walls and a jungle of plants in pots and hanging from the ceiling – and then, before I could get a chance to begin a proper conversation with him, he made his excuses and left.

Everything was very fine; but I was filled with a horrible sense of loss and loneliness. I wanted my Callipo to be with me. I wanted to share with him my delight in all this extravagance.

In a melancholy spirit, therefore, I undressed and took a bath. The warm water lulled my senses and I felt overwhelmed by a desire to sleep. Accordingly, when I was done and had dried and perfumed myself with some of the gorgeous array of talcums and scents, I slipped between the silk sheets of the bed, lay my head on the gloriously soft pillow and was asleep in a matter of moments.

When I awoke, several hours later, there was a small table beside my bed spread with a white lace cloth and bearing a glass jug of lemon juice, white rolls, green olives and soft cheese. I was ravenous, and ate the food gratefully, swallowing in gulps like a greedy puppy.

The notion that when one is asleep there is another who has given thought to your needs is profoundly comforting. You are once more the child cared for by the loving mother, or the child of God at last offered tangible proof of His benevolence.

Having eaten, I felt soft sleep once more steal upon me. All creatures like to sleep following their food; I was no exception. Feeling curiously like a warm, well-fed colt I slid back down beneath the sheets. Wrapped securely in Michelangelo's Heaven I shivered deliciously and was soon once more asleep.

This time I dreamt, and was in a land of clouds, moons, stars, floating cheeky angels and flying musical staves.

'Ramon!' a voice whispered. 'Ramon!' It might have been a seductive angel, one of those tumbling naked in the mists of Heaven. I searched, but could not see. 'Ramon! Ramon!' The name repeated over and over finally hooked me back into consciousness.

I opened my eyes to see myself surrounded by a troop of heavily built men. They wore baggy white tracksuit trousers and were naked from the waist up. Their identities were hidden behind black eye masks.

One of them tugged at my silk covering and it slipped off my naked body softly as a cloud. I knew that I could do nothing, and was not expected to do anything, so I merely lay still and awaited my fate.

Surprisingly soft hands caressed my smooth skin and my cock began to stir like a thick bud coming to life in spring sunshine. I was lifted up – so gentle were the carriers my movement was like levitation – and carried to the bath where all the scents I had gaudily applied were washed away by two of the men. After they had dried me, they applied warm oil to my skin.

I could not hide my erection – strong and firm it pulsed hard against my stomach pointing straight upwards – but the men ignored it; or, at any rate, gave no hint of being stirred themselves.

Next, they tied my hands behind my back with silken cord, and I was blindfolded with a silken sash.

I was led gently from the room. Blind and helpless, my only indication as to where I was being taken was in the different quality of the air and the feel of the floor beneath my bare feet. At first my feet were on soft carpet, then marble; then, judging by the echoing of the creaks, across a large, bare, wood-panelled room.

We came to stone steps and the hands holding me became more solicitous for my safety. I imagined that perhaps we were descending into a chamber very like the one beneath the Castello Caccini. How long ago all that seemed now!

Finally, I was lifted up and hung in a kind of harness, my hands and feet outstretched. Although this might sound uncomfortable, it was not. My blindfold was removed, and a strange, unearthly music began: a low, steady pulsing intertwined with a singing as of angels.

We were indeed in a place very like a dungeon. Burning sconces were held in brackets all round the room, so far as I could see, and the air was thick with a sweet yet also pungent scent.

Now I felt a warm presence inside my arse crack. At first, I thought that yet more scented oil was being poured delicately on to my body; but gradually I came to realise that this was the skilful, gentle working of a tongue. I groaned and, with this groan, came the lightest of sensations around my cock. It was a mouth so careful and subtle as to be almost unnoticeable: indeed, it seemed like mere warmth until with infinite delicacy the slightest pressure of tongue and lips was applied to my glans penis.

Tongues caressed every inch of my body, hands gently pinched and stroked and teased and devilishly sensuous words – whose meaning I could not fathom, they being in medieval Italian – were whispered in my ears and seemed to inhabit my body like live creatures imparting a type of eroticism all their own. My skin was all the tighter and more sensitive for the actions of these words, and the nerve endings in my cock all the more receptive.

When the first cock slipped inside my arse, it took several men to hold me steady. There was a little awkwardness in the beginning, then a rhythm was established whereby each thrust pushed my cock deeper into another man's mouth. I was being fucked to fuck.

And always that music! Going round and round and round! Unearthly yet somehow also belonging to a very earthly, pagan sensibility. Teeth bit into my neck and shoulders and I loved the pain, crying out for more and yet more. The cock of my fucker pushed hard against my prostate deep in the very depths of my being and the joy was indescribable. This was everything. This was the world revealed.

I would have come there and then had not my fellator removed his mouth just in time. I was lowered into a position across a bench, turned around and had my legs hoisted high. Now I could see the strong, hairy-chested man who was fucking me, although his exact identity remained hidden behind the mask. A succession of cocks was presented in turn for me to lick and suck, whilst a tongue somehow found its way to work against my own cock.

The next position saw me as part of a near sandwich. I was hoisted above one man and eagerly sank my cock into his arse, whilst another man fucked me.

Time could only be measured by my exhaustion. Finally, I was hauled away in my harness and hung like a slab of meat whilst they in turn ejaculated over me. Come spilled down my thighs, across my chest, over my face. I twisted my head and reached for as much as I could with my tongue. Eventually, I was allowed my own release by the simple facility of a willing hand. I bucked and shook as the spunk shot from me in half a dozen powerful judders.

I was kept in that chamber for, I believe, many days. I was well-fed and allowed sleep. But no one ever spoke to me, and I knew that I must not question any of the things that might happen to me.

I fucked and was fucked. My arse knew dildos of every shape, size and delight, a chain of silver balls, a soft-gloved hand. I submitted to everything and was glad so to do.

Finally, one day, I was unshackled and led back upstairs. Again I was bathed and scented and then laid back into that beloved, soft bed.

I slept. Perhaps for days. I know that I woke several times to drink water and sometimes it was dark, sometimes light. I cared not. All I wanted and needed was glorious sleep.

And then Tonio appeared. He brought a simple repast and, after I had eaten, helped me dress in colourful, loose-flowing silks.

'Signor Morlacchi wishes to see you now,' he said.

I nodded.

'But your trials are not yet over. There is one last to come.'

'That's fine,' I said. I was confident, now, that I could cope with anything that anyone could dream up.

'But,' he lowered his voice confidentially, 'this trial is by far the hardest. Very few men have gone through this unscathed.'

What tortures could I not endure? I laughed lightly.

'Tonio, I am not afraid. If you could but know what I have undergone in the past few days and, before that, with my Maestro Cavallo, you would know that nothing can possibly hold any terror for me.'

'You do not know,' he said solemnly.

And, alas, he was perfectly correct.

The worst was yet to come.

Twenty-Three

M y days were idle, but within that aimlessness lay a grey mist of awful uncertainty. I knew that something terrible was going to happen: a trial so severe, Tonio warned me, that others, of a highly sensitive disposition, had quite lost their sanity; but he refused absolutely to give me details. Always he repeated that I was free to go at any time. I need not remain. But, of course, I could not go. I had come so far, to turn back now would be something that I would surely regret all my life. And, besides, Tonio's companionship was giving me increasing delight. Each day he visited me in my rooms. We talked, played chess (a gorgeous set with figures of gold and silver) and made love.

Another daily visitor was Signor Crivelli and with each recital of his I learnt something new.

Most of my time, however, was tedious. I paced my rooms, gazed out of the window longing to be able to return to my cello.

Then it happened.

One day, without warning, I was taken again by the masked men and subjected to the same treatment as before. Following this, I was left naked in a dark cell for what seemed like a week, or perhaps even longer. Delicious food was brought to me each day, but my bed was hard and the only light came from high barred windows. How sweet that light seemed! And how delicious the sound of birdsong coming from outside! In all the time I was there, no one spoke to me, nor I to anyone else other than myself. I became perhaps a little schizophrenic. It was instructive, though, to separate my character into some of its component parts and to realise how much my personality was divided. 'I hate Bruckner!' I told myself, at one point. And then promptly disagreed with myself, pointing out all the qualities in his music that I most admired. I came to the conclusion that character and firm belief are merely conveniences: it is impossible for a fully rounded personality to possess either.

On the day of my release, Tonio came for me. He wrapped a cloak around me and took me back to my rooms where, after a bath and a breakfast of calf's liver and bacon, I climbed once more into my delicious bed and slept the long sleep of the just. I dreamt that I was in the Kalahari desert playing an instrument that consisted of one string only. The music, simple as it was, was balm to my soul. Tears poured down my cheeks so that when I awoke I found the pillow quite damp. It was the deep of night and a full moon shone in at the window washing everything in a pale yellow glow. I sat up and looked about me. Somehow, the moonlight seemed to impart a quality of timelessness and stillness. The silence was broken only by the gentle lapping of water and a frail hollow metallic clanking from somewhere far off. This could have been the fifteenth century. Still deeply tired, I slid back beneath the sheets and was soon asleep again.

Tonio woke me with a kiss. The room was full of daylight.

'Today is the day,' he said with a sad smile as, sitting on the bed, he brushed the hair from my temple.

'You mean I get a cello?' I burst out enthusiastically.

His eyes told me that this was not going to happen. He shook his head. 'No. Today is the day for your trial. If you are still willing to go through with it?'

'You mean that last spell in the dungeon was not the last trial?'

'No. Not at all.'

Suddenly, I felt as though I had no strength. Oh, what was this all about? It was like being trapped in some bizarre Byzantine labyrinth turning now one way, now the other, and never getting anywhere but deeper into confusion.

Seeing my distress, Tonio climbed, fully clothed, into bed beside me.

'Don't worry!' he whispered, holding me tight.

'But what is this test? What is this trial? I mean, I have been through so much, surely this can be no worse?'

'It will be difficult.'

'Am I to be blinded? Castrated? Maimed in some way?'

'No. Nothing like that.'

'Then what?'

Instead of an answer, Tonio kissed me on the lips and ran his hand over my body. We made love, and I was as vicious as I was passionate. I bit his neck until I drew blood, pulled his hair, pinched and twisted his limbs until I could no longer distinguish his cries of pain from those of his pleasure: perhaps there was no difference. Finally I fucked him with such a fury that every object in the room rocked and a glass fell from my night table and shattered on the floor. When I was done, my cock was black with bruises.

'Tell me,' I said, breaking the post-coital silence. 'Tell me now.' Surely our fucking had smashed through that barrier.

Tonio sighed. 'I must not,' he said. 'Please don't make me. But ... But you will remember that Signor Morlacchi instructs us that Art, the composition of Art and its perfect realisation is the greatest good. It is eternal and, when true, is the tangible manifestation of God on this earth. Nothing must stand in its way. Signor Morlacchi's greatest sense of pride came from a student a decade ago. He, too, was a cellist; and when he had been through all the stages here he was awarded with the Silver Mandala. With the token around his neck, he played Bach's G Minor cello suite with a perfection such as Signor Morlacchi had never heard, and then he expired. He died. His spirit knew that it had reached the end of its earthly journey. To touch earthly perfection, and then die! What could be better?'

I wasn't quite so sure on that one. The sentiment echoed something Signor Cavallo had once told me, in what seemed now like another age. So many things seemed to be falling into place. But Tonio would not be drawn further on my fate.

Tonio and I spent a happy day together. We played chess, cards and backgammon, talked on the philosophy of Schopenhauer, sang part songs and shared a simple supper of paella with a good wine brought to us by an amiable ancient servant.

That night we slept in the same bed. And I knew the happiness of true consummated love. But, after I had gasped my final orgasm, I unexpectedly recalled Callipo. Dear Callipo. Whatever had become of him? Unbeknownst to me, I was to discover the answer to that question before very long.

The summons came at dawn.

Twenty-Four

I was awoken by Tonio getting out of bed. He padded over to the windows and pulled back the heavy curtains. The morning was overcast and the light that came into the room was grey and melancholy. Tonio stood at the window, gazing out; and, as I watched him in profile, I saw for the first time imperfections in what I had hitherto believed was a stupendously perfect body. His buttocks were not quite the rounded peaches I had imagined, and his chest was a touch on the bony side. His shoulders were not quite straight and his cock and balls were not remarkable. All this was a curious revelation, because I had imagined hitherto that I knew his body intimately: had we not already made love countless times, and had I not gazed at him long and hard? So we can look and not yet see. Tonio's imperfections – if such they were – served, however, to deepen my affection for him, because here was a real human being rather than some pornographic fantasy.

I rose also and went to join him at the window. I stood behind him, wrapping my arm about his neck and pressing my chin into his shoulder.

A light drizzle was scratching the air and the low clouds seemed to drain all colour from the vista of canals and palazzi. Raindrops slithered down the long windows.

My cock was beginning to firm against the warmth of Tonio's buttocks, when he suddenly pulled away (I was quite hurt) and went into the bathroom. Not wanting to join him (he had rejected me, I was not going to trail after him like a lost puppy), I went back to bed.

Twenty minutes later, Tonio emerged, wrapped in a bathrobe, fresh and sweet-smelling from the shower. He said, 'Today is the day.'

And there came a knock at the door.

Tonio looked at me, and in his eyes there was an expression of deep sadness. He hesitated and for a moment I doubted that he would answer the door.

But he did. He talked with whoever it was in a low voice so that I could not make out the words. Then the visitor went away and Tonio turned to me.

'Time to get ready,' he said.

When I had bathed, I emerged from the bathroom to find Tonio laying out a dark suit of new clothes on the bed.

When I was dressed (Tonio adding the finishing touches, straightening my collar, tightening my tie, smoothing away the odd crease) I felt as though I were heading for a Mafia funeral. The feeling was compounded when Tonio led me downstairs and out of the front entrance of the academy and I saw, at the landing stage, a black gondola waiting. We stepped in. Signor Morlacchi was already installed. He gave us no greeting, but merely signalled to the gondolier to get underway.

After ten minutes we were at the mainland. I had already seen the black limousine and somehow knew that it was intended for us. The gondolier became our chauffeur.

Tonio and I stepped into the back. In the front seat, next to the driver, sat Signor Morlacchi.

The car was wonderfully spacious, and so comfortable that we started our journey without my at first being aware of it. Only when I looked out of the window did I see that we were actually moving – and at some speed.

'Where are we going?' I asked. My seat was as comfortable as an armchair. I hoped for a long journey.

'You'll see!' came the reply.

Tonio patted my knee and gave me a light kiss on the cheek.

It was indeed a long journey. Despite my uncertainty as to our destination and my fate when we got there, I felt quite at ease and, for a time, fell asleep.

The car stopped by a desolate sea coast.

I got out. The clouds hung low over the grey wrinkled surface of the water. Towards the horizon it was impossible to make out which was sky and which sea. The wind blew flecks of rain against my face. On one side of the road was a muddy field, on the other sand dunes. The tide was out revealing a large expanse of sand.

The whole aspect was bleak.

Another car drew up behind us. Three men in dark suits got out and approached Signor Morlacchi. There was a quietly whispered conference.

The atmosphere was horrible. Suddenly I wanted to go home.

And then who should step from this second car but Callipo! I let out a cry of welcome and opened my arms to him.

But instead of running towards me, he turned away with a slight shake of his head.

'Callipo?' I called.

'Hush!' Tonio took my arm. 'Come back into the car for a moment.'

I duly obeyed. Once inside, Tonio asked that I shut my door as he had shut his.

'Listen,' he said, putting an arm around me. 'What I have to say is very difficult and perhaps I should not be telling you right now, but if no one stops me then I think we can judge that I have permission.'

In a level voice, Tonio explained what was to happen. The awarding of the Silver Mandala, he explained, was now dependent on this last test. I must shoot Callipo. My old friend was to be tied to a stake and I would be required to execute him.

'I won't do it!' I said, straightaway. 'To hell with the Silver Mandala!'

'Go through this barrier and you will penetrate to the very soul of Art. You will have proved that nothing can stand in your way. Compare it to those aesthetes who live their lives in a state of total celibacy and silence in order that they might reach God. It is an extreme, but true Art, the true God is an extreme. The gun may or may not be loaded. The trial is not about the execution per se, but whether or no you can actually go through with it.'

'I don't care. I'm not going to do it.'

'You're saying the temporary pleasure of friendship is greater than the eternal joy of Art?'

'Not friendship, but love. And love is certainly greater. For a start it's not temporary. It is eternal. What we put into the air through our affections lasts beyond the mere presence of our bodies. Love is more eternal than Art. Look at the music of the ancient Pharaohs – what do we know of that? But we certainly know that the Egyptians loved one another in exactly the same way as we do. I will never murder one whom I love. I will never murder anyone.'

My argument defeated Tonio and he could say nothing to counter it. He was as puzzled as a child. He simply could not understand why I would reject the possibility of becoming a true musician. He was a believer, and believers can never be swayed by argument. So, too, was I a believer.

We got out of the car and I explained my philosophy over again to Signor Morlacchi. As I held conference with him, his burly companions stood close behind, constantly eyeing the road and the field as if looking for possible assassins.

When I was finished, Signor Morlacchi said, 'I cannot persuade you otherwise. As you well know, my argument is beyond the mere reach of words. If you have not understood by now, you will never understand.'

'Then that is how it must be.'

'The loss to the world is inestimable. Signor Cavallo told me that no one, in his opinion, had ever come so close as you to realising the true spirit of music. Do you realise what might come about if you could pass through this final barrier: if your spirit could only be released by this last, great act? Such music could literally heal the world.'

'No,' I said. 'Music alone can never be capable of that. Only love can truly heal.'

'There has been plenty of love, and much good has it done thus far in our history!' he said sharply. I could tell he was struggling to maintain an even temper. 'And how much true music has there ever been? Almost none by comparison. Ramon, do not let this opportunity pass. Never again will you have another chance to prove yourself. Do you want to return to mediocrity? Do you want the world to carry on as before with its massacres and murders and its indifference to God?'

'Music cannot save the world.'

'You know that to be untrue.'

He was right. I had to modify my statement.

'Music alone cannot save the world,' I corrected.

'You pathetic weed,' he sneered.

'If I were to become a murderer how could I ever play Bach?'

'You misinterpret our philosophy deliberately.'

'No, signor. I speak what I believe to be the truth. It is what music itself has taught me. If my argument cannot sway you then it is because it is, like your own, beyond words. Let us both go back to music and listen anew.'

'You fool!'

He gazed at me as if in amazement and then abruptly turned on his heels and got back into his car, followed by his driver. His henchmen returned to their vehicle and in a matter of moments both cars were speeding away down the lonely straight road.

Leaving me, Tonio and Callipo stranded in the middle of nowhere.

Callipo now came up to me and put his arms around my

shoulders. We hugged. When finally he released me, he said, simply, 'I think you should have done it, Ramon.'

'No, you don't!'

He did not reply, but simply tilted his head.

Tonio, who had been sitting on a dune, now approached.

'It's all over, then,' he said. 'Perhaps we'd best be getting along.'

'How far are we from the nearest town?' I asked.

'About forty kilometres. We have a long journey ahead.'

So began the long journey home. It was taken for granted that Tonio would accompany us. He said that Signor Morlacchi would surely blame him for my 'failure', and would not welcome him back at the academy. Had he not briefed me in the car, I might have been persuaded by Signor Morlacchi.

'Nonsense!' I protested.

'It's true,' he insisted, and I said no more. I did not want him to think that I did not want him to be with us.

But would Signor Cavallo welcome us back at Castello Caccini? I had, after all, surely failed in his eyes also.

Twenty-Five

W e need not have worried.
    'No,' said Signor Cavallo, as he and I walked alone through the garden on the evening of the day of our return. We had washed, rested and eaten a simple but utterly delightful repast. 'No. Your test with Signor Morlacchi was one thing. You failed in his eyes: but, judging by what you have told me, you have passed in mine. Love is, indeed, the one thing stronger than music. That is what I had hoped you would come to understand.'

We paused by a rose bush. The white flowers glowed wonderfully in the dusk and the air was moist with their sweet scent. Bending to savour a particular flower, our cheeks touched. With a small turn, Signor Cavallo moved his lips towards mine. We kissed lightly at first, then more passionately. At last I found myself in the arms of my beloved. All my other loves had been a mere prelude to this. This was what I had wanted from the first, but only now was I truly ready for it and could properly appreciate it.

The years passed. We four lived on in the Castello Caccini. We were friends and lovers, perfectly balancing each other with our respective needs and strengths. My career flourished. I was much in demand for international tours, and the like. But always I was glad to return to the place that I called home – and still call home.

Sometimes, Callipo, Tonio and I go on a ghost-hunt; but we haven't found anything yet. And, likewise, we search for the Indians in the glasshouse; again, we can find no sign of such people. When pressed, Maestro Cavallo will only smile and say, 'But, ah, Ramon, you know that they were there at one time!'

Our greatest joy is to sit on the lawn of a summer's evening and make music. Myself and Maestro Cavallo on cellos, Callipo playing a spinet and Tonio with his flute. A night of music is perfectly followed by a night of lovemaking. The four of us together in Maestro Cavallo's vast bed in his bedroom which is, perhaps, the most glorious room in the entire *castello*. I do not believe I have described that room. And neither have I described how it is with the four of us. Some things may be best left to the imagination when a book is set aside for the last time.

IDOL NEW BOOKS

STREET LIFE
Published in March Rupert Thomas

Ben is eighteen and tired of living in the suburbs. As there's little sexual adventure to be found there, he decides to run away from both A-levels and his comfortable home – to a new life in London. There, he's befriended by Lee, a homeless Scottish lad who offers him a friendly ear and the comfort of his sleeping bag.

£7.99/$10.95 ISBN 0 352 33374 X

MAESTRO
Published in May Peter Slater

A young Spanish cello player, Ramon, journeys to the castle of master cellist Ernesto Cavallo in the hope for masterclasses from the great musician. Ramon's own music is technically perfect, but his playing lacks a certain essence – and so, Maestro Cavallo arranges for Ramon to undergo a number of sexual trials in this darkly erotic, extremely well-written novel.

£8.99/$10.95 ISBN 0 352 33511 4

FELLOWSHIP OF IRON
Published in July Jack Stevens

Mike is a gym owner and a successful competitive bodybuilder. He lives the life of the body beautiful and everything seems to be going swimmingly. So when his mentor and former boyfriend Dave dies after using illegal steroids, Mike is determined to find out who supplied his ex with drugs.

£7.99/$10.95 ISBN 0 352 33512 2

Also published:

CHAINS OF DECEIT
Paul C. Alexander

Journalist Nathan Dexter's life is turned around when he meets a young student called Scott – someone who offers him the relationship for which he's been searching. Then Nathan's best friend goes missing, and Nathan uncovers evidence that he has become the victim of a slavery ring which is rumoured to be operating out of London's leather scene.

£6.99/$9.95 ISBN 0 352 33206 9

DARK RIDER
Jack Gordon

While the rulers of a remote Scottish island play bizarre games of sexual dominance with the Argentinian Angelo, his friend Robert – consumed with jealous longing for his coffee-skinned companion – assuages his desires with the willing locals.

£6.99/$9.95   ISBN 0 352 33243 3

CONQUISTADOR
Jeff Hunter

It is the dying days of the Aztec empire. Axaten and Quetzel are members of the Stable, servants of the Sun Prince chosen for their bravery and beauty. But it is not just an honour and a duty to join this society, it is also the ultimate sexual achievement. Until the arrival of Juan, a young Spanish conquistador, sets the men of the Stable on an adventure of bondage, lust and deception.

£6.99/$9.95   ISBN 0 352 33244 1

TO SERVE TWO MASTERS
Gordon Neale

In the isolated land of Ilyria men are bought and sold as slaves. Rock, brought up to expect to be treated as mere 'livestock', yearns to be sold to the beautiful youth Dorian. But Dorian's brother is as cruel as he is handsome, and if Rock is bought by one brother he will be owned by both.

£6.99/$9.95   ISBN 0 352 33245 X

CUSTOMS OF THE COUNTRY
Rupert Thomas

James Cardell has left school and is looking forward to going to Oxford. That summer of 1924, however, he will spend with his cousins in a tiny village in rural Kent. There he finds he can pursue his love of painting – and begin to explore his obsession with the male physique.

£6.99/$9.95   ISBN 0 352 33246 8

DOCTOR REYNARD'S EXPERIMENT
Robert Black

A dark world of secret brothels, dungeons and sexual cabarets exists behind the respectable facade of Victorian London. The degenerate Lord Spearman introduces Dr Richard Reynard, dashing bachelor, to this hidden world.

£6.99/$9.95   ISBN 0 352 33252 2

CODE OF SUBMISSION
Paul C. Alexander

Having uncovered and defeated a slave ring operating in London's leather scene, journalist Nathan Dexter had hoped to enjoy a peaceful life with his boyfriend Scott. But when it becomes clear that the perverted slave trade has started again, Nathan has no choice but to travel across Europe and America in his bid to stop it. Second in the trilogy.

£6.99/$9.95   ISBN 0 352 33272 7

SLAVES OF TARNE
Gordon Neale

Pascal willingly follows the mysterious and alluring Casper to Tarne, a community of men enslaved to men. Tarne is everything that Pascal has ever fantasised about, but he begins to sense a sinister aspect to Casper's magnetism. Pascal has to choose between the pleasures of submission and acting to save the people he loves.

£6.99/$9.95 ISBN 0 352 33273 5

ROUGH WITH THE SMOOTH
Dominic Arrow

Amid the crime, violence and unemployment of North London, the young men who attend Jonathan Carey's drop-in centre have few choices. One of the young men, Stewart, finds himself torn between the increasingly intimate horseplay of his fellows and the perverse allure of the criminal underworld. Can Jonathan save Stewart from the bullies on the streets and behind bars?

£6.99/$9.95 ISBN 0 352 33292 1

CONVICT CHAINS
Philip Markham

Peter Warren, printer's apprentice in the London of the 1830s, discovers his sexuality and taste for submission at the hands of Richard Barkworth. Thus begins a downward spiral of degradation, of which transportation to the Australian colonies is only the beginning.

£6.99/$9.95 ISBN 0 352 33300 6

SHAME
Raydon Pelham

On holiday in West Hollywood, Briton Martyn Townsend meets and falls in love with the daredevil Scott. When Scott is murdered, Martyn's hunt for the truth and for the mysterious Peter, Scott's ex-lover, leads him to the clubs of London and Ibiza.

£6.99/$9.95 ISBN 0 352 33302 2

HMS SUBMISSION
Jack Gordon

Under the command of Josiah Rock, a man of cruel passions, HMS *Impregnable* sails to the colonies. Christopher, Viscount Fitzgibbons, is a reluctant officer; Mick Savage part of the wretched cargo. They are on a voyage to a shared destiny.

£6.99/$9.95 ISBN 0 352 33301 4

THE FINAL RESTRAINT
Paul C. Alexander

The trilogy that began with *Chains of Deceit* and continued in *Code of Submission* concludes in this powerfully erotic novel. From the dungeons and saunas of London to the deepest jungles of South America, Nathan Dexter is forced to play the ultimate chess game with evil Adrian Delancey – with people as sexual pawns.

£6.99/$9.95 ISBN 0 352 33303 0

HARD TIME
Robert Black

HMP Cairncrow prison is a corrupt and cruel institution, but also a sexual minefield. Three new inmates must find their niche in this brutish environment – as sexual victims or lovers, predators or protectors. This is the story of how they find love, sex and redemption behind prison walls.

£6.99/$9.95   ISBN 0 352 33304 9

ROMAN GAMES
Tasker Dean

When Sam visits the island of Skate, he is taught how to submit to other men, acting out an elaborate fantasy in which young men become wrestling slaves – just as in ancient Rome. Indeed, if he is to have his beautiful prize – the wrestler, Robert – he must learn how the Romans played their games.

£6.99/$9.95   ISBN 0 352 33322 7

VENETIAN TRADE
Richard Davis

From the deck of the ship that carries him into Venice, Rob Weaver catches his first glimpse of a beautiful but corrupt city where the dark alleys and misty canals hide debauchery and decadence. Here, he must learn to survive among men who would make him a plaything and a slave.

£6.99/$9.95   ISBN 0 352 33323 5

THE LOVE OF OLD EGYPT
Philip Markham

It's 1925 and the deluxe cruiser carrying the young gigolo Jeremy Hessling has docked at Luxor. Jeremy dreams of being dominated by the Pharaohs of old, but quickly becomes involved with someone more accessible – Khalid, a young man of exceptional beauty.

£6.99/$9.95   ISBN 0 352 33354 5

THE BLACK CHAMBER
Jack Gordon

Educated at the court of George II, Calum Monroe finds his native Scotland a dull, damp place. He relieves his boredom by donning a mask and holding up coaches in the guise of the Fox – a dashing highwayman. Chance throws him and neighbouring farmer Fergie McGregor together with Calum's sinister, perverse guardian, James Black.

£6.99/$9.95   ISBN 0 352 33373 1

THE GREEK WAY
Edward Ellis

Ancient Greece, the end of the fifth century BC – at the height of the Peloponnesian War. Young Orestes is a citizen of Athens, sent to Sparta as a spy. There he encounters a society of athletic, promiscuous soldiers – including the beautiful Spartan Hector.

£7.99/$10.95   ISBN 0 352 33427 4

BOOTY BOYS
Jay Russell
Hard-bodied black British detective Alton Davies can't believe his eyes or his luck when he finds muscular African-American gangsta rapper Banji-B lounging in his office early one morning. Alton's disbelief – and his excitement – mounts as Banji-B asks him to track down a stolen videotape of a post-gig orgy.

£7.99/$10.95
ISBN 0 352 33446 0

EASY MONEY
Bob Condron
One day an ad appears in the popular music press. Its aim: to enlist members for a new boyband. Young, working-class Mitch starts out as a raw recruit, but soon he becomes embroiled in the sexual tension that threatens to engulf the entire group. As the band soars meteorically to pop success, the atmosphere is quickly reaching fever pitch.

£7.99/$10.95
ISBN 0 352 33442 8

SUREFORCE
Phil Votel
Not knowing what to do with his life once he's been thrown out of the army, Matt takes a job with the security firm Sureforce. Little does he know that the job is the ultimate mix of business and pleasure, and it's not long before Matt's hanging with the beefiest, meanest, hardest lads in town.

£7.99/$10.95
ISBN 0 352 33444 4

THE FAIR COP
Philip Markham
The second world war is over and America is getting back to business as usual. In 1950s New York, that means dirty business. Hanson's a detective who's been dealt a lousy hand, but the Sullivan case is his big chance. How many junior detectives get handed blackmail, murder and perverted sex all in one day?

£7.99/$10.95
ISBN 0 352 33445 2

HOT ON THE TRAIL
Lukas Scott
The Midwest, 1849. *Hot on the Trail* is the story of the original American dream, where freedom is driven by wild passion. And when farmboy Brett skips town and encounters dangerous outlaw Luke Mitchell, sparks are bound to fly in this raunchy tale of hard cowboys, butch outlaws, dirty adventure and true grit.

£7.99/$10.95
ISBN 0 352 33461 4

---------×---------------------------

Please send me the books I have ticked above.

Name   ....

Address   ....

            ....

            ....

            .... Post Code ....

Send to: **Cash Sales, Idol Books, Thames Wharf Studios, Rainville Road, London W6 9HA.**

US customers: for prices and details of how to order books for delivery by mail, call 1-800-805-1083.

Please enclose a cheque or postal order, made payable to **Virgin Publishing Ltd**, to the value of the books you have ordered plus postage and packing costs as follows:

UK and BFPO – £1.00 for the first book, 50p for each subsequent book.

Overseas (including Republic of Ireland) – £2.00 for the first book, £1.00 for each subsequent book.

We accept all major credit cards, including VISA, ACCESS/MASTER-CARD, DINERS CLUB, AMEX and SWITCH.

Please write your card number and expiry date here:

....

Please allow up to 28 days for delivery.

Signature ....

---------×---------------------------

WE NEED YOUR HELP . . .

to plan the future of Idol books –

Yours are the only opinions that matter. Idol is a new and exciting venture: the first British series of books devoted to homoerotic fiction for men.

We're going to do our best to provide the sexiest, best-written books you can buy. And we'd like you to help in these early stages. Tell us what you want to read.

THE IDOL QUESTIONNAIRE

SECTION ONE: ABOUT YOU

1.1 Sex *(we presume you are male, but just in case)*
    Are you?
Male	☐	
Female	☐	

1.2 Age
under 21	☐	21–30	☐
31–40	☐	41–50	☐
51–60	☐	over 60	☐

1.3 At what age did you leave full-time education?
still in education	☐	16 or younger	☐
17–19	☐	20 or older	☐

1.4 Occupation _____

1.5 Annual household income _____

1.6 We are perfectly happy for you to remain anonymous; but if you would like us to send you a free booklist of Idol books, please insert your name and address

_____

_____

_____

_____

_____

SECTION TWO: ABOUT BUYING IDOL BOOKS

2.1 Where did you get this copy of *Maestro*?
Bought at chain book shop ☐
Bought at independent book shop ☐
Bought at supermarket ☐
Bought at book exchange or used book shop ☐
I borrowed it/found it ☐
My partner bought it ☐

2.2 How did you find out about Idol books?
I saw them in a shop ☐
I saw them advertised in a magazine ☐
I read about them in _____
Other _____

2.3 Please tick the following statements you agree with:
I would be less embarrassed about buying Idol
books if the cover pictures were less explicit ☐
I think that in general the pictures on Idol
books are about right ☐
I think Idol cover pictures should be as
explicit as possible ☐

2.4 Would you read an Idol book in a public place – on a train for instance?
Yes ☐   No ☐

SECTION THREE: ABOUT THIS IDOL BOOK

3.1 Do you think the sex content in this book is:
Too much ☐   About right ☐
Not enough ☐

3.2 Do you think the writing style in this book is:

Too unreal/escapist ☐   About right ☐

Too down to earth ☐

3.3 Do you think the story in this book is:

Too complicated ☐   About right ☐

Too boring/simple ☐

3.4 Do you think the cover of this book is:

Too explicit ☐   About right ☐

Not explicit enough ☐

Here's a space for any other comments:

SECTION FOUR: ABOUT OTHER IDOL BOOKS

4.1 How many Idol books have you read?

4.2 If more than one, which one did you prefer?

_____

4.3 Why?

SECTION FIVE: ABOUT YOUR IDEAL EROTIC NOVEL

We want to publish the books you want to read – so this is your chance to tell us exactly what your ideal erotic novel would be like.

5.1 Using a scale of 1 to 5 (1 = no interest at all, 5 = your ideal), please rate the following possible settings for an erotic novel:

Roman / Ancient World ☐

Medieval / barbarian / sword 'n' sorcery ☐

Renaissance / Elizabethan / Restoration ☐

Victorian / Edwardian ☐

1920s & 1930s ☐

Present day ☐

Future / Science Fiction ☐

5.2 Using the same scale of 1 to 5, please rate the following themes you may find in an erotic novel:

Bondage / fetishism ☐
Romantic love ☐
SM / corporal punishment ☐
Bisexuality ☐
Group sex ☐
Watersports ☐
Rent / sex for money ☐

5.3 Using the same scale of 1 to 5, please rate the following styles in which an erotic novel could be written:

Gritty realism, down to earth ☐
Set in real life but ignoring its more unpleasant aspects ☐
Escapist fantasy, but just about believable ☐
Complete escapism, totally unrealistic ☐

5.4 In a book that features power differentials or sexual initiation, would you prefer the writing to be from the viewpoint of the dominant / experienced or submissive / inexperienced characters?

Dominant / Experienced ☐
Submissive / Inexperienced ☐
Both ☐

5.5 We'd like to include characters close to your ideal lover. What characteristics would your ideal lover have? Tick as many as you want:

Dominant	☐	Caring	☐
Slim	☐	Rugged	☐
Extroverted	☐	Romantic	☐
Bisexual	☐	Old	☐
Working Class	☐	Intellectual	☐
Introverted	☐	Professional	☐
Submissive	☐	Pervy	☐
Cruel	☐	Ordinary	☐
Young	☐	Muscular	☐
Naïve	☐		

Anything else? _____

5.6 Is there one particular setting or subject matter that your ideal erotic novel would contain?

_____

5.7 As you'll have seen, we include safe-sex guidelines in every book. However, while our policy is always to show safe sex in stories with contemporary settings, we don't insist on safe-sex practices in stories with historical settings because it would be anachronistic. What, if anything, would you change about this policy?

_____

_____

SECTION SIX: LAST WORDS

6.1 What do you like best about Idol books?

_____

6.2 What do you most dislike about Idol books?

_____

6.3 In what way, if any, would you like to change Idol covers?

_____

6.4 Here's a space for any other comments:

_____

_____

_____

_____

Thanks for completing this questionnaire. Now either tear it out, or photocopy it, then put it in an envelope and send it to:

Idol Books/Virgin Publishing
Thames Wharf Studios
Rainville Road
London
W6 9HA